"YOU TEMPT ME BEYOND REASON."

"Surely you know that," he said harshly. "You cannot be that innocent. You are not a child."

She looked ridiculously pleased, and Alexander let out a groan of frustration. "You want to kiss me," she said, rather too happily.

"Yes, I want to kiss you. I'm a man and you are a beautiful girl sitting next to me night after night in her bedclothes." He ended on an exasperated note.

"I give you permission."

He pressed his fingers to his temples and muttered a prayer. "Have you not heard a single word I've said, girl?"

"You said you wanted to kiss me." She sat on the bench and smiled up at him.

"What are you doing to me?" he asked, looking at her almost beseechingly. As she watched, desire and something like resignation flickered in his gaze. And then in one quick, desperate motion, he grabbed her upper arms and brought her against him, their lips only a breath away. "This is a mistake. A mistake . . ."

Other Books by Jane Goodger

Marry Christmas

A Christmas Scandal

A Christmas Waltz

Published by Kensington Publishing Corporation

When a Duke Says I Do

JANE GOODGER

ZEBRA BOOKS
KENSINGTON PUBLISHING CORP.
http://www.kensingtonbooks.com

ZEBRA BOOKS are published by

Kensington Publishing Corp.
119 West 40th Street
New York, NY 10018

All Kensington titles, imprints, and distributed lines are available at special quantity discounts for bulk purchases for sales promotion, premiums, fund-raising, educational, or institutional use.

Special book excerpts or customized printings can also be created to fit specific needs. For details, write or phone the office of the Kensington Special Sales Manager: Attn.: Special Sales Department. Kensington Publishing Corp., 119 West 40th Street, New York, NY 10018. Phone: 1-800-221-2647.

ISBN-13: 978-1-4201-1151-4
ISBN-10: 1-4201-1151-5

First Printing: December 2011

10 9 8 7 6 5 4 3 2 1

Printed in the United States of America

ACKNOWLEDGMENTS

I am always extremely grateful to the people who help me with my research. In particular, I would like to thank Gail Kervatt, M.Ed., who gave me needed insight into a rare disorder called selective mutism. While this is a disorder that affects children, the impacts of this condition are often felt into adulthood, especially if untreated. In selective mutism, a child cannot physically speak in front of strangers, but easily speaks with people he or she is comfortable with. It's an extremely complex disorder, and one that can be devastating to a child who has it.

I would also like to thank Tiffany Cooper, who bravely and graciously gave me her first-person account of the affects of botulism, referred to as Kerner's disease in this book. Tiffany's courageous battle with this disease was inspiring to me, as she was far more ill than my heroine. Here's hoping you're doing well, Tiffany.

Lastly, I would like to thank the great late Kate Duffy for having faith in me, for being one of my biggest fans, and for making me laugh at this sometimes crazy business of writing romances.

Chapter 1

Nottinghamshire, England, 1862

One of the more harrowing tasks of the servants of Mansfield Hall was searching for Miss Elsie, who had a tendency to fall asleep in the oddest places. They once found her balancing precariously on the edge of a fountain, one hand dangling in the water as carp nibbled curiously and painlessly upon her fingers. Though the servants always began their search in her rooms, it was almost inevitable that they would find her where she oughtn't to be—and never in her bed.

"Don't she look like an angel, though," Missy Slater, Elsie's personal maid, said, gazing down at her employer as she slept like the dead curled up in an oversized leather chair in her father's library.

Mrs. Whitehouse, the housekeeper, was far less charitable, and scowled down at the sleeping girl. "As if I have time for this," she grumbled, then cleared her throat loudly in an attempt to awaken her.

"You has to give 'er a good shake," Missy said,

doing just that. She was rewarded when Elsie's moss-green eyes opened drowsily, and she smiled. She nearly always woke up smiling.

"What am I missing?" she asked, as she always did. She was feeling a bit groggy, for she must have been sleeping for at least an hour. The servants had been instructed to never awaken Elsie unless something of importance had happened.

"That Frenchie painter is here," Missy said. "I know you wanted to be in the ballroom when your father met with him."

"Monsieur Laurent Desmarais, Miss Elizabeth. He arrived not ten minutes ago," Mrs. Whitehouse said, glaring at Missy for her familiarity. Missy made a face behind the housekeeper's back and Elsie found herself trying not to smile at her maid. Just because she knew she should, she gave Missy a half-hearted stern look, which only caused the little maid to shrug innocently.

"Thank you, ladies," she said, bouncing up, as if she hadn't just been sound asleep. She patted her golden-brown hair, which was none worse for having been slept upon, and headed off to the ballroom. Having the great Laurent Desmarais paint a mural on their ballroom wall was a great coup for the Stanhope family. Usually, the famous muralist painted for no one beneath the level of a viscount, but her father, Baron Huntington, had more pounds than the typical baron, and apparently that income was more than Monsieur Desmarais could resist.

The Stanhope estate was in close proximity to the Dukeries, an area of Nottinghamshire that had an excessive number of dukes, making it a rather fortunate place for any family with girls of marrying age. Elsie had the good fortune of having been engaged to a future duke from the time she was an infant. At least, her father insisted it was good fortune. Elsie thought the idea of having her future laid out before her rather uninspiring.

Which was why having Monsieur Desmarais agree to paint their ballroom was so very exciting. So little of anything nearing excitement happened at Mansfield Hall.

Elsie lifted her skirts and ran, her slippers tap-tapping on the marble floor, as she hurried to the ballroom, a fairly new addition to their sprawling old home. There she found her father in deep discussion with a rather rotund-looking man, whose mustache was so thin, it looked as if it had been painted upon his face. His hair had too much pomade and his clothing looked about to burst away from his porcine body.

"Ah, this must be the beautiful Mademoiselle Elizabeth," he said in his delightful French accent, and instantly Elsie forgave him his rather dubious charms. She'd conjured up a far more romantic image of the famous painter and felt rather ridiculous about that now.

Elsie dipped a curtsy. "Monsieur Desmarais, *un plaisir*," she said, in impeccable French. "*Veuillez m'appeler*, Mademoiselle Elsie."

"Of course. Mademoiselle Elsie. Lord Huntington was telling me a bit of your wishes. You require a large mural, no?"

"Yes. I would like it to cover this entire wall," she said, indicating a large barren wall that had been stripped of all decoration in preparation for the muralist. A man was there, his back to them, laying out a drop cloth to protect the ballroom's marble floor.

"My assistant, Andre," Monsieur Desmarais said, nodding toward the man, who froze momentarily at the muralist's words before continuing his work. "He does not speak, but he hears perfectly fine, the poor soul. He's been with me since he was a boy. His English name is Alexander, but I call him by his French name."

"How very charitable of you," Elsie said.

Monsieur Desmarais puffed up a bit, seeming pleased by Elsie's comment. "Do you have anything particular in mind for the mural?" he asked. "I understand you admired Lady Browning's mural last Season."

"Indeed I did. But I was thinking of something else. I was thinking of perhaps a lake." She gave him an impish smile, acknowledging her whimsy. "A magical lake."

"Magical?" Monsieur asked, with obvious skepticism.

Elsie smiled, her eyes full of merriment. "A secret lake might be a better description. Or one long forgotten. With a gazebo, at the far end." From the corner of her eye, she could sense the assistant turning his head a bit as if to hear better what she was planning. "It's painted white, but with paint chipping and rotted wood, perhaps. But I want it to look enchanted, not neglected, if you know what I mean. And in the center of the small lake"—she closed her eyes—"a rock formation, jutting out."

At that moment a loud clatter sounded and Elsie opened her eyes. The mute had apparently dropped a supply of brushes. In rapid French, Monsieur chastised the younger man. "He is not usually so clumsy," he said apologetically. "Usually as silent as a little mouse, that one."

"Do you think you could paint that? I remember such a lake from my girlhood. There were no swans, but you may add some for visual interest or whatever you like."

"Just a lake?"

"A secret lake," she said, teasing. "I wonder if it would be possible to paint it as if someone is seeing it through branches or trees?"

"This would be difficult," he said slowly, staring at the wall, his eyes falling briefly on his assistant. "But I think it can be done."

"Wonderful," Elsie said, clapping her hands together. "And will it be done in time for my birthday ball? I'll be twenty-two on September the fourteenth. Is that enough time?"

"I will endeavor to complete the mural for you in time, Mademoiselle Elsie."

"It shall be the best of all balls," Elsie said, grabbing her father's arm and hugging it to her. "Thank you, Father."

Lord Huntington gazed down affectionately at his daughter, and Elsie smiled, a bit guiltily, up at him. She knew she could ask her father for the moon and the man would try to give it to her. And since her mother died three years before, he'd been even more indulgent. Even though she was already engaged—and had been for seventeen years—her father had given her a Season in London to introduce her to the society she would soon be an integral part of. Since her fiancé seemed to be in no hurry to marry, Elsie wanted to experience as much fun as she could before the daunting duties of being a duchess claimed her.

"It shall be a lovely mural," Elsie said, watching as Monsieur Desmarais donned his smock. With a fine charcoal pencil, he began the barest outline of what Elsie knew would be a work of art. She knew, because Lady Browning's rose garden mural was quite the most beautiful thing she'd seen. She'd half expected the air in the lady's ballroom to smell of roses, so real and life-like was that fanciful garden. Lady Browning's only complaint was that Desmarais had included a few fading blooms, which the countess claimed her gardener would never allow.

When Elsie saw that painting, the exquisite detail, the realness that made her feel as if she could walk right into that garden and touch a pointed thorn, she knew she had to have a mural of her own. She knew, without even thinking, what she wanted the subject matter to be. It had to be of that secret lake at Warbeck Abbey, where she and her sister had played, making believe they had discovered something truly magical. They'd never told a soul about the lake, about how they'd dangled bare toes into the cool water while sitting on a dock that was beginning to sag rather dangerously. Elsie and Christine had always dreaded their visits to Warbeck Abbey, for it was such a dour, strict place where the laughter of children seemed out of place. But after they'd discovered the lake, their visits had become far more tolerable.

The mural would be a happy reminder of her sister, who she still so desperately missed. They'd been twins, identical in nearly every way and inseparable, and her death twelve years earlier had affected Elsie profoundly.

"Let's leave them to their work," Elsie said, leading her father out of the ballroom. "I have about a dozen letters to write before meeting with the chef. Are you planning any dinner parties in the next few weeks, Father?"

"No, dear. Nothing special."

Elsie frowned, and started to say something but stopped herself. Her birthday ball would be the first large social gathering they'd had at Mansfield Hall since her mother's death. While many a man would have remarried already, Michael Stanhope missed his wife desperately and only recently had begun accepting invitations. If not for her aunt Diane, Elsie was quite certain she wouldn't have had a Season at all. Her father simply had no interests other than wandering the countryside and collecting unusual lichens. They were quite beautiful, but his preoccupation with them was at times a bit worrying. He carried a magnifying glass and sketchbook with him and would disappear for hours at a time. He seemed content enough, but Elsie did worry about him.

Perhaps as much as her father worried about her. What a pair they were—a father who wandered the forest and a daughter who was afraid to fall asleep.

Chapter 2

Like a dutiful girl, Elsie went to her room just after ten o'clock and donned her nightclothes as if she had every intention of going to bed. And like most nights, after Missy had said good night, she stared at her bed, that most hated of all places, and sat in a chair by the fire with a book, feeling her eyes burn from weariness.

Christine had died in her bed. Not the one that sat in Elsie's room now; her mother and father had removed it long ago thinking that would help their remaining daughter rest. They'd even allowed her to change her room, but Elsie could not bring herself to do it, to lie in a bed without thinking about Christine, her sister and her heart, smiling over at her.

They were ten years old, and that night they had whispered to each other in the dark about how they would go into the forest and search for the haunted cottage one of the village children had told them about. Even though it sounded suspiciously like the German fairy tale, *Hansel and Gretel*, they convinced themselves that the cottage did, indeed exist. Hadn't they found a secret lake by themselves? Certainly they could find a haunted cottage.

They fell asleep just as the moonlight was beginning to edge up her bed, but only Elsie woke up the next morning. She tried not to think about that moment, the awful realization, the instinctive, stomach-dropping knowledge, that her sister was gone. Christine had been cold and lifeless and even though Elsie had screamed for help, and screamed and screamed, she'd known her sister was dead. The loss was fathomless, and even now, years and years later, Elsie would sometimes miss her sister so much it was a physical ache.

So, no, Elsie did not go to bed that night. She hadn't slept in a bed in twelve years. Christine was her twin, her second half, and when Elsie was still a child she'd decided that if she fell asleep in her bed, she would die, too. Someone would come into her room in the morning and find her cold, lifeless body, just as she had found Christine. Elsie knew she was being silly, but the fear was so ingrained, so much a part of her now, she simply could not do it. She'd tried, only to break into a cold sweat, then break down and cry. Over the years, her father had given up and let her wander the house at night, knowing it was the only thing that gave her comfort. When she was still a child, the servants would find her curled up in the library, fast asleep. She would awaken, frightened, confused until she realized where she was and that she was still breathing. And that Christine was still gone.

"You can be sure if I had a bed as comfortable as

yours, I'd be sleepin' in it," Missy had told her once after spending a good deal of time looking for her.

"Don't scold," Elsie had said. "Perhaps I will tonight." But she never did.

Elsie stared at her bed and told herself as she had every day since Christine's death that nothing would happen to her if she just lay down, pulled the covers up to her chin and closed her eyes. But whenever she did that, she began to be aware of her breathing—in, out, in, out—so aware that it was difficult to breathe at all. With a little sigh of frustration, Elsie grabbed her wrap and pulled it on, then tip-toed to the door separating her room from the small one where Missy slept each night. Pressing her ear to the door, she could hear her maid's soft snores, and smiled. A cannon could go off in her room and Missy would not hear it. Still, she opened her door quietly and stepped into the hall, lit only by a half-moon.

No one could navigate the house in the dark as well as Elsie. It wasn't much of a talent, but she was rather proud of this ability anyway. She moved down the hall to the main staircase, walking quickly and quietly down the grand curving stairs on tip-toe.

Then stopped cold.

A light shone from the ballroom. A light never shone anywhere in this house at night. Ever. Elsie stared at that slice of light for a moment before deciding that perhaps Monsieur Desmarais must have left a lamp lit. She would have to talk to him about that, as a lit lamp could easily lead to a fire, especially in a home with a cat. Even though Sir Galahad was put out most nights, sometimes the servants could not find him and he remained indoors.

A noise from the room made her heart skitter. Certainly Monsieur Desmarais could not be working at this time of night. It was well after midnight. The ballroom could only be accessed from a set of double doors and several French doors that led to the outside terrace but which were always kept locked. Elsie considered sneaking outside and seeing who was in the room, but she'd not donned her slippers and the grass outside was sure to be cold and wet from dew. Holding her breath, she moved to the door, her hand on the latch, listening intently. Yes, there was someone—or something—in that room scratching about and it sounded much too large to be Sir Galahad. She pulled on the door latch, squeezing her eyes shut, and gave silent thanks to their well-trained staff who regularly oiled the doors to eliminate squeaks. A small slice of light lit her hand, hit her face, and she peeked inside. At the far end of the ballroom was a man, tall and powerful, making sweeping gestures along the wall. It took her a moment before she realized it must be Monsieur Desmarais's assistant.

How curious. She watched as he drew on the wall, fine lines, outlining what would eventually be the mural. For long minutes she watched, fascinated with the sure way he worked, almost as if in a frenzy, slashing, moving about with controlled grace, hardly paying attention to what he was doing. Monsieur Desmarais was nowhere in sight. The room held only the couch and table she'd had placed there so she might read in the sunlight on cold days, for the ballroom was the sunniest, warmest place in the house in winter. In fact, the book she'd been reading still lay upon the table where she'd sat just that afternoon after the artist and his assistant had stopped for the day. Why was this man here now? And why was he doing what Monsieur Desmarais should be? For long minutes she watched him, and saw a vision slowly appearing before her—the lake, the rocks, the gazebo, and around it all the twining branches and vines. It was only the outline and already it was magnificent. And it had not been there this afternoon when she'd picked up her book. At that time, the wall had only a very few lines upon it, a grid of sorts and nothing more.

Elsie thought of the beautiful mural in Lady Browning's home, and wondered if this man were the artist, not the famous muralist and knew, instinctively, that she was right.

She stepped into the room, not bothering to hide her entrance. "Good evening," she said, and he froze, one hand poised to draw. He stood that way for several seconds before he slowly lowered his hand to his side. He was completely still, unnaturally so, as if he didn't even dare take a breath. His loose white shirt was untucked, his sleeves rolled up revealing a strong, sinuous upper arm.

"Please don't stop your work. I'm just fetching my book." He continued to stare at the wall in front of him unmoving and she wondered if his face were disfigured in some way. "I won't tell. I promise."

Then he turned to her, as if curiosity overcame

him, and stared in such an oddly intense way, Elsie felt uncomfortable. He was rather amazingly, disturbingly handsome. His hair was a deep chocolate brown, thick and unruly and far too long for convention. His eyes were some light color; she couldn't quite tell in the lamplight. And his mouth was . . . Elsie had to look away. She shouldn't be thinking about his mouth or the color of his eyes or anything else about him. As Monsieur Desmarais's assistant, he was little more than a servant.

"I don't care who paints the mural just as long as it gets done," she said with measured casualness. "Did you do Lady Browning's rose garden?"

He nodded slowly.

Elsie grinned, proud of her perception. "Oh, marvelous," she said, clapping her hands together. "Please do continue to work. Don't mind me and I won't mind you. I'm afraid I find it difficult to sleep and often end up here. Quite improper, I know." She grinned again and he simply stared at her. He couldn't be daft. Certainly a man with such artistic talent had to be highly intelligent. Finally, he turned back to the wall, gripping the charcoal so tightly, she could see the tendons in his arms.

Alexander could not believe his misfortune. No one, in all these years, had ever discovered Monsieur Desmarais's secret. Once, Monsieur *had* been the finest muralist in all of Britain, but rheumatism had made holding a pencil or paintbrush for more than a few minutes excruciatingly painful. It had been an insidious thing, taking away his ability a little at a time. By the time Monsieur could no longer do anything but supervise, Alexander had discovered his own talent, which was easily perfected with such a wonderful mentor.

Alex loved Monsieur Desmarais like a father and would die before the older man was shamed. He didn't know if he could trust this girl, but it looked as if he was being forced to. If only she would go away. If only she would stop that incessant chatter.

"I think it should be rather nice to have company," she said, sounding rather wistful.

He would not be good company for anyone, particularly not a girl who was apparently lonely and given to wandering about her house at night.

"I don't sleep," she said. He tensed again, as he always did when a stranger spoke to him. But he found himself relaxing a bit when he realized she did not expect him to respond and didn't seem to care one bit whether he did or not. "Well, I *do* sleep, just not at night. And not in my b . . . my room," she said, as if simply saying the word "bed" were naughty. Which it was, and he almost smiled.

Alexander had discovered there were two kinds of women: those who thought him a eunuch simply because he didn't speak, and those who thought him good sport. When he was younger, he rather liked the latter. But this one was perhaps simply young and naïve. No good girl would spend time alone with a strange man in the middle of the night unless she was looking for a bit of naughtiness or was so innocent those naughty thoughts hadn't entered her head.

He began working as she prattled on about her

sleeping habits. He stared at the wall and frowned. Most of the detail would come later when he was painting, but now he was creating the scene, the perspective. He was used to doing pretty landscapes, fanciful castles in clouds, or mountain scenes. This mural, however, was different, and far more personal. No one could know, of course, what painting this lake was doing to him. It was like a knife to his soul, every slash of his charcoal tearing further into his damaged heart.

It was perhaps not entirely shocking that this girl would have seen the lake, that place he remembered with an odd mix of happiness and horror. Mansfield Hall was not far from where he'd grown up near a lake very much like the one the girl described. Enough time had passed that he very much doubted anyone would recognize him. He'd rarely been brought out into society even as a child, for fear he would humiliate himself. And, of course, his father. While his brother would bow and say all the proper things a boy should say to adults, Alexander never could. He would stand there, his eyes wide open, frozen as if a lump of ice around his throat prevented him from speaking. Such a scene had played out more than once, followed by a thrashing, before his father had given up on him entirely. The last time, the worst by far, didn't bear thinking about at all.

His father had been deeply ashamed of his second son, but Alexander had still been surprised when his father had committed him to an asylum for the mentally deficient one month after his brother's death. And there, he'd been forgotten. They probably still thought him there, that sad place where the aristocracy placed their unwanted offspring, the deficient ones that were an embarrassment.

He'd been so lost in thought, he hadn't heard the girl come up next to him. She traced a line he'd drawn with one finger. "The rock," she said, a smile on her lips. She oughtn't to be so close to him. She smelled sweet and looked sweeter. Her wavy red-gold brown hair falling down her back, her green eyes sweeping along the line he'd drawn. He hadn't seen what she looked like that afternoon, and she'd been in the shadows this evening. Now that she stood bathed in the soft light of his lamp, he realized she was beyond exquisite. "It looks exactly as I pictured it." She gave him a curious look, a small tilt of her head before returning to the couch and her book.

"It's special to me, that lake," she said, her voice echoing in the emptiness of the vast room.

He wished he could tell her to stop talking, to leave him alone. But he knew from painful experience that once someone who thought him mute discovered he could talk, their reaction was humiliatingly jubilant, as if they had somehow "cured" him. Other times people felt angry and betrayed, and he supposed that was how his father had felt. For he could easily talk to his mother, even to his tutor, but in front of his father, he froze. He never spoke to someone who knew he could not speak, and he rarely got a chance to speak to anyone else. He liked his silent world of paint and charcoal and beauty—a world this girl was disrupting.

"My sister and I discovered the lake," she said. "It's surrounded by a huge hedge and shrouded with mystery. We found it at Warbeck Abbey. Have you ever been?"

Alexander ignored her, ignored the fear that sliced through him at the mention of that terrible place.

"No one ever speaks of the lake and why there's a large hedge surrounding it." He willed himself to keep working, even as nightmarish images filled his head. "Of course, we were children and told in no uncertain terms that we should stay away from the hedge, that there were monsters on the other side. We couldn't resist," she said, laughing. "We walked around it until we discovered the smallest hole in the hedge. How brave we were, for we actually thought there might be a monster. Christine went first. She was my twin, but she was always far braver than I. We were exactly alike in every other way." She paused and Alexander thought she was finished.

"On the other side of that huge hedgerow was the lake. It was beautiful and yet somehow so forlorn, as if it hated being surrounded so. I never did find out why that lake was hidden."

Alexander heard her sigh and the sound of her picking up her book. My God, how long was she going to stay here? All night? He glanced back at her and gave her a pointed look, fighting the urge to tell her to leave him alone.

"I'm bothering you," she said, sounding completely unrepentant. "To be honest, I find it quite refreshing to talk to someone who doesn't interrupt. It's almost as if I'm holding you captive to my conversation."

Alexander fought a smile, turning back to the

wall before she could see. He decided, then and there, that she could talk all night if she wished. No woman had ever told him she liked his silence.

After a while, her chatter stopped and Alexander was so consumed with his work, he was unaware of how much time had gone by. It wasn't until he noticed the sky was lightening that he realized he'd worked the entire night. Monsieur would be angry with him, for he'd not be able to sleep and the old man needed him to be attentive. For all his bluster, Monsieur rarely got angry, and when he did, it was like a summer storm, violent and short and soon forgotten. Their relationship had become a careful dance for they both knew how their roles had experienced a subtle shift the day Alexander began doing most of the painting. Alexander didn't mind the pretense because he loved what he did, was content to create beauty, and knew he would not have been able to charm customers the way Monsieur did.

It was imperative that no one ever discover Alexander was the true artist. The life he'd grown to love so much would end instantly, and a man he loved like a father would be humiliated beyond bearing. Which was why Alexander was angry with himself for working so late; it increased the possibility of discovery. And then he remembered the girl, and his foolish, foolish belief that she would keep his secret. He should have feigned confusion and put his charcoal away, he should have sought his bed and left her alone with her book. What had made him think he could trust her?

He looked back and saw her sleeping form on

the small couch, the lamp long out, the book lying next to her hand. *Damn.* It would not do for someone to find her here, with him. He pulled out his watch and saw it was only five in the morning, too early for even the servants to be up and about. He walked over to Miss Stanhope and felt his gut wrench oddly at the vision before him. She wasn't the most classically beautiful woman he'd seen, but there was something about her, a vulnerability that he understood. She was lonely, so lonely she'd spent the night talking to a man who could not talk back to her. Her gold-tipped lashes lay like delicate shadows on her soft cheek, and her lips, slightly open, were a bit wider than they ought to be. His hand hovered over her shoulder for a moment before he gathered the courage to touch her. He was about to lay a hand on her shoulder, but frowned when he realized his hands were smudged with charcoal and would certainly leave a mark on her pristine white wrap. And so he nudged the entire couch with one knee, hoping the movement would awaken her.

She sat up so quickly, he stumbled back in surprise, letting out a small sound. She pushed her hair from her face and did something so unexpected, he flinched. She smiled, a glorious, heart-wrenching smile. "Hello."

He backed up another step and nodded. She squinted at the far clock, hidden in the early morning shadows, and pursed her lips. "What time is it?"

He held up his hand, showing her five fingers.

"Goodness. I haven't slept so long in years." She looked truly amazed. "How wonderful." She stood and walked to the mural, letting out a small gasp. "Oh, my. Alexander, is it?"

He nodded.

"You are quite gifted," she said, staring at his light charcoal drawing. "Truly gifted. It's precisely as I imagined it. Precisely." She turned back to him, where he stood as if fastened to the floor. "I must go. Good day." She walked to the door, but stopped as she touched the handle. "I shan't tell. A promise is a promise. So, it's our secret."

And then, as if it were a common occurrence for a young woman to have spent the night on the couch in a room with a strange man, she simply walked out the door.

Chapter 3

Elsie felt better than she had in memory, and wondered how on earth she'd been able to fall asleep in the ballroom as a strange man worked. Likely because she'd talked herself into exhaustion. Poor man had no doubt wanted to scream to her to stop talking. She actually giggled at the thought.

She went up two flights to the nursery, where her little sister still spent so many hours. Mary was her parents' last attempt at creating an heir for Mansfield Hall. After Christine died, Mama had suffered several miscarriages, something Elsie had only recently discovered. At the time, she'd only known that her mother was ill and her parents inconsolably sad. But when her mother was close to having Mary, she'd confessed about the anguish of losing so many children, which made this baby so much more a miracle.

Her mother had been nearly forty years old when she'd died just a week after pushing Mary into the world. At least she got to hold her perfect little baby girl before finally drifting away. That was three years ago.

Mary was one of the reasons Elsie was in no hurry for her wedding. Marriage would only take her away from Mansfield, and most especially away from Mary. It was not lost on anyone in the Stanhope household that Elsie was of an age that Mary could have been her own child.

"Look who's up," Elsie said, going over to the tiny bed where her sister sat playing with a small rag doll. Mary had the finest toys money could buy, porcelain dolls from France and little German wooden figures, but her sister adored the rag doll appropriately called "Baby."

"Elsie," Mary said with a pout. "Look. It's boken."

"Baby is broken? Oh, no. Let's take a look." Baby did, indeed, have a small tear. "That's easy to fix. I just need some needle and thread and we'll have her as good as new in no time at all."

Elsie handed the doll back to her sister, who held it as if it had been out of her hands for a week. "Come with me to my room and I'll fetch my sewing kit." Mary jumped off her bed and held up her hand with the assurance of a child who knows someone will always be there to take it.

On the way out they encountered Mary's nanny, Miss Lawton. "I'll take her, Nanny," Elsie said, ignoring the slight sigh from her employee. "I promise not to fall asleep. I slept wonderfully last night and believe I won't even need a nap at all today."

"How wonderful, Miss Elsie," Miss Lawton said with a little curtsy. Poor Miss Lawton was often asked to help with the search.

Elsie picked her sister up at the stairs, impatient to get to her room and change so they could both go down to the breakfast room. Mary was supposed to eat all meals in the nursery, but Elsie hated sitting in that room alone, day after day. Her father rarely ate breakfast, and if he did, it was a simple roll and slab of ham that he could eat while trekking through the woods in search of lichen.

"What shall we do today, Mary? Shall we play hide and seek with Nanny?"

Mary nodded her head and beamed a smile at her big sister. Mary always hid in the same place and giggled loudly as Elsie went in search of her, which the big sister duly ignored. It was Mary's favorite game and usually wore her out rather quickly.

"I get to hide first," Elsie said.

"In the cupboard?"

"We shall see, shan't we?" Elsie always hid in the cupboard and pretended surprise when Mary found her. She gave Mary an extra squeeze, feeling sadness wash over her, for soon would come a time when she wouldn't be around to hide in the cupboard and give her little sister hugs.

Life at Mansfield Hall was sedate and unchanging, especially since the death of its mistress. Having Monsieur Desmaraìs in residence was as much excitement as the old house had had in three years.

And now, just one day after that excitement, came the letter that would alter Elsie's life forever. She saw it on the silver tray in the entrance hall, that thick velum with a ducal seal. Her stomach plunged, for she knew what it was. She was twenty-two, Lord Hathwaite was twenty-five, and it was past time they married. Now the time had come.

With a hand that trembled, Elsie picked up the message and broke the seal, praying it was an innocuous invitation and not the dreaded summons she believed it to be. She handled all the family's correspondence of late, for her father was too distracted by his studies to worry about such mundane matters as invitations and bills. She'd been running the household for years now, without complaint. But at that moment, she wished she could simply hand off that letter to someone else, someone who would deal with whatever it said. She had a sudden and sharp longing for her mother.

The letter was short and to the point. The wedding day was set for May, the announcement to be made at her birthday ball. Tears welled up in her eyes as she looked around at her beloved home as if it were one of the last times she'd ever see it. She didn't want to leave and be mistress of that huge palace the Duke of Kingston presided over. She wanted her country home, with its warm yellow stones and overgrown gardens.

"Oh, dash it," she said, wiping away her tears. How silly she was being. She'd known since she was a child that this day would come. If she was honest with herself, she should be grateful that it hadn't come far sooner. Most young women would have traded places with her in an instant, for Lord Hathwaite was not only to be a duke, he was also rather handsome. He was infinitely polite, a fine dancer, a good conversationalist. And boring beyond tears.

She didn't love him and he certainly didn't love her; she doubted he could produce such an emotion for her. Even though she knew she was probably being unfair to a man she truly didn't know that well, she'd never seen so much as a flicker of interest in his dark eyes about anything. She was merely the conclusion of an agreement made years ago between their fathers. It wasn't as if such an unemotional match were unheard of. In fact, she could not think of one couple she knew who could say they'd had a love match, other than, of course, her own mother and father.

She remembered talking to her mother about Lord Hathwaite, about how she might come to love him. And if she didn't, at least he seemed like a kind man who would treat her well. What did she truly know of him? She'd danced with him a handful of times, sat next to him at a total of three dinner parties, gone to the opera and sat nervously in the ducal box ten feet away from her intended.

When she'd visited Warbeck Abbey as a child, she'd spent most of her time with her sister, not the solemn little boy who lived there and rarely was allowed out to play. As far as she knew, they had nothing in common other than the fact that their fathers had once agreed to pair them up over some political matter that at the time was of utmost importance. It all had something to do with trade and China.

"May the tenth. I shall become a marchioness on May the tenth," she whispered.

* * *

Oscar Wilkinson, Marquess of Hathwaite and future Duke of Kingston, emptied his stomach into his chamber pot in anticipation of an audience with his father whilst cursing the bad luck of having two dead older brothers. Oscar would have been more than happy to have had the option of military service; it seemed a far less hazardous thing to face any enemy than to face his father. But His Grace would have none of it. Having lost two sons already, and at a very young age, his father would do nothing to put his final heir in jeopardy.

"Sir, your father awaits." These nervous words came from the long-suffering Mr. Farnsworth, whose face seemed to sag more every year as if His Grace's ill treatment of his loyal secretary were dragging him down.

Oscar rinsed out his mouth and gazed at his reflection in the mirror, hating what he saw: a frightened little boy. Damned if he was going to show it. His father could no longer have him whipped, could no longer touch him with anything but his scathing verbiage. Oscar shouldn't let it bother him, but it did. Lucky dead brothers.

Of course, Oscar knew nothing of them, only that they had both died when he was three. He had no memory of either boy, having spent the first four years of his life in the nursery. Henry was the oldest, the shining star, the only child his father had ever been kind to. Henry had stood up to his father like a man, had been more ready at twelve years old to be duke than Oscar was now at age twenty-five. At least that was what he'd been told time and again.

Oscar dragged a hand through his hair. "Walker,"

he shouted, and was gratified that his valet was at the ready to make his appearance impeccable. Walker, grimacing, brushed his suit, fixed his necktie, and gave his shoes one last quick buffing before nodding his head.

"Wish me luck," he said.

"Good luck, sir," Walker said with heartfelt sincerity. It was a sad thing, indeed, when a man's servants pitied him, Oscar thought disparagingly. He knew what this meeting was about and had been dreading it for nearly his entire life. There could be no other reason to meet with his father, for he'd done nothing wrong and nothing right. The only thing left to discuss was his imminent marriage or the duke's own death, which, unfortunately, did not seem to be in the offing. The man was sixty-two but could easily have passed for someone ten years younger.

Oscar took a deep breath and headed out the door, his face set. It would not do to have his father sense his fear of what this meeting would bring. Hell, marrying Elsie Stanhope should bring nothing but joy—and likely would have if he'd had the opportunity to make a single decision about the girl. He didn't object to her, per se, he simply objected to the fact that every detail of his life thus far had been carefully, tediously mapped out by his tyrannical father. Right down to their wedding trip. No doubt the old man would hover over his bed on their wedding night, telling him where to put what.

He'd not been allowed the raucous excesses of youth, but rather had been constantly under the careful watch of His Grace. The only time he'd ever gotten any freedom was the single summer he'd spent with his former schoolmates drinking and carousing. What a glorious summer it had been. It had lasted approximately two weeks before His Grace got word of his activities and brought him home. He hadn't *lived* yet, and now he was to be shackled for the rest of his life to a girl who was about as exciting as a piece of lightly cooked toast.

A footman stood sentry outside his father's offices and Oscar requested permission to enter, as he was always forced to do in this house.

"One moment, Lord Hathwaite." The efficient servant disappeared into the room, only to appear moments later, opening the door wide enough for him to make entry into his father's lair.

His father was obviously waiting for him, for he sat in his leather-bound chair, glowering darkly. Oscar gave his father the bow he was due.

"You wanted to see me, Your Grace?"

The duke snapped open his watch, no doubt placed on his desk like a prop in a badly written play. "I wanted to see you ten minutes ago, Hathwaite."

His father never called him by his Christian name, and Oscar never called the man with whom he shared lineage Father. They treated each other like acquaintances—who didn't much like one another.

Edgar Wilkinson, the seventh Duke of Kingston, eyed his son with open disdain. "You need a better valet," he said finally.

Oscar tried not to let his scathing tone lower him, but it was a difficult task. Despite everything, a sick and weak part of him still strove to please this man. He hated that most of all.

"Take a seat."

Oscar eyed the uncomfortable and rather small chair indicated by his father and stifled a grimace. He longed to lounge in it insolently, to put on an air of boredom, but he simply lacked the courage to do so. He sat, back straight, shoes planted firmly and flatly on the floor in front of him and awaited his father's pronouncement.

"The wedding is set for May the tenth. It should be the event that launches the Season. Your fiancée is having a birthday celebration in September and we will formally announce the engagement then."

Oscar felt his stomach give yet another sickening twist. He had been right about this meeting, so he didn't know why it should shock him so much to hear those words.

"Have you informed Elsie, Your Grace?" It was such a small victory, to see how calling his future wife by her nickname irked his father.

The duke wrinkled his nose in distaste. "Lord Huntington shall be informed today. I just sent a missive to him and expect an answer will be forthcoming. In the meantime, I wish you would cease calling Miss Elizabeth that ridiculously common name and use her proper Christian name."

"Yes, sir."

The duke took a deep breath, his nostrils flaring as if he'd just picked up a nasty scent. "I have a request to make of you."

That was, perhaps, the oddest thing his father had ever said to him. His father didn't make requests, he made demands. He ordered, he did not ask. "I would request that you name your first born son Henry." His voice was like steel, but his eyes flickered with enough emotion that he almost looked vulnerable for the briefest moments.

Oscar couldn't help himself. He laughed. The sound burst from his throat before his brain could stop it. And then he did something much worse. Using the disdainful tone he'd learned so well from his sire, he said, "You have no right to make such a request."

"No right?" the duke asked, with menacing softness. "I have every right. My son will not have died in vain."

"Sons. You had two sons."

The duke's face turned livid. "You are dismissed," he bit out.

Even though Oscar was shaking, he stood and walked out of the room without another word, feeling as if he'd finally won a victory over the old duke. He just wished the victory tasted sweeter.

Chapter 4

Elsie meant to avoid the ballroom, for she sensed the man was uneasy with her presence. But when she found herself wandering the main floor and spied that narrow strip of light beneath the ballroom door, she simply couldn't resist spying to see what Alexander was doing.

Monsieur Desmarais had demanded complete privacy, claiming that he could not work with disruptions and wanted to surprise Miss Elizabeth with the final creation. Elsie had been slightly amused, knowing precisely why no one was allowed into the room, but she remained silent. There was something about his assistant, a compelling combination of strength and vulnerability that made her want to protect him.

It had been two nights since she'd discovered Monsieur's secret. She found it was beyond her control not to peek into the room, knowing Alexander was hard at work on her mural. Besides, she liked the company, such as it was, in these lonely, dark hours when the rest of the world lay asleep. Her bare feet were soundless as she walked across the cool marble, and she was about to reach for the door when an odd sound stopped her cold. Her entire body became attuned to a noise coming from within the ballroom that sounded painfully familiar.

Silently, she opened the door, hardly daring to breathe, until she could better hear the heartrending sound of a man's despair. Alexander stood, one arm straight against the mural wall, one hand dangling, fisted tightly, by his side, his head bent, his body shaking. He was weeping.

She could not count how many times she had heard such a sound coming from her father's room, the quiet agony of a man whose heart was breaking but who was trying desperately not to let anyone know.

In a moment, Elsie was by his side, looking helplessly up at him as he stared with anguish at the wall. "Alexander, what is it?"

He startled, as if he hadn't sensed her there, then rubbed his face against his sleeve in one quick motion.

"Are you all right? Is there something I can get for you? Monsieur?"

He shook his head, his cheeks suddenly ruddy with embarrassment or perhaps anger that she'd discovered him in his weakness. He didn't look at her, still stared at the wall, and finally, Elsie followed his gaze and gasped.

"Oh," she breathed, taking in what he'd drawn in fine detail. Two little boys climbed up the rock, the smaller one holding out a sturdy hand to help up the bigger lad. It was the expressions that were so moving; that little boy's eagerness tinged with hero-worship, the older one's accepting help he probably didn't need. It was there, in a few finely executed lines of charcoal, living, breathing boys that she could almost hear; she could almost picture the water glistening on their skinny little bodies.

"My goodness," she said, staring in disbelief at the drawing. She knew it would be even more magnificent when he painted the scene. It was almost painfully beautiful. No wonder it brought him to tears, for there was something about those boys that tore at the heart, some intangible quality she couldn't define. "They're beautiful, Alexander."

He looked at her sharply, then almost as quickly looked back to the mural with a strange intensity. Elsie stared at his profile, and realized she was in the presence of a masculine beauty she'd never before seen. His jaw was well-defined, sharp and finely sculpted, his nose aristocratic, his mouth almost too perfect, as if an unattainable ideal manufactured by an artist. His cheeks, still slightly damp from his tears, were ruddy, and his eyes, which stared so intently at the wall in front of him, were framed by a strong brow and shadowed by thick, straight lashes.

"I shall never tell your secret," she said fervently, wanting to put an end to some of his torture. "And I'll tell you why. First, I made a promise to you, one that I will honor. Second, if I did reveal your secret, my beautiful mural would never be finished."

He seemed to relax, but still made no move to continue working. Always when she spoke to him directly, he seemed to tense, as if her words were battering him and he was bracing himself for the blows.

Elsie suspected she made him nervous, that he was not used to working in front of clients.

"Do you mind my visits? I imagine it gets rather lonely here working by yourself. Do you wish me to leave? I'd quite understand if you did."

His finely carved mouth moved slightly, almost as if he were trying not to smile. And he shook his head.

"Good then. I shan't bother you any more. I'll just read and, well"—she said impishly—"does my talking bother you? I would like to talk to you." She walked over to her couch and sat upon it in a lady-like pose, part of her knowing she should leave. "Would you like to know why I wander about the manor house at night like some manner of ghost?"

He inclined his head, which Elsie took as an affirmative. "I had a twin sister and she died in her sleep. *In my bed*," she said with dramatic emphasis, for she didn't want his pity. "Ever since then, I simply cannot bear to sleep in a bed. I drive the poor staff here quite crazy, for I seem to fall asleep in the most unlikely places."

Alexander listened as the girl talked about her sister, about their adventures, and found himself becoming enchanted by her. She shouldn't be here, in this room, with him, wearing her very virginal nightclothes. She shouldn't stand so close to him, close enough that he could smell her sweet scent. She seemed so utterly unaware that she should not be alone with a strange man in the middle of the night. How could a girl be so completely innocent? Or was she one of those women who thought him a boy because he could not speak, someone without a man's needs or thoughts or lust?

She certainly wasn't dressed seductively in that nightgown and robe that covered her from beneath her chin to her toes. But he couldn't stop his thoughts from moving in a carnal direction. She might be innocent, but there was a woman with a woman's curves hiding beneath that silly nightdress and he couldn't stop his mind from imagining what she looked like, what she would feel like.

It had been a long time since he'd been with a woman and she'd been far too tempting, standing next to him, looking up at him in concern as he shed his shameful tears.

What a fool he was, crying all these years later, crying for the boy he'd been, for the life he'd had. Those two boys were long dead, that life long gone, but it still hurt like hell when he allowed himself to think of it. What had possessed him to paint the figures, he did not know. He only knew he had to. It wasn't a choice. He *had* to. Sometimes it happened like that. He'd be drawing or painting and stand back and see something he wasn't even aware was there. It was magical, when it overcame him, as if someone else were inside him, taking over, creating a beauty he was not even aware he was capable of.

When he'd seen what he had drawn on that rock, he was as moved as Miss Elsie had been. Moved to humiliating tears, it would seem.

Monsieur would be furious, but at the moment, Alexander didn't care. He needed those two boys, their smiling faces, their innocence. He needed to capture that moment, that last bit of happiness. He didn't know why it was so important, he only knew it was.

"Alexander?"

He stiffened, then forced himself to relax, reminding himself that she was one of the few people who didn't care if he never uttered a word. He turned to face her and caught his breath. She should leave. Now. He wasn't certain he'd ever seen anyone more lovely than the girl sitting there with her knees drawn up and her toes peeking beneath that lacy hem. He knew it was foolishness, for he'd been seduced by women wearing filmy nightdresses that left nothing to the imagination. He'd been waylaid by women who threw off their robes, revealing gloriously naked bodies. And yet, nothing had ever affected him the way this girl did, sitting on that couch, arms wrapped around her knees, looking at him as if . . . as if he were normal.

"Would you care for something to eat? I get famished in the nighttime and cook always leaves something for me in the ice box. Are you hungry?"

She was not only lovely, she was *nice.* He nodded, smiling broadly, for no one other than Monsieur had ever asked after him, had ever wondered if he were hungry or cold. Or lonely.

She padded off, her long braid bouncing from side to side like a metronome. He immediately felt her absence, and scowled. He liked working alone but last evening when she'd not appeared, he'd missed her presence. Any dream he'd had of a normal life, of falling in love, having a family and children, had been beaten down over the years. But once in a while, he felt a longing in his heart, a weakness in his soul, that made him dream about a home with a wife and children and happiness. A girl like

Elsie could cruelly make a man long for things he would never have. Which was why he almost hoped she'd get distracted and not return. Ever.

Still, he couldn't stop his smile when she returned with a plate laden with cold chicken and two apples. Two.

God help him.

Elsie startled awake from the breakfast table when a hand touched her arm.

"Miss Elizabeth, there's a terrible row," Mrs. Whitehouse said, looking worried. "In the ballroom. I know the staff has been banned, but I thought I should tell you. And Lord Huntington isn't in the house."

Elsie squeezed her eyes shut and shook her head to awaken herself. She hadn't fallen asleep at the breakfast table in months. "I'll see to it," she said, wiping her face delicately with a napkin to remove any crumbs that might remain.

"It's Monsieur Desmarais, and I think he's yelling at that poor mute boy."

Suddenly, Elsie's heart began slamming in her breast. How dare Monsieur berate Alexander, when that poor man was doing all the artist's work and he was taking all the credit. Elsie smoothed her skirts as she walked, giving her reflection a quick check just to be certain her simple coif was still intact, and marched to the ballroom. Indeed, there was yelling coming from inside the room.

"I do not do the people. You know this is true.

This could ruin me. You have put everything in jeopardy. If you do not remove the boys, I will."

Elsie barged into the room without knocking, her heart beating wildly in her chest as she took in the scene. Monsieur held a wet cloth in his hand and was approaching the mural, hellbent on removing the two boys. Alexander stood stiff, his body shaking with anger or frustration or agony, watching silently as Monsieur stalked with determination toward the wall.

"Monsieur Desmarais," Elsie yelled pleasantly. "My goodness, what is all this hubbub?" She walked up to where Alexander stood, still stiff, breathing hard through flared nostrils. His hands were by his sides, his fists clenched so hard his arms shook.

"Ah, Miss Elsie," the Frenchman said with forced pleasantness. "I am angry with myself, that is all. The eccentric artist in me. I never add the people to my scenes. Never. And I am angry that I have. It is not what you asked for, no? So I remove it immediately."

Alexander's jaw clenched again and again and his hands shook even more. Elsie stepped slightly in front of him and reached back, grasping one of his shaking hands in a desperate attempt to calm him. She could almost feel his agony, his desperation, his impotent rage.

"But you cannot," Elsie said. "The boys are charming. A wonderful addition. I shall be heartbroken if you remove them, Monsieur. In fact, I insist they stay."

She could hear Alexander's breathing calm a bit,

feel his fist relax slightly. She gave his hand one more reassuring squeeze before letting go and approaching the muralist. "Monsieur, they are so charming. I shall have the only original Desmarais mural with children. I adore it, I truly do." She pouted for good effect, and Monsieur let out a long, beleaguered sigh.

"But now everyone will insist I do the same for them. I am known for my landscapes, not portraits."

"The boys are such a small part of the mural, one tiny little bit of whimsy. Please, Monsieur."

He shot Alexander one last dark look, then gave Elsie a courtly bow. "As you wish, Mademoiselle."

Elsie beamed a smile. "Thank you, Monsieur." Then she turned, still smiling and nearly had the breath knocked out of her by the intensity of the look Alexander gave her. She couldn't read it, only knew it affected her on a strangely physical level, as if someone shot a bolt of lightning through her entire body. Her smile faltered slightly as she walked by, stunned by the unsettling feeling.

Behind her, she heard Monsieur Desmarais mutter in French, "You have nearly betrayed me, my boy. Do not do it again." Apparently, Monsieur had forgotten Elsie spoke excellent French.

Chapter 5

For some reason, that night Elsie was shy about entering the ballroom. She opened the door and peeked in, giving a small sigh of relief when she saw Alexander was there hard at work. He turned and lifted his head in greeting when she moved toward the softly glowing lamplight.

"Are you all right?" she asked, moving into the light.

He gave her another of his uncomfortably intense looks, before looking back to the mural. And he did something rather remarkable.

"Thank you."

The words, spoken softly in a clear baritone, seemed to echo in the nearly empty room. He stared at the wall, that familiar tension making his entire body stiff.

"You're welcome," she said, acting as if it was not unusual for a mute person to speak. He gave her a quick look, as if assessing her reaction, and slowly relaxed. "I worried about you all day, after that verbal slashing Monsieur gave you. Are you in terrible trouble?"

"No."

"Well, good, then. May I stay for a while?"

For the first time, he looked at her and grinned, a full smile that lit his beautiful eyes. "You may," he said, still smiling.

"I'm going to a house party next week. Would you like to hear about it?"

He nodded, and Elsie walked back to the couch, her heart singing with unexpected joy. And then, as if he'd never spoken a word, she talked about the upcoming house party she and her father and aunt were planning to attend.

"It's at Stapleford Hall. Have you heard of it?" She didn't wait for an answer, but forged on. "The Wrights are absolutely marvelous and have a rather large and boisterous family. I've often wondered what it would be like to have many brothers and sisters. Of course, I have Mary. Oh, you haven't met Mary, have you? She's a darling. You'll adore her if you can meet her. I suppose you will after the mural is done and Monsieur lifts that ridiculous ban on allowing us into the . . ."

Alexander worked, half listening to Elsie, and knowing he was in the presence of a miracle. And Lord above knew that was a frightening thing, indeed. If she had gasped or gaped or peppered him with questions when he'd spoken, it would have been far better. He would have been angry and humiliated and it would have been a good deal easier to ignore her. But she had only smiled and said "you're welcome" as if the fact that a mute man had spoken was of no consequence whatsoever.

He had finished with his sketch and would start painting the mural's intricate border tomorrow. Monsieur was a genius at mixing paint to the precise colors and consistency necessary and it was one aspect of the mural painting that he insisted on continuing. Alexander was glad to let that particular job go to Desmarais so he could concentrate on the mural itself.

"You begin painting tomorrow?"

She had walked up next to him silently, and stood now looking up at the mural, the soft glow of the lamp bathing her in its light.

"Yes." He could feel her eyes on him, almost as tangible as a touch.

"Do you mind if I watch?"

"I don't mind." He didn't. In fact, if she didn't come, he would miss her. They stood together in silence, as he gathered the courage to ask her a question. He swallowed, trying to dislodge the growing knot in his throat. "Why didn't you react when I spoke?"

She smiled, in that impish way he already recognized as being uniquely hers. "I did. On the inside. I was shouting for joy. Couldn't you tell?"

"No," he said, unable to stop a smile of his own. All these smiles felt so odd on his face.

"Well, I'm brimming with curiosity and I'm confident that some day you'll share your story with me. In the meantime, you may listen to my stories. I imagine when you get tired of hearing about me, you'll tell me yours."

He nodded, feeling his heart swell in the oddest way. What a singular girl she was, he thought.

"One question," she said, holding up one finger, her eyes sparkling with curiosity. No doubt she was simply dying to know why he remained mute for so long. "Does Monsieur know you can speak?"

He could feel his cheeks flush, as if he'd been caught in a great lie. "He does not know and I cannot tell him. It would hurt him, and that is one thing I have vowed never to do."

Her delicate red-gold brows creased. "I don't understand."

"He believes me to be mute, to need him. It would crush him, I think, to know I've kept this secret from him for so long."

"I should think he'd be pleased."

"Perhaps," he said, but he shook his head, struggling to explain to this girl about the delicate balance he had with Monsieur. He needed Monsieur nearly as much as the older man needed him. Alexander knew he could never obtain new clients, solicit work, and negotiate a price. The thought of going into strange homes and talking to people was enough to make him physically ill. He felt far, far more comfortable around strangers now than he had as a child, but he dreaded such confrontations. It was a weakness he had struggled with his entire life. The nightmare of his childhood had eased over the years. He could speak, but it was something he must force, a subtle torture he must sometimes endure to communicate.

The relief that this beautiful girl had accepted his ability to speak with almost no curiosity was nothing short of astounding. If he'd been charmed by her before, now he was completely and unalterably smitten. A completely ridiculous state to find himself in, but there it was.

Every day for a week, she would come into the ballroom and talk—she far more than he. But as each day passed, Alexander became more and more comfortable, until someone listening to the pair of them would have noticed nothing odd about the young painter. He told her about his days traveling around with Monsieur, learning how to paint, the years they'd spent in Rome repairing ancient murals. Alexander hadn't spoken so much since he was a child, and he realized he could not remember such pure happiness as the hours spent with Elsie.

On the fifth day, he'd been working for nearly two hours before he realized Miss Elsie had not made an appearance. Disappointment stabbed at him. He'd become so used to her presence, he found he missed her happy chatter, missed her, in fact. The border along the bottom of the mural, an intricate twining of leaves and vines, was nearly done. Monsieur and he would have to build a scaffold soon so he could continue painting. He stepped back, lamp held in hand, and examined his work, frowning. Working by lamplight was always more difficult than painting in the full light of day, and he constantly made adjustments when he joined Monsieur in the ballroom after his rest. He wanted this mural to be magical for Elsie and for himself.

"Good evening."

As always, she entered the ballroom silently and smiling.

"Good evening," he said, giving her a small bow, which for some reason made her smile broaden.

"I've a surprise for you," she said, skipping over to a dark corner of the room. He could hardly see her, only the faint glow of her white nightdress. She sat, and he heard the sound of a match being struck, and then she was illuminated by a lamp sitting upon a piano that had not been there earlier that day. Music, soft and vibrant enough to fill the large room, hit him like a cool breeze after a sweltering day.

"Chopin," he whispered almost reverently, and had the sudden and rather embarrassing urge to weep. He'd played this piece, Chopin's Nocturne No. 9, in his teenage years, long after he'd joined Monsieur, making music when he could not speak. Oftentimes, he and Monsieur would work in a house where the residents were not at home. Monsieur would let him seek out a piano, for most great homes had one, and he would lose himself in the music for hours at a time.

He still remembered sitting at one such piano and discovering the Chopin nocturne sitting on the music stand, and his joy when he'd heard the music Chopin had written. Alexander had been such a quiet boy, and the piano had allowed him to express himself in a way he never could verbally. It was now two years since he'd touched a piano, because he simply had had no opportunity.

The music, the woman, drew him and he stood and watched her play. She grinned at him when she made a small error, but forged on, giving a competent rendition of the beautiful piece.

"You're quite good," he said, and she laughed.

"I suppose you could do better, then."

"Perhaps."

Elsie lifted her eyebrows in surprise. "Do not tell me that in addition to being a master painter you also play the piano."

"A bit."

Elsie moved over and made a gesture for him to sit next to her. He hesitated only a moment before taking a seat, giving her that shy smile she found so completely charming. If Elsie were honest, she could admit she found everything about Alexander charming.

"No one will hear?" he asked uncertainly.

"The ballroom is an addition and quite separate from my father's suite. He won't hear a thing."

He placed his hands, strong and only slightly paint-stained, on the keys almost reverently. "I haven't played in years."

And then he began, and Elsie felt her skin prickle with overwhelming emotion, as if what she was hearing was so beautiful it could not be contained. She played well. He played masterfully.

She looked at this man next to her and knew, deep inside, that he was something special, something undiscovered and far, far more than a muralist's assistant. She'd already noticed he spoke like an educated man, his rich baritone sounding almost aristocratic. His manners were impeccable. And she could not overlook his raw beauty, his quiet strength. In Elsie's world, men were not kind or passionate, or beautiful. They were polite and, frankly, quite boring. Who was he? Where did he come from?

As he played, he grew more confident, and lost himself entirely in the piece, his eyes closed, his strong hands creating nuances she was not capable of. When he finished, she clapped softly, but with exuberance.

"Marvelous. Oh, that was lovely. I shall never play that piece again," she gushed, and he looked down at the keys and smiled.

"I'm out of practice," he said.

"Really, Alexander, you cannot be modest when you play like that." She stared at him, this puzzle next to her. "Who are you? You're more than you seem, aren't you?"

His smile slowly disappeared. "I am Monsieur's assistant. Nothing more." And he stood abruptly. "I must get back to work."

Elsie reached out and grabbed his arm, touching his sleeve but feeling the heat of his skin beneath the well-worn cotton. "I'm sorry. Please. Play something else." His arm was rigid beneath her hand, and he closed his eyes as if he were in pain as he drew his arm slowly out of her grasp. "Alexander, I'm sorry. I've no right to question you or demand anything of you. Except perhaps to play for me again."

He looked at her almost unwillingly, that handsome face hard, his expression implacable. "I don't think you should continue coming here at night," he said. "I have work to do and you are nothing but a distraction to me. Besides that, it is highly improper.

Surely you understand that as an unmarried woman you should not be here, alone, with a man."

"Oh. I suppose not. I just . . . I never . . ." Elsie felt unshed tears stinging her eyes. He'd just given her the harshest set down she'd had in years.

"You never what? Considered me a man? Because I am a servant? Or because I cannot speak in front of people."

Elsie shook her head. "No. I just thought you were nice." *And I'm so very, very lonely.* She twisted her hands in her nightdress, suddenly realizing how terribly improper it was to be alone with any man in only her nightclothes.

He let out a sigh, his anger deflating, and he sat at the edge of the piano bench staring at the keys again. "I was raised in an affluent family, but my affliction caused my father to abandon me to an asylum when I was ten years old. I was there only a short time when one of the doctors helped me to escape and introduced me to Monsieur. That is my story. That is all you need to know."

"I'm sorry. You don't need to tell me anything. It's really none of my business." She sat there feeling simply awful, and finally asked, "Do you still want me to leave?"

Another sigh. "No." But it sounded most begrudging.

"I don't think of you as a servant. I think you are wonderful," she said, daring a quick look at him. "But you are right, it is highly improper and for that reason, I won't tell if you don't."

"Another secret, then?" His mouth quirked as if he were trying not to smile.

She nodded. "Can I tell you something? A confession? I don't want to go to that house party, because I shall miss our visits and I will think of you working in here all alone."

His expression grew pensive. "You shouldn't think of me at all. Nor should I, you."

"But do you?" Elsie held her breath, knowing she had crossed a line that should never have been crossed. She knew she thought about Alexander far too much, she knew she shouldn't visit him each night. She knew she shouldn't touch him or even talk to him, but these nighttime visits were all she looked forward to.

Alexander lowered his head as if in defeat. "I do. Far more than is proper."

"Are you so very proper, then?" she asked with a teasing lilt.

"I must be," he said forcefully. "You must be."

"Why?" Elsie breathed, even though she knew why. She'd never in her life felt so strange, so alive when with a man. She had never before kissed a man, never wanted to, truth be told. But she found herself staring at his mouth and wondering what it would feel like to press her lips against his. Just that thought made her stomach twist, made her want something she didn't understand.

"Miss Elsie, you should go." His hands gripped his thighs so hard, she could see the indents of his fingers in his trousers.

"Do you know Badinerie by Bach?" Elsie looked at him cautiously and thought she detected the smallest of smiles. "It's a duet."

"Yes, I know. I've never had the opportunity to play a duet," he said.

"Here is your chance."

His expression was one of disbelief. "Have you any idea the sort of danger you are courting, Miss Elsie?"

She looked him straight in the eye. "Duets are not dangerous. Now, get up so I can find the music. It's in the bench."

He got up with an air of impatience, and waited until she found the correct sheet music.

"Here it is," she said unnecessarily. "Now sit and play with me. Please."

He sat as far from her as possible and Elsie beamed a smile at him, which apparently had no effect on his mood for he simply stared at her darkly. Nodding her head, she began to play, and he played his part without hesitation. It was a short piece, and lively, and when they were done, Elsie clapped.

"Well done," she said. "Now, how dangerous was . . ." She looked at him and felt a sudden rush of heat, of desire, that she'd never felt before in her life ". . . that." Elsie swallowed, her eyes drifting down to his mouth, her breath coming out in shallow spurts. *Kiss me. Please, kiss me.*

Never before had a man looked at her like this, as if he were angry and dangerous and untamed.

"I think. You. Should. Leave," he said softly.

Elsie swallowed, then blinked, feeling as if she was coming out of a trance. "Until tomorrow, then," she said, forcing a politeness, a distance, she didn't feel. What she wanted was to throw herself into his arms, but she feared if she did, he would push her away, and that would be far too humiliating to bear.

Alexander waited until the door clicked shut before muttering a vile curse. That girl could tempt a saint, he thought, rubbing his hands through his hair. He didn't know what the hell he was going to do, because God only knew he wasn't a saint.

He'd thought she might be frightened by his desire, but curse him, she welcomed it. Elsie was no child, but he had a feeling she was experiencing a woman's desire for the first time, an intoxicating and perilous mix. He could hardly think of her without becoming aroused. The last thing he needed was a nightly concert sitting next to her soft body with only two thin layers of cotton between her and his hands. When she touched his arm, it took strength he didn't know he had not to drag her into his arms and kiss her and release some of the awful tension that had been building since the day she walked into the ballroom.

"Please, God, give me strength," he whispered fervently. Nothing good could come from kissing her, from allowing himself to feel anything for her. He feared it was already too late for his heart, but he'd be damned if he allowed himself to touch her with his body. The best thing for both of them was to push her away, tell her to leave him alone. He couldn't risk a scandal and he couldn't bear to hurt her.

And he knew he could never have her, just as he knew that the life he was supposed to have had was gone forever. The day his father put him in that asylum and walked away without looking back, without an ounce of sadness or regret, was the day he knew that other life was over.

Elsie walked quietly and determinedly to the piano and lit the lamp, completely ignoring the man who painted so diligently. She knew, knew, knew she shouldn't be here. She knew she wanted something she could never have. And yet, when nighttime came again, she found herself unable to keep away, as if Alexander was a drug, the only cure to her terrible loneliness. All day she thought of him, how his eyes looked when he stared at her in that intense way of his. How his hair curled, unruly and unkempt, onto his brow, how his firm lips always seemed to be fighting a smile. She felt truly alive for the first time in her life and knew she was in the throes of an infatuation she didn't even want to try to stop.

When she walked to the piano, she didn't look at him, but she felt his eyes on her. Oh, she loved this feeling of knowing a man looked at her with something other than bland disinterest. It was intoxicating, wonderful, exhilarating and so completely welcome. She began playing Chopin's Étude "Winter Wind" quite badly. She played and watched Alexander cringe over and over again. This piece was far beyond her skills, and yet she doggedly forged ahead, murdering the piece and no doubt making Chopin roll in his grave, poor man. Finally, blessedly for both of them, she came to the end and looked up, laughing silently as he continued to ignore her.

"How was that? I've been working ever so hard on

those runs and I think I'm finally getting them as dear Mr. Chopin wrote them."

Alexander's shoulders shook, and Elsie wasn't quite sure whether he cried or laughed.

"Oh, surely it could not have been bad enough to make you cry," she called. She'd never been one to flirt, but found she had quite a talent for it—at least when it came to Alexander. "Please, Alexander," she said softly. "Play it for me."

He turned and stared at her a long moment before letting out a sigh and putting down his brush and pallet. "One song," he said firmly. "As it is, this mural may not be completed for your birthday."

"You can catch up the next few days when I am gone." She moved off the bench and allowed him the seat. "Have you ever played this?"

"Not well."

"But better than I?"

He gave her one of his half smiles. "Perhaps." He did play the piece nicely, but Elsie could tell he needed practice.

"Bah," he said when he'd finished. "This piece is beyond my skills."

"I expect perfection when I return."

"How long will you be gone?" he asked with what seemed to her like forced nonchalance. He stared at the piano keys, lightly running his fingers over them so that they produced nothing more than muted thumps instead of notes.

"Three days. And I'll miss you, too," she said, teasingly.

His answer was a frown.

"You wound me, sir."

He gave her a quick, angry look. "Please stop, Miss Elsie. I am not one of the boys you flirt with at balls. I think you do not know how cruel you are."

Elsie felt her cheeks burn in mortification. "No, no," she said, rejecting his conclusion. "I'm sorry. I . . . I'm awful at flirting. I've had little practice, you see, and I don't know what I'm doing."

"You shouldn't even speak to me. And certainly you should not flirt. To do so is . . ."

"Is what?"

His nostrils flared slightly and she could tell he was angry. "It's beneath you. There have been other women who wanted me. Who had me. I know I'm a novelty of sorts. I *know* this. And I haven't been above taking what they freely offered. I'm not a fool. I know what you are doing."

Elsie let out a sad laugh. "Then could you please tell me because I don't know. I only know that I cannot stop thinking about you, that the only thing I look forward to is nighttime so that I be with you."

He looked at her, searching her face for mendacity, then apparently finding none, let out a weary sigh. "Go to your party, Elsie. And when you come back, leave me alone."

"Why?"

"Because you tempt me beyond reason," he said harshly. "Surely you know that. You cannot be so innocent. You are not a child."

She looked ridiculously pleased, and Alexander let out a groan of frustration. "You want to kiss me," she said, rather too happily.

"Yes, I want to kiss you. I'm a man and you are a

beautiful girl sitting next to me night after night in her bedclothes." He ended on an exasperated note.

"I give you permission."

He pressed his fingers to his temples and muttered a prayer. "Have you not heard a single word I've said, girl?"

"You said you wanted to kiss me." She sat on the bench and smiled up at him.

"What are you doing to me?" he asked, looking at her almost beseechingly. As she watched, desire and something like resignation flickered in his gaze. And then in one quick, desperate motion, he grabbed her upper arms and brought her against him, their lips only a breath away. "This is a mistake. A mistake," he said fiercely, giving her a small shake.

"No. It's not." And she pulled him to her, until their lips touched and she thought she'd die of pure happiness. She was kissing him, Alexander, and it was wonderful and freeing. At first, he resisted, even as his lips pressed against hers, even as she let out a sigh. Then, as if something broke or snapped, he moaned and moved his mouth against hers in a way that was so incredibly carnal and unexpected, she nearly swooned. It was as if this kiss turned her entire body to a strange liquid that pooled high between her legs in a delicious sensation that was purely wonderful. Never would she have dreamed that a single kiss could make her feel so. It was stunning.

He pulled away, looking anguished. "Oh, God," he said, his hands clutching her upper arms convulsively. "I'm done for now." And then he brought his mouth against her jaw, her neck, and Elsie learned the bliss of a man's rough beard against a woman's delicate skin. She let out sounds she wasn't even aware she was capable of, and felt sensations she didn't know existed. It was insane, but she wanted him to touch her—everywhere, anywhere. He brought his mouth against hers again, and placed one hand gently on her chin, his thumb on her lower lip. Pulling, he opened her mouth and he kissed her, touching his tongue against hers, creating so much heat between her legs, she thought she might explode. She not only welcomed him, she moved her own tongue against his, exploring the wonderful sensations such a carnal action created. A low sound came from deep within him as they deepened the kiss, as her hands moved to the back of his head and kneaded through his thick hair.

"Oh, God, Elsie," he said, moving his hands along her sides, with nothing to stop the heat of him except two thin layers of cotton.

"Please," she whispered, not even knowing why, only knowing that her body ached for him to touch her. She felt his hand on one breast, a thumb moving across a taut nipple, and couldn't stop the sound of pure pleasure that came from her parted lips. Nothing could have prepared her for the intense sensations his touch invoked. His breathing was harsh as he cupped her breast, as he dipped his head and kissed her aching nipple through the layers of her nightclothes. He let out a strange sound, almost a moan of pain, as he stopped and laid his head against her breast.

Then he exploded off the bench, leaving her nearly toppling over on to the floor without his support. He strode over to the mural and picked up his brush, and stood there staring blindly at the painting. She stayed on the bench, her hands bracing herself, her breath hard, her eyes glazed with desire, her body aching for more. She finally knew what it was like to feel a man's touch, to ache for more.

"Oh," she said, small and nearly silent. She understood, now she finally comprehended what he'd been trying to say, why a kiss could be the cruelest of all fates. It *had* been a mistake, a terrible one. For now Elsie knew passion, and knew that she would likely never have it in her married life. She never should have kissed this beautiful man. He had warned her, practically begged her to leave him alone. He'd been right, right, right.

For Elsie had a terrible feeling she was falling in love with him, with this silent man whom she could never have.

Chapter 6

"What is wrong with you, niece?" Aunt Diane asked. "You've done nothing but mope around ever since we arrived."

Elsie stared out at the expansive lawn where many of the Wrights' guests were gathered for a game of croquet, a game Elsie had just learned to play and had previously found to be rather delightful. But Lord Hathwaite was playing and she simply couldn't bring herself to join him.

This was the extent of their conversation in the first two days Elsie had been at the house party.

"So good to see you, Lord Hathwaite."

"Yes. And good to see you."

"We received your father's missive about the wedding." This said simply to garner some reaction.

"Indeed."

She wanted to bash him over the head with his mallet just to see if he'd react to that. *Indeed.*

"Is this to be my future, Aunt? Do you see anyone laughing or enjoying life?" Of course, at that very moment, one of the female guests let out a rather unseemly laugh, which only made Elsie scowl more.

"Your father told me about the wedding date," her aunt said knowingly.

Elsie stared mulishly at Lord Hathwaite, knowing that her future was set in stone before her and also knowing there was nothing she could do about it. At least her overbearing future father-in-law was not at the party. She was terrified of him and he knew and probably expected it. She half suspected Lord Hathwaite was terrified of the old duke, as well.

She knew she was being difficult, but it was as if she'd awakened after a long sleep only to realize her entire life had passed her by. Though she hadn't looked forward to her marriage, she'd never actually dreaded it. And now she did.

Because of one—or perhaps two—kisses.

If only Lord Hathwaite had shown even the smallest interest in kissing her . . . or talking to her or looking at her or walking with her. She supposed when you knew who you were going to marry since the time you could think, the idea of pursuit never entered one's head. Perhaps if she pursued him, it might be fun.

With determination, she said, "I'll go play."

When she reached the group, she called out, "Can you have one more player?" They agreed and she took up the ugly yellow mallet that was left. "You'll have to refresh my memory as I've only played once. Lord Hathwaite, perhaps you can be my mentor."

He looked slightly put out, but maybe Elsie, in her contrary state, was simply imagining things.

"Of course," he said, giving her a graceful bow. Ever proper, ever polite.

She looked up at him in what she imagined was a coquettish manner. "How does one hold the mallet?" she asked, purposely holding it wrong.

"That's fine," he said, distracted. "Hey, good shot, Whitmoore." Then he looked back at her. "You'll be fine. It's a simple enough game and it doesn't matter who wins, after all, does it?"

And off he went. Elsie stared after him, then gave her aunt a pointed look, as if to say: See what I mean? Aunt simply laughed and waved her hand at her niece as if all was well in the world, which it was. Her niece would be a duchess some day. What could possibly be wrong with that?

"You look particularly glum, Hath," Lord Whitmoore said to his old school chum. "And your father isn't even here."

"But he hovers like a black specter in my life," Oscar said, pulling back a long drink of fine French brandy. He stared at the rich, amber liquid, swirled it about, then placed it firmly on the mantel. It wouldn't do to get drunk before lunch. "He's set the wedding date."

"Ah," Whitmoore said. He stood by a large bank of windows overlooking the Stapleford gardens where several young ladies were examining the Wrights' prize-winning roses. Among them was the lovely Miss Elizabeth. "She's grown into a beauty. That's some luck there."

Oscar grunted. "I suppose."

Whitmoore laughed. "I still wouldn't trade places with you for a harem of beautiful women."

"Thank you for your encouraging words," Oscar said dryly.

"Hell, Hath, we all know what a miserable codger your father is. And we probably don't know the half of it. But this marriage is your escape. You can move to your town house in London and never speak to him again until he's on his deathbed. You can start the life of idleness and debauchery you've always wanted to lead."

Oscar smiled grimly. "I was thinking of going to Northumberland. Or Scotland. But I fear his tentacles will find me no matter where I go."

Whitmoore looked suitably shocked. "You cannot drag a new bride to Northumberland. She'd leave you in a day."

Oscar actually looked happy for a moment. "Precisely."

"It's not as if she's a shrew. She seems rather nice to me," Whitmoore said with clear puzzlement.

"Then you marry her."

"Too late for that, you know."

"Nothing is more disgusting than a happily married man."

Whitmoore grinned. "You might be happy, too, if you'd put your mind to it." He peered out the window again. "She seems to get on with my Agnes. We could have dinners together and attend the opera in Town."

"And raise our heir and a spare together," Oscar said bitterly. He hated this, hated feeling sour and sad and angry all the time. He'd hated his life, every single minute of it, except for the times at school and those glorious two weeks that single summer. He felt as if he were suffocating, as if something heavy was pressing down on him, making it impossible to breathe. Why did his brothers have to die. Why?

And then Oscar heard his father's voice and felt his body convulse.

"Hell, Hath, what's he doing here? Sorry, old chap," Whitmoore said with real concern.

God, he wanted to cry. Instead, he straightened and schooled his features to betray no emotion as he watched his father walk into the room.

"Drinking already? Isn't it a bit early for that, Hathwaite? Is this your bad influence, Whitmoore?" he boomed.

"No, sir. I mean, yes, Your Grace. In fact, that is mine," he said, indicating the abandoned drink on the mantel. Whitmoore, the most confident of men, lost all poise in the face of the Duke of Kingston.

"And the one in your hand?"

"They're both mine," he said weakly. "Good day, sir." And he was gone before Oscar could blink, not that he blamed his friend.

"Still need your friends to lie for you, I see."

"The drink is mine, Your Grace."

Kingston ignored his son's comment. "Why aren't you out in the garden with your intended? I've heard you're ignoring her completely."

"No, sir."

"There have been rumors about you. Ugly ones. The sooner you are married, the better."

Oscar gave his father a look of complete confusion. He never did anything or went anywhere. How could there possibly be rumors about him? "I don't understand, sir."

His father looked at him with the purest disgust. "Is there a reason you don't wish to spend time with your intended? A reason you haven't shared with me?"

Oscar thought back on every moment he'd spent in the company of Elizabeth and could not recall one thing that would cause his father distress. He had not been attentive, that was true, but neither had he ever put them in a compromising position. He'd never even kissed her cheek.

"No, sir. We played croquet yesterday, as a matter of fact. She's quite good. Rather a vicious player," he said, with a small note of appreciation. In fact, her aggressive play was one of the most memorable times he'd spent with her, giving him a small glimpse into a woman who might not be a complete timid mouse.

"I never hear of any escapades about you and females." The words were innocuous enough, but his father's tone was incongruous, as if this were some sort of strange interrogation.

"That is because you forbid it."

His father threw back his head and laughed, but it was an ugly, evil sound. "Good God, Hathwaite, you must be the only son in the kingdom who has obeyed that particular edict. Unless there is something else keeping you from females."

Oscar stared at his father in disbelief as it finally occurred to him what the duke was suggesting—that he didn't like women, but preferred men. "Rest assured, Your Grace, I greatly enjoy the company of women," Oscar said, feeling his temper rise. "It is only my restrictive and oppressive life that has made any debauchery quite impossible. In addition, I am a Christian man and an honorable one."

"It doesn't matter whether you are or not or whether you enjoy women or not. Just know that you will be married and you will produce an heir. I, too, am a man of honor and will obey the agreement I set down with Lord Huntington. Nothing will prevent your marriage. Nothing."

The duke turned on his heel, leaving Oscar behind seething with impotent rage. By God, when the old man died he'd dance on his grave and not care who saw him.

Elsie, of course, was completely unaware of the tension and drama between Oscar and his father, and picked an unfortunate time to request her first kiss from the man she would one day marry.

After dinner, Oscar, looking even more tense than usual, requested that she join him for a walk in the garden. Although he'd asked politely, there was no mistaking him for a man who was doing this voluntarily, something that was confirmed when she saw his father give his son a subtle and curiously arrogant nod of approval.

They walked in silence for a time, an uncomfortable, tense silence, until Elsie had to talk. "It's a lovely night, is it not?"

"Yes, it is."

She looked up at his profile and acknowledged dispassionately that he was handsome. "Is your mother expected tomorrow?"

"I have no idea."

Beneath her hand, she could feel his arm flex until it was almost like holding onto an oak pole. "Lord Hathwaite, are you angry with me?"

He stopped suddenly, his jaw flexing, which for some reason reminded her painfully of Alexander. "No. I apologize. I'm not good company this evening. Perhaps we should go back inside."

"Perhaps, instead, we should talk about why this marriage of ours is as unwanted by you as it is for me."

He looked at her with complete surprise. "I beg your pardon."

"If I'm wrong, please tell me. I shall beg forgiveness."

"You are not wrong," he said, sounding rather miserable. "But please, do not take it personally."

Elsie laughed, and was happy to finally see a real smile on his handsome face. "How else am I to take it?" Then she waved her hand at him when he began to explain. "Please, do not apologize. We hardly know each other and yet we are expected to marry in a matter of months. I'm quite content with my life right now. I have a little sister, if you remember, and I shall miss her terribly when I'm married."

They continued on with their walk, more relaxed.

"And you? Why do you not want to marry?" Elsie asked. Even though she was not looking forward to their union, she had to admit she was slightly unsettled knowing that he wasn't either.

"I feel like a cad."

"Please don't," Elsie said, giving his arm a squeeze. "We are simply pawns, you and I. I think that is part of it, is it not?"

"Yes. That's it precisely. When I was younger, I wondered if I could breathe without my father's permission. And now I am a man and he still maintains a stranglehold on my life. Sometimes I wish . . ." He stopped, bending his head as if the ground would offer up an answer.

"You wish?" Elsie urged.

"I wish I was not the Marquess of Hathwaite. I wish I could do as I pleased in life."

Elsie laughed. "I imagine there is no one in Christendom who has not made that wish."

He looked at her strangely a moment, as if seeing her for the first time. "Have you wished it?"

"Of course. While there is a certain amount of comfort in knowing I shall marry into a good family, a part of me wishes it were my choice."

"Should I feel insulted?" he asked with a rare smile.

"No more than I." They continued walking side-by-side, no longer arm-in-arm, as if by unspoken agreement. "I suppose it has been difficult for you. Your father is a bit . . ."

"Overbearing?"

Elsie smiled guiltily. "A bit."

"I'm afraid it's much more than that. He's even demanded that our first son be named Henry. Can you fathom it?"

"He's naming our children?" Elsie said, aghast. "Goodness."

"Hardly good," Lord Hathwaite said dryly.

They walked until the shadows grew long, stopping to admire a pretty arbor completely covered with ivy. That arbor, its leaves, reminded her of her mural, which reminded her of Alexander. She missed him and felt a frisson of happiness at the thought of returning home on the morrow and seeing him again.

Yes, that kiss had been a mistake, but Alexander was her friend. Certainly they could remain friends.

"Have you ever been in love?" Elsie asked, then added, "Don't worry, I am not looking for a declaration."

He smiled, and again Elsie was struck by how handsome he was. "No. I have not."

"I imagine you have kissed a girl, though."

His smile remained. "Yes, indeed I have."

"Then I suppose you wouldn't have any objection to kissing your intended?" Part of her wanted to erase the memory of Alexander's kiss, to prove that any kiss would send her head spinning and set her body afire.

He looked momentarily embarrassed but recovered nicely enough. "It would be my pleasure," he said gallantly, then leaned forward, stopping abruptly, almost angrily. "Have you spoken to my father?" he demanded.

Elsie stepped back, startled by his sudden fierceness. "Do you mean privately?"

"Yes, that's exactly what I mean."

"Do I look as if I've been browbeaten by anyone other than you today?" she asked, raising one eyebrow.

Lord Hathwaite let out a small sigh, his anger disappearing as quickly as it had come. She hadn't been aware of his temper until that moment. "I do apologize. My father has a way of getting beneath my skin and festering there." He shoved his hands in his pockets, which made him look rather like a petulant boy. Elsie stood beneath the arbor, wishing she were back in the Wrights' home with the others. Her fiancé was such a gloomy sort.

"Shall we go back?" she asked, after what seemed like an interminably long time. She'd never understood some women's fascination with quiet, brooding men. Quiet was fine, she thought, thinking of Alexander, but brooding *and* quiet was simply tedious.

The first day without Elsie was blissfully quiet. Alexander got an enormous amount of work done and he could almost convince himself that he was glad she was gone. And then, the second night, he gave in and sat at the piano, not playing, but remembering her soft, warm body, the way she'd been so responsive, her smell, her sounds. He was filled with a sharp pang of loss. The loneliness of his days and all the days to come covered him like a shroud.

He missed her. He missed having someone to talk to, who would not judge, who would laugh at his humor such as it was, who would look at him without pity. Even Monsieur, for all his kindness, thought of Alexander as someone to pity. And he wanted things, desperately so, that he could never have. He wanted to love her, be in love with her, wake up next to her every day of his life. It could never be. He was unable to give her the life she deserved, for he was only half a man, one who humiliated himself in public even now.

He touched the middle C lightly, smiling at the sound. He tried not to think of his past, but for the first time in years, he felt its loss. First the lake and the boys, and now Elsie making him feel for a few days as if he could jump up and touch the moon. The fall was so, so far.

When Elsie returned, she would not find him, for he'd already told Monsieur he would work only during the daytime. It was critical to the mural, he'd told his master, that he be able to paint in daylight anyway, even though the painting had not suffered from working in lamplight. Monsieur's ban had been obeyed by everyone in the household, including Elsie. She had enough honor, he knew, that she would never put Monsieur in danger of discovery.

He knew when she returned, for he heard the carriage's arrival, and heard her voice through the door. That his entire body felt her presence with such intensity only validated his conviction that they must stay apart. *Nothing good can come of seeing her*, he told himself again and again. His heart, good God, his heart hurt so damned much.

That night as he lay in bed in the small cottage he and Monsieur shared, he pictured her entering the ballroom and finding it empty. He knew she would be disappointed and it took all his resolve not to go, not to wait for her. He could tell himself he could not touch her, that it was wrong, but he knew if they were together again he would not be able to resist.

He ached for her, his heart, his body, but he spent the night staring at the ceiling, listening to Monsieur snoring in the next room.

Chapter 7

Elsie walked into the ballroom on the third night after her return from the Wrights' house party, allowing her heart to hope that Alexander would be there. Instead she felt a now-familiar pang of disappointment. No, it was more than that. It was pain, raw, physical pain.

It didn't matter that he was merely an artist's assistant. He had become something more to her and to have him purposely avoid her was—unendurable. She needed to see him, to explain how sorry she was that she had allowed that kiss. It was wrong of her, wrong of them, even if it had been the most wonderful thing that had ever happened to her. What she'd thought had been a beautiful kiss she now remembered with a bit of shame. Engaged girls did not wander about their houses in the night and kiss men who were not their intended. She should not have allowed it, should not have encouraged it. It could never be more than a dalliance, a spoiled girl's infatuation with a man she could never have. Thought of like that, she was completely in the wrong.

Still, no matter how she chastised herself for her foolishness, she pined around the house, hovering outside the ballroom door just on the hope she might glimpse him. And he, no doubt, was simply relieved that the house's naughty little heiress had finally left him alone. Even as she tortured herself with such thoughts, she knew, deep down, that Alexander didn't think of her so.

She wished they could go back to how they'd been, simply two lonely souls finding friendship. But that kiss, the one she'd so fervently wanted, had been such a terrible mistake. Why her heart should feel so empty, she didn't know. Certainly, she wasn't in love with Alexander. That was impossible. But she knew she missed him, knew the thought of never spending an evening talking and laughing with him left her feeling hollow and more than a little wretched.

She sat at the piano and tapped at a single note, sighing out loud, sounding very much like what she was: a young woman in the throes of her first infatuation. She began to play a song that captured the grief in her heart, another Chopin piece that never failed to make her throat close on tears even when she was not already feeling sad.

As she played the *Tristesse*, she closed her eyes, letting the music flow from her fingers, losing herself, until she realized she was crying. Abruptly, angrily, she stopped and dashed away the tears.

"That was beautiful. Chopin would be proud."

She gasped, and smiled, seeing Alexander standing at the entrance of the closest French door.

"I don't know why I'm playing such a sad song," she said. It was so clearly a lie, she let out a watery laugh. She'd been looking at him, but turned to stare blindly at the piano keys. "Why have you stayed away, Alexander?"

"I think you know," he said, his voice low. How she'd missed the sound of his voice. "I shouldn't be here now."

Elsie twisted her hands in her lap and smiled uncertainly at him. "I'm glad you are here, for I need to apologize to you. I have been putting you in a terrible position, forcing you to entertain me when you should be working."

"I could have told you to leave. Even that first night. The fault is mine. I knew it could only lead to a bad end."

Alexander watched silently as Elsie moved her hand back and forth upon the ivory keys, almost a caress. Lamplight bathed her in a golden glow that made her seem impossibly beautiful. Her long hair, pulled back loosely from her face, seemed almost afire in the light even as her face was cast in a shadow. She literally took his breath away.

Alexander had never been drawn to a woman the way he was drawn to Elsie. He wasn't a stupid man, or one driven by his baser needs. But as he'd lain abed earlier that night, he'd let his mind wander to the ballroom where he knew she would be. He vowed he wouldn't touch her, though God above knew he wanted to. But he simply needed to see her, to listen to her voice, to be with someone who didn't judge or pity.

He closed his eyes, willing away the loneliness that for some reason he was only just now starting to recognize.

"I should go," he said.

She could have had any number of reactions. She could have been defeated or angry. Instead, she leapt up from the piano bench, her white teeth visible even in the gloom of the ballroom, and smiled brightly at him.

"No, please stay," she said. "I promise not to put you in a compromising position."

He stayed at the door, staring at her, as if unsure whether or not to enter. He knew he should not. He knew he should turn around and go back to the little cottage he shared with Monsieur, but she drew him to her, made his heart long for things he'd never even let himself dream of.

"I have apologized and you have accepted, so all is well," she said. "It was completely uncharacteristic of me. Honestly."

He smiled slightly. "You don't often kiss workers who come into your home then?"

She blushed, two spots of red in her otherwise pale face, and let out something that sounded very much like a snort of mirth. "Not usually. It was terribly forward of me. My mother certainly would have scolded me and my father, well, he would have been shocked by my behavior."

"I did kiss you back," he said, wishing she hadn't apologized—again—for something he'd wanted so much. It only confirmed his belief that he should not touch her again. She was a baron's daughter and he was nothing. No one. He must continue to tell himself that lest he let himself think impossible thoughts.

"Yes, but how could you resist?" Elsie said, laughing. She was fighting hard to turn this conversation into something light and trivial, and he decided to let her.

"True. But I fear I cannot let you take the blame, not entirely," Alexander said. "I should have forbade you to come here. I could have ignored you or sent you away. But I didn't."

Elsie stood and walked to the little sofa set nearer to the mural. She sat, then turned so that she could look at Alexander, who still hovered near the door, still uncertain whether he should stay. "You've been getting a lot of work done, I see."

"No distractions."

"Would you come sit by me?"

He hesitated only a moment before joining her on the sofa, pressing his large body as far away from her as possible. No need to test himself too much.

Elsie stared at him while her mind went over and over what she wanted to say. The truth of it was, she liked him, quite a lot, but she also knew that they could never be anything more than friends. After all, she was practically engaged; true, the announcement hadn't been made yet, but that was only a formality and she knew it well. He didn't know she was engaged, and to blurt it out now would seem somehow presumptuous. How mortifying if he was simply enjoying a little dalliance and she was thinking he wanted something more meaningful. She'd done that once before. A young man had asked her for two dances, and she had felt she must tell him she was engaged. He'd been rather confounded by her announcement. "I only asked for a dance, not for your hand." She still burned in mortification from that set down.

"You told me I was being cruel, and I understand that now," she said. "But I acted foolishly. And hurtfully. I understand that I am a baron's daughter and you are . . . you are . . ."

"Nothing," he said, without inflection.

"Not nothing, you know that," Elsie said, her tone chastising. "You are, in fact, one of the most wonderful, intelligent, talented men I have ever met in my life. But I am also a realist, and I think you are, too." She took a bracing breath, praying that he would understand what she said next. "So for that reason, I believe we should agree to be friends only."

He looked at her sharply, then let out a rather humorless laugh.

"I do recognize that there is a certain attraction between us. Would you agree?" she said, trying to sound sophisticated even though her heart beat madly in her chest. To suggest such a thing was quite unlike her.

He tilted his head as if examining her. "I would."

"But I, for one, believe I can restrain myself from thinking of you as anything other than a friend." She ended this last with a sharp nod. He raised one eyebrow and gave her one of his half-grins, as if everything she uttered was charming and not entirely serious.

"You could try to think of me as a servant," he said in that same amused tone. Why he thought this was funny was beyond her comprehension.

"Is it impossible for a man and woman to be friends?"

Alexander could not quite believe what she was asking of him, and his old assessment about how incredibly naïve she was seemed to be true. All he could think of when she was gone was how he wanted to hold her, how he longed to bury himself inside her, how she would taste, sound, feel when his mouth closed around her taut nipple. It had been pure agony staying away from her when he'd known she'd returned and he knew she was wandering about the house alone wearing only her nightclothes. He was not a saint, he was nothing close to a saint and he hadn't had a woman in far too long to be able to sit by one this beautiful and be able to tolerate it with a smile. And yet, if he wanted her company, if he wanted the privilege of talking to her, looking at her, it would seem he would have to accept her olive branch of friendship and pretend he didn't want to lay her down on this couch and taste every inch of her delectable body.

"No, it is not impossible," Alexander said slowly and completely disingenuously, though part of him wished it were true. It would be far less torturous if he could think of her as some asexual being.

"So. We are agreed."

He decided that he was willing to suffer through his unfulfilled desire simply to be with her. A frighteningly telling thought, indeed. "Yes. Agreed."

"Oh, marvelous," she said with a little clap. It was an adorable habit of hers when she could not contain her happiness, that little clap. "Good, then. Now that we are friends, I want you to tell me about your childhood."

"A very boring story," he said, feeling his entire body heat.

"But it is your story and I am interested."

Alexander swallowed. He'd never told anyone about the pain of his childhood, the humiliations, the beatings. He had never told a soul who he really was, and God willing, she would never find out.

"My father was an important man," he said. "And I was a shameful embarrassment to him." He stopped to gauge Elsie's reaction, and was gratified that he saw no pity on her lovely face, only curiosity. "I suppose it was maddening to him that I refused to speak to him."

"Why didn't you?"

Alexander shook his head, for it was a question he'd asked himself a thousand times over. "He was a stranger to me and I could not speak to strangers. He spent most of his time in London, coming home only rarely. My throat would freeze up. I tried so hard so many times. In my head I screamed to myself, but nothing would come out. It was only after I knew someone well that I felt brave enough to speak."

His father had been a large and frightening man, especially to a little boy who constantly lived in fear of him. It became so bad that all Alexander needed was to hear his father's footsteps and he would freeze up, putting on what his father called "that idiot look." He'd hated himself nearly as much as he hated his father.

It was always the same. His father would demand something, and he would stand there, stiff and unmoving, unable to utter a sound, and his father would have his secretary cane him. He never laid a hand upon Alexander himself, but always delegated the task as if even touching his son would somehow contaminate him.

One of the worst beatings came when his father had quietly come up to the schoolroom to observe his sons being taught. Alexander had been reading aloud, proud of his ability, glad to impress their tutor, Mr. Thoresby. And then, when he'd finished, his father had entered the small room, clapping, but Alexander knew he was furious. Like every time before, his throat closed and he shut down while he furiously begged himself to speak. Anything. One word. One syllable to show his father he was not the failure he thought he was.

But he could not.

"How terrible for you," Elsie said when he was finished.

"Yes. It was."

Somehow during the telling of his terrible tale, she'd moved over until she was sitting next to him. She clasped one of his hands in both of hers, holding it firmly in her soft grip. "Who is he? I should like to throttle him."

"That," he said, giving her hands a squeeze and pulling away, "is something I shall never divulge."

"The Earl of Derby," she guessed, frowning.

"No. Do you think I come from something so grand as an earl?"

"Lord Shelton? I've never liked him much. He seems like the kind of man who would hurt an innocent child."

Alexander laughed. "Stop. It is unimportant. That is part of my life that I do not care to think about."

"It's hard for me to think of you like that, so helpless. You don't seem helpless to me at all." Her hand was back on his arm, foolish girl. Did she not know what that simple touch did to him, how it made it difficult not to drag her into his arms, especially with her looking so fierce and protective? He might have expected pity, but the thought that she wanted to throttle his father was rather heartwarming.

Then she laid her head on his shoulder, as if it were something she did every day. He looked down at the top of her head, at the messy part down the middle, and wished he had the strength of character to push her away. But her head resting on his shoulder felt so completely right that he couldn't bear to send her away. Not just yet. He could behave, he didn't have to think carnal thoughts, he could ignore the sudden tightening in his groin at the sound of her deep, contented sigh.

"See?" she said, lifting her head and looking up at him. "We can be friends."

She looked so beautiful in that moment, her lips parted slightly, her moss-green eyes completely guileless. "Can friends kiss?" he asked, just to tease, and her eyes widened, then narrowed.

"No. They cannot," she said firmly, but he caught

her smile as she lowered her head. She tucked her arm beneath his and held his hand. He moved his thumb against the silky softness of her hand, not able to stop the simple caress.

"I do believe friends can kiss," he said, staring at their joined hands.

"Not if they wish to remain *only* friends," Elsie pointed out with maddening logic.

"All right," he said, giving in for the moment. "I've told you about my painful childhood. Now you must divulge something about yourself."

"I've already told you everything. My life has been rather boring up to this point. You know about my sister, my mother's death, my little sister Mary. I have no secrets," she said, then added, just for total honesty. "I do have one secret."

"One, I take it, that you are not going to divulge."

"Not until the day you tell me who you really are."

Chapter 8

Elsie awoke wonderfully rested, feeling safe and warm . . . and snuggling against a very large, warm, male body. Her head was tucked beneath his arm, which lay draped down her side, ending at the swell of her hips where his hand curved around her curves. She really ought to be horrified, but instead she smiled. The sun was just hinting at rising and she had gotten a full night's rest.

"Alexander?" she whispered, not wanting to startle him. "We fell asleep."

He jerked suddenly, then slowly relaxed. "It's still early, sweetheart," he muttered. "Go back to sleep."

"Alexander, I really should return to my rooms. I find the idea of being ruined not quite to my liking."

Alexander's eyes came fully open, and he sat up abruptly, nearly pushing Elsie from her seat. He rubbed his hands over his face briskly. "Good morning," he grumbled.

"Good morning, sir." She stood up, then bent over and kissed his cheek, laughing when he scowled at her.

"Must you always be so infernally happy? Do you realize the fix we'd each be in if someone had come in here and found us sleeping together?"

Elsie refused to let him ruin her fine mood. She was wonderfully happy and well-rested and nothing was going to make her angry, not even this ill-mannered man. It didn't matter if he was right. "I slept wonderfully in the arms of my best friend. Now why on earth should I be anything but ecstatically happy?"

"You are dotty," he said darkly, but with a hint of humor.

"You needn't worry. I hardly think my father would force us to marry," she said and wished immediately that she could call her words back. "I didn't mean that the way it sounded."

"You sounded like a snob," he said, and though his tone was light, she thought she sensed an underlying anger.

"Something I am not," she said. "I am simply being pragmatic."

"Then there is nothing to keep us from our attraction."

She was slightly outraged. "Nothing but God and my morals."

He shook his head and laughed. "Do you truly think God is up in heaven looking down upon you and judging your every move, your every thought?"

"I hope not," she said in a small, mortified voice. "I'm afraid He would find me severely flawed." She grinned again, erasing any dark thought from his brain. "I'll wish you good day, sir, and see you tonight?"

Elsie thought he would say no, but he nodded instead and her smile grew ever wider. "I shall ask you about the asylum. I confess I'm very curious about your time there." With that, she fairly skipped from the room, as if they were nothing more than friends, as if he hadn't lain awake for at least an hour, savoring the feel of her in his arms before weariness finally let him sleep.

"You are distracted today, *mon fils*," Monsieur Desmarais said, looking curiously over at Alexander. "That is the tenth time you have checked your watch. Do you have an appointment later? Perhaps with one of the maids?"

Alexander could feel his cheeks burn, and he shook his head. He was a man in his third decade, and he could still blush from a bit of teasing. Impatient with himself, he bent and examined a section of the mural's border. He liked to put a bit of whimsy into his paintings, little hidden objects or animals that most people wouldn't even notice. He'd put a fairy in this one, a tiny little wood pixie fluttering above a ladybug. He doubted anyone would ever notice her or her interesting resemblance to the daughter of the house, but he didn't do this for anyone but himself.

"The red head, I am thinking. She is the one who makes the excuses to come in ten times a day. Oui? She is a pretty thing and if I were a younger man . . ." he said wistfully. Then Monsieur chuckled, enjoying his teasing. "It has been a while, non?"

Alexander gave him a dark look, which only caused Monsieur to laugh even harder.

"It is not good for a man, you know, to not use the gifts God has given us." Alexander smiled, and Monsieur seemed satisfied enough with that reaction to stop the teasing.

He silently chastised himself for being so transparent. The hours seemed to drag by, only because he knew he would see her again, talk to her, hold her hand. And maybe he would sneak a kiss. Or two.

She wanted to know about the asylum, and he would tell her.

Wickshire Asylum had been a small, private institution tucked away in the Cotswold Hills. It was a place where the wealthy placed their unwanted children, those deficient creatures they had little use for. It was considered a better alternative than to simply lock such nuisances away, which was what so many people had done in years past. The staff was caring and kind and did their best to teach the children a skill that they might someday use to improve their lot in life. While some of the children could not communicate in any way, many were happy and affectionate and thought themselves part of a large and unique family.

Alexander, however, did not. He was very afraid and very alone, having been cast out of a place he loved in the midst of a terrible turmoil. He wanted nothing more than to return home where his mother would be there to lay a gentle hand on his head and kiss his cheek and tell him none of what had happened had been his fault. He had a small room to himself, a window to peer out of, but nothing else. There were no books, no tutors, and he was so very frightened, he didn't utter a sound at all. Not one. Not even when he cried.

He'd been in the home for nearly a month when one of the doctors took a particular interest in him. He was in the main parlor, a place with a large fire crackling merrily, where the best behaved of the children were allowed to socialize in the evenings before bed. Alexander hated it. He hated that they had tried to make it homey, hated that everyone smiled at him as if he were an imbecile. He would have broken something if there had been anything to break. But the shelves and tabletops had been cleared of anything that would harm the more clumsy of the children.

So he sat sullenly staring at the fireplace, not even bothering to look up when he heard a strange squeaking sound, though it took a great deal of tenacity not to when the other children gave out happy shouts and ran toward whatever it was making such a racket.

And then he heard it. The piano, played rather inexpertly, by a young doctor. Dr. Stelton banged away, making Alexander wince, but drawing him to the shabby old instrument. The doctor looked up, smiling, and asked Alexander if he would like to make the same noise.

For the first time, the smallest hint of a smile touched his lips, and he nodded solemnly. With a great flourish, Dr. Stelton stood up and offered the stool to Alexander, who felt, for the first time in weeks, that he might not die of grief.

He played his favorite Mozart sonata, stunning the doctor and drawing all the adults who worked in the asylum into the room. He hardly noticed, for his eyes were closed and his mind was lost in the music. When he finished, the room was filled with onlookers who gave him a rousing round of applause.

That night, Dr. Stelton went to his room, tucking him in and making him feel, if not loved, then worthy of kindness. He would never forget what the doctor had said that night.

"You don't belong here, Alexander, do you?"

He shook his head, warmth spreading through his skinny little body and causing tears to prick at his eyes.

"Well, sir, I shall endeavor to fix that."

Four weeks later, he was secreted out of the asylum and introduced to the famous muralist, Monsieur Desmarais, who as it happened, was about to move to Italy. It would be years before he returned to England, years that turned Alexander from a young boy to a young man.

Alexander was completely lost in his thoughts, staring without focus at his woodland fairy, and did not hear Monsieur come up next to him.

"A little nymph, non? She is charming, mon fils, but I fear you spend too much time on these little details." Then he shook his hand in front of him, as if to erase his words. "Non. *Non,*" he bellowed. "Do not listen to this old man. You are a master, and now

I am the assistant, and you are a far better painter than I ever was."

Alexander frowned fiercely and shook his head, making Monsieur laugh aloud. "You protect me too well, mon fils."

Then he pulled out a flask and took a deep drink from it, letting out a sigh of satisfaction. Monsieur did not always drink, but the pain of his rheumatism was often unbearable and the brandy he favored cut that pain a bit. He would often fall asleep in one corner as Alexander worked, waking up only if someone knocked on the ballroom door. Monsieur had laid down strict rules to all that no one was allowed to enter the room without permission.

They stopped for the day, Alexander rousing his old friend from a drunken sleep by gently nudging his shoulder. Then he helped him stand, putting an arm around Monsieur until he was steady enough to walk to their cottage. Even when drunk, Monsieur cared about their project, and he looked over the mural with a satisfied nod. "You did well today," he said, as he always did. There was a time when Monsieur would praise Alexander, then point out some flaw, but the older man had stopped doing that years ago.

They walked together to the small cottage once used by the gamekeeper. It held just two tiny bedrooms and another main room. Every night at seven o'clock, a footman would arrive with their nightly meal and the two would eat silently and companionably. And then, Monsieur would take out a cigar and his flask and within one to two hours, would be sound asleep, leaving Alexander alone with little to do. When he was still a boy, Monsieur would teach him the classics, as well as any mathematics he remembered from his own schooling. Alexander had been a voracious reader, finding solace in the written word. And, of course, on those occasions when they were in an empty home, he would find a piano and play until his fingers ached.

At eight o'clock, Monsieur was already abed, their meal cleared away, and Alexander was left alone with his thoughts, which of late always turned to Elsie.

"You seem unusually happy tonight," Lord Huntington said, gazing fondly at his daughter. They were dining in their cozy breakfast room, as they always did, forgoing the much grander formal dining hall. The etched-glass gaslight sconces cast the room in a cheery glow, but Elsie kept on her mother's tradition of lighting tapers for added elegance.

"I am happy," Elsie said, thinking of Alexander and smiling down at her plate of roasted pheasant.

Her father wiped his brow with a handkerchief. It was stuffy in the room, for the day had been unusually warm and sticky, even for August, and Elsie considered blowing out the candles, which only made the room seem hotter.

"I am about to make you even happier. While you were out wandering the grounds, I received an invitation to a ball today from Lord Browning. Miss Olivia's birthday, as it happens and her first real ball. A come out of sorts."

"Olivia is sixteen already?" Elsie said, slightly shocked. Olivia had always seemed like a small girl, it was hard to believe she was coming out and would be in Town for the Season husband-hunting. It made Elsie feel rather ancient.

"Yes, and apparently quite the young lady. Lord Browning has already had an offer for her, but he's waiting until she's a bit older and had at least one Season. He does indulge that girl."

"He reminds me of another father I know," Elsie said, smiling at her father, who gave her a rather sheepish grin.

"Yes, well, I'm glad you're all settled on Hathwaite. Lord Browning was beside himself with worry about his daughter's future. But, Olivia is a lovely girl and will no doubt attract much attention on the marriage mart."

Elsie's smile faded slightly. "Yes, it is lovely to have it all settled."

Her father paused and set down his fork. "You are unhappy, my dear?"

"Oh, no. No, not at all. Perhaps there are times when I wish my life was not so mapped out for me, but Lord Hathwaite is a perfect gentleman and I'm sure we will suit."

"Then what is wrong? Two minutes ago you seemed to glow from happiness, but I do believe I put out that light when I mentioned Hathwaite."

Elsie looked down at her plate, wishing she hadn't revealed her true feelings. "Please don't worry, Father." She pushed a small, boiled potato with her fork, a frown marring her face. "I just wonder sometimes.

What if I had fallen in love with someone else during my Season?"

"We have a marriage contract, my dear."

Elsie forced a smile. "Yes, of course, but what if I'd fallen madly in love with someone else? Would you have permitted me to marry that person?"

"Let's just thank God you did not," he said with a frustrating note of finality. But Elsie would not be deterred.

"Father," Elsie said with a bit of exasperation. "Please answer my question."

Lord Huntington gave his daughter a sharp look. "Have you fallen in love with someone?"

Elsie laughed. "No. Of course not. I was simply wondering. That's all."

"Good, my dear, because we do have the contract, you see."

"I know, but marriage contracts are broken all the time. They are not binding, not really, are they?"

Her father looked extremely uncomfortable and actually squirmed a bit in his chair. "Your contract is a bit different. I don't want to get into the particulars of it, but suffice it to say there is a reason we've been living so well these past years that has nothing at all to do with the estate's income nor my investments, such as they are."

A sick feeling came over her, making her fear that she might actually lose her supper. "And if I didn't marry Lord Hathwaite?" she asked quietly.

"Please, Elizabeth, this is not something I wish to discuss with you," her father said, his voice tinged with anger.

"But it's my life we are discussing. Surely I should

be aware of the details of the business dealings that decided my entire future."

"I will tell you only this: If you were to renege, we would lose the estate and I would be ruined. Kingston is a very powerful man."

Elsie stared blindly at the plate.

"It was a mutually beneficial agreement," her father persisted. "Kingston got what he wanted and I was promised my daughter would one day be a duchess. It was a very important vote on the China trade. Vital to Kingston at the time."

"Obviously," she said softly. Elsie had never felt trapped, but for some reason she felt for the first time as if walls were closing in on her, leaving her no escape. Strangely, it was a prison from which she'd never before wanted to escape. She swallowed heavily, confused by her sudden resistance to what had always been an accepted and even anticipated future.

"Elsie," her father said kindly. "Look at me." Elsie tried to school her features so as not to worry her father. "Has something happened, my dear? Has Hathwaite said or done something I need to address?"

"Oh, no, Father. No. He is always a gentleman."

"*Is* there someone else?" he asked, clearly baffled by her questions.

Elsie thought of Alexander, then immediately abandoned that thought. Even if she was not engaged, her father would never agree to such a marriage. "No, Father. There is no one. No one at all. I think I am simply getting nervous now that the wedding is only months away." She forced a smile and was gratified when her father relaxed. "Now, tell me, when is the ball? I do hope you plan to go, Father. It's been so long since you've had a bit of fun."

Lord Huntington spent a few moments busily carving a piece of pheasant before answering his daughter. "The ball is in one week and I do plan to attend. I'm beginning to believe people are thinking I've gone a bit batty, wandering about collecting my lichen."

"Oh, no, Father. They don't, truly."

"Regardless, it's time. Lord and Lady Browning have given us short notice, but apparently they are in the midst of a renovation and were not certain it would be ready in time for Olivia's birthday. I hope I still fit into my formal wear."

Elsie shook her head. "I still cannot believe Olivia's ready to be married. I feel so . . ."

"Old?" her father said with a wicked gleam she hadn't seen in years.

"Oh, you are terrible, Father," Elsie said, laughing. "I am a bit long in the tooth, but will be married soon enough." Elsie would not let the sick tumble of her stomach at the thought of her marriage to Lord Hathwaite ruin their meal.

"Anything else interesting in the post?" Elsie asked.

"Only an invitation for Monsieur Desmarais to attend the same ball," her father said, with obvious pride. It was rather a significant development that the great artist was in their home.

Elsie smiled, as if this news was of no consequence. She was the only person other than Alexander and Monsieur Desmarais himself, who knew that the true artist would not be attending a ball that night.

"We shall have to invite Monsieur to come with us in our carriage," Elsie said.

"I have issued that invitation already, but he has asked that he not inconvenience us so. He is not expecting to stay long, as I understand it."

Elsie enjoyed her father's company, and was very pleased to see he was acting more like himself lately. Despite her misgivings about her upcoming nuptials, she knew in her heart that her father had only her future in mind. Her mother's death had cast a pall on their home, one that the two of them were still trying to push through. They finished their meal, telling each other the doings of the day, the minor events that only the two of them would find remotely interesting. It occurred to Elsie as they said their good nights, that her father and Alexander were the only two people she knew who were delighted to listen to her talk about nothing.

Chapter 9

Elsie felt like a child anticipating a wonderful birthday party. Her stomach was all a-jumble, but there was another feeling, one still new and fresh and intoxicating, one she didn't have a name for.

It was stiflingly warm in the ballroom, for the late afternoon sun had shined relentlessly through the bank of French doors. Monsieur Desmarais and Alexander had kept several of the doors open while they worked, but now they were closed and the room was nearly unbearably hot. She immediately ran back to her room and put on a simple day dress, the one she wore when she was assisting the servants to clean out a dusty, unused room. It was loose-fitting and didn't require a corset, but she certainly couldn't go wandering around outside with a man in her nightclothes.

Donning her slippers, she flew down the stairs, skidding to a halt outside the ballroom door, pausing to catch her breath. *He is simply your friend*, she thought to herself. *Nothing more.* But she couldn't stop her smile or her happy anticipation, no matter how she chastised herself, no matter how fruitless such a friendship must be.

She entered the room to find him already on the couch, but he stood the moment he heard her.

"I hardly recognize you dressed," he said, smiling.

Elsie looked down at her plain dress and fluttered the skirts a bit. "I thought we could walk outside. It's dreadfully hot in here."

"It is a bit cooler outside," Alexander said. He walked to the still-open door that led to the large terrace, then waited for her to precede him, as only a gentleman would.

"Oh, it's lovely out here," Elsie breathed, taking Alexander's hand and pulling him to the edge of the terrace. "If I close my eyes I can picture the night of my ball, the couples dancing, the orchestra playing, and everyone admiring the stunning mural upon the wall."

"I wish I could be there."

Elsie opened her eyes, and grasped his other hand, so they stood facing one another. "But you must be there. I shall insist."

Alexander stiffened, and his expression turned stony as he withdrew his hands. "It doesn't matter that you insist. I will not be there. It is impossible."

"I see," Elsie said, unable to keep the hurt from her voice.

"It's not that I wouldn't want to be there," Alexander said, letting out a frustrated sigh. "Don't you understand that I do not belong in a ballroom with your guests? Besides, I . . . I cannot attend such public events. Do not ask it of me, for I will only disappoint you."

"No doubt you and Monsieur already have another commission," Elsie said, trying to keep her tone neutral, as if the thought of Alexander leaving, of him not being with her for her ball, did not crush her.

"We do."

Elsie did not want to think on it. It was still so far away, weeks and weeks before her ball, before the mural would be completed. "Let's walk," she said with forced cheerfulness.

To her delight and relief, Alexander gave her a small bow then presented his arm for her to take. "I am at your command," he said gallantly.

They walked down the shallow steps to the lawn, where dew immediately darkened her silk slippers. The night air was filled with the thick sound of crickets and the distant croaking of bullfrogs. A nightingale, its silhouette plainly visible atop an oak sapling, sang incessantly from its perch. Such wonderful summer sounds reminded Elsie painfully of the times Christine and she would sneak out of their rooms and into the summer night.

"I love walking about at night," Elsie said wistfully. "But I must confess that I have a slight fear of being alone outside at night in the dark. I'm always expecting a wolf to come bounding out and gobble me up."

Alexander muttered something under his breath.

"Beg pardon?" Elsie said, suspecting he'd said

something about how it was even more dangerous to be walking about with him.

"I said something to the effect that you're in no danger from wolves," he said, sounding as if he were trying not to laugh. "There hasn't been a wolf in Britain in more than one hundred years."

Elsie narrowed her eyes. "That is not what you said, sir."

Alexander chuckled. "Smart girl."

"Hmph." Elsie pretended to pout for perhaps ten seconds, before tugging on his arm and leading him to a large tree with odd foliage sprouting on it. "Tell me about your time in the asylum."

"I don't know why you insist on making me relive my unfortunate past," he said lightly. "It's rather heartless of you."

"Indulge me, please. I am interested, truly. You are, in fact, the most interesting person I've ever met."

"You have led a sheltered life to be sure."

Elsie ignored his quip, even as she was pleased by it. "You've been locked in an asylum, for goodness sakes. Not many people can say that, you know."

Alexander shook his head, but he was smiling so Elsie knew he was not bothered by her demands. "I'm afraid I'm going to have to disappoint you if you've had visions of Bedlam in that imaginative head of yours. It was nothing like that. In fact, it was a private institution that presented itself as a home for children who were deemed untrainable." He told her his story, his words measured and dispassionate, ending with his being introduced to Monsieur Desmarais.

Though it was not a tragic story, at least not to his

thinking, by the time he finished, Elsie had tears running down her face.

"Oh, Alexander," she said, and threw herself into his arms, very nearly sobbing out a grief he didn't understand.

"Darling, please don't cry for me. It wasn't a terrible experience at all. And it allowed me to find Monsieur, something for which I am grateful."

She looked up at him, clearly distressed. "But you were just a child and were abandoned and you'd done nothing wrong. Your father is monstrous and if I ever chance to meet him I shall tell him so."

"No doubt you already have met him," Alexander said, "and probably found him charming."

"Never. I wish you would tell me who he is," she said, moving out of his embrace.

Alexander smiled down at her. "So you could throttle him, no doubt."

"It does sound silly when you say it aloud. I would give him the cut direct."

"Which, no doubt, would have little or no effect on him."

Elsie tilted her head. "Is he so very powerful then?"

"In some circles, yes."

"In my circle?"

"Enough, Miss. I shall not tell you more lest you discover my great secret."

"Who you truly are is not important, I suppose. You would still be my friend if you were a butcher's son or a prince, would you not?"

"I would."

She smiled, and he let out a small groan. "What is wrong?"

"Must you be so beautiful?" he asked, sounding flabbergasted. "It would be so much easier not to kiss you if you were homely."

She lifted her nose in mock affront. "I had no idea you were so shallow."

"I suppose I'm as shallow as any other man who is standing in front of a beautiful woman he wants to kiss."

"Well," she said, putting her hands behind her back and pacing in front of him, furiously trying to hide a smile. "It just so happens I may have discovered a bit of a loophole in our kissing ban."

"Oh?"

Elsie looked up into the misshapen tree and giggled. "It just so happens, sir, that we are standing beneath a rather large cluster of mistletoe."

Alexander looked up at the large bush-like growth sprouting so incongruously from the tree. "Mistletoe," he said slowly. "Have you lured me out here, Mademoiselle, under false pretenses?"

"Absolutely, I have."

"How very naughty of you, Miss Elsie."

"I do have one rule, however," she said with mock sternness, looking so utterly adorable he had to stop himself from sweeping her into his arms. "You must put both hands behind your back."

"Like this?" he said, putting his hands immediately behind him.

"Just so," she said with a satisfied nod. "And I should do the same."

Alexander's mouth went dry when she thrust her own hands behind her back, which only served to accentuate her lithe body and its wonderful curves.

"Now we may kiss."

They leaned toward one another, each grinning like a fool, so that when they did kiss, their teeth touched, making them laugh. "That will never do," Alexander said softly, his smile fading as he stared down at her upturned face in the moonlight.

He leaned forward again, this time his lips touching her soft, pliant mouth, breathing in on her exhale. He clutched his own wrist so tightly, it was nearly painful, but it was either that or pull her to him. He moved his mouth expertly over hers, taking her bottom lip and sucking gently. Her tongue darted out to taste him and that was nearly his undoing. He was painfully aroused, his body screaming for him to take her into his arms, to press against her. Instead, with a low groan, he pushed his tongue into her mouth, exploring the sweetness there. His knees nearly collapsed when her tongue began to meet his, matching his rhythm, one so erotic he wondered if she was aware what she was doing.

He was losing the battle with his self control, and he let go of his wrist, only to fist his hands by his sides, still not touching her with anything but his mouth, his tongue.

With a small sound, she stepped back, her breathing shaky. "It is not fair," she said, her voice low and trembling. "It should not be like this. I should not have to suffer this."

Alexander stiffened. "I don't understand."

"It is not fair that I should be forced into . . ." She stopped abruptly. "It is best left unsaid." She swallowed, and he could see her throat moving as if she were trying not to cry.

He put his hands upon her upper arms. "Tell me."

"It is best left unsaid," she whispered, looking up at him as if her heart were breaking.

"Very well." His tone was cool, his expression stony.

She just shook her head. "We shouldn't have kissed. I shouldn't have allowed it. But you are all I can think of from the moment I wake up to the moment I fall asleep. This is wrong and I should not be here."

"Elsie," he said, giving her a little shake when she refused to look at him. "It is the same for me. The same. Do you understand what I am telling you?"

"No," she said, nearly shouting. "Please don't, Alexander. Don't say another word. I can't bear it."

Alexander stepped back, his breathing hard, his stance angry.

"Oh, please don't be angry. One of us must be strong, must face reality."

"Then it is I who must be strong, for I am not the one who led us beneath a large growth of mistletoe," he nearly shouted, all the anger and frustration he felt coming out. "It was not well done of you, Miss Elsie, not well done at all. You cannot play the coquette, then back away angry that your own actions have resulted in unwanted consequences."

"I know," she said softly. "You must think me a terrible sort of girl."

"Not terrible. Just very, very young."

"I don't much care for reality and I suppose, for just a little while, I wanted to pretend I was simply a girl kissing a boy. It seems I am forever apologizing and I fear I must do so again. Please don't be angry."

He let out a harsh breath, ashamed that he was making her feel distressed. He knew better, but it was so excruciatingly maddening to know, to *know* she wanted him and to be able to do nothing about it. And yet, that was not entirely true. He could do something. He simply chose not to, he realized, as a wave of self-loathing nearly knocked him to his knees.

"I am not angry with you," he said harshly, then softened his tone when he realized he did, indeed, sound angry. "I am angry with myself. You are such an innocent and I have no right to touch you."

Elsie bowed her head. The night had become so quiet, he imagined he heard her tears hitting her dress, soft little taps of misery.

"Let me walk you back to the house."

She dashed away the tears and nodded. "I've ruined everything," she said. "Stupid, silly mistletoe."

"No," he said quietly. "We were the silly stupid things. You and I both."

At the ballroom door she turned to him and bravely lifted her chin. "Good night, Alexander," she said, holding out her hand.

"I can't, Elsie," he said, staring at her hand, as if she were saying a casual good night to an acquaintance of little consequence. He felt his heart wrench at the look of sadness in her eyes. And then her face crumpled.

"I don't want to lose you. You are my best friend. Can't we simply pretend tonight didn't happen? Please?"

A stronger man would have walked away, but Alexander was not a strong man, not when it came to matters of the heart. "As you wish."

She gave him a tremulous, watery smile. "See you tomorrow night, then?"

"Until tomorrow."

Chapter 10

Monsieur Desmarais was a man of great pride, which was why it was so difficult to rely more and more on Alexander with each passing day. He was also a man of compassion, who worried that one day he would no longer be able to paint, leaving his fostered son with no way to make a living.

For years now, ever since it became clear that Alexander was fast becoming a master, guilt had gnawed at the Frenchman. The young man was a prodigy and deserved a far better education than he was able to give him. He should be in Paris displaying his work at the Salon; his work was that good. An artist such as Alexander was wasting his talent on these bourgeois English, who didn't know a master painting when they saw it.

And, of course, he himself was a fraud, claiming credit for work he hadn't done. It had started with Alexander helping him to paint when his hands grew too painful to hold a brush. Then, Alexander began to paint entire sections of the murals.

Now, Desmarais was nothing more than the assistant, the companion of one of the greatest painters he had ever had the privilege to know. And no one even knew.

It gave Desmarais no pleasure to propagate this deception. But he was a pragmatic man who knew his livelihood and his reputation rested on the broad shoulders of the man he'd thought of as son for years. He was still vain enough to go to a ball and bask in the accolades thrown at him, false though they were. He still needed to be admired, needed his patrons. He knew he was becoming a pathetic parody of himself, knew it but wouldn't change it.

"I don't know how much longer I can continue this ruse," Desmarais said the night of the ball as Alexander expertly tied his formal necktie. Alexander simply shook his head. His face was uncommonly expressive and Desmarais over the years had developed a rather uncanny way of understanding the most subtle changes in his eyes, the set of his mouth, the position of his jaw. "Don't worry, mon fils, I can continue a few more years. And the dancing with the pretty ladies? As long as I am en vogue, I will not say no."

Desmarais had rejected both Lord Huntington's generous offer of joining his carriage and the offer of a driver. Desmarais was a prideful man, but he also knew himself rather well. He very rarely remained sober, and when he was drunk, it was not uncommon for him to say something unfortunate. Alexander would drive him to the ball, would watch over him, would remove him when he became dangerous to himself.

"You have not been yourself lately, mon fils. Are you feeling well?"

Alexander smiled at his friend and nodded. But no, he was not feeling well. These past few nights his visits to the ballroom had been brief and kept purposefully impersonal. He knew he was being cruel, was hurting Elsie with his indifference, but he was also hurting himself. And tonight he would be forced to watch his beloved in the arms of other men, enjoying a world that he could never be part of. Even if things were different, the thought of entering a ballroom full of people was enough to make him ill. It was better, he told himself, that he remained apart, that he continue to live the quiet life he'd been living. The alternative, while intoxicatingly tempting, was impossible.

As the two men climbed aboard the smart little phaeton, Desmarais nodded toward the main house where a small party was climbing aboard the carriage. Alexander caught a glimpse of Elsie, enough to see she looked far more elegant and far more beautiful than he'd ever seen her before.

Lord and Lady Browning's estate lay in Sutton in Ashfield, less than an hour's drive from Mansfield Hall, on a well-traveled road that skirted Kings Mill reservoir where King Henry II was said to have gotten lost for a time during a hunting trip. Elsie didn't know if the story were true, for it was the stuff of fairy tales, but it was said King Henry got separated from his hunting party and stumbled upon a home, requesting food and lodging without divulging his identity. The kind couple fed the king, let him share a room with their son, finding out only the next day who their guest was. The king knighted the mill owner, gave the owner's daughter to one of his lords in marriage, and promised the young son marriage to a court lady.

She let her mind wander, giving in to fanciful thoughts of Queen Victoria elevating Alexander to some high rank that would make him a suitable husband for her. It was unusual for Elsie to daydream for she was ever realistic about what life would bring. At least she had been until Alexander. She lived, after all, in a world where beloved sisters died and mothers too. There could be no fairy tale for her. If she were honest with herself, many a young girl in her position would see her engagement to a future duke as fairy tale enough.

She realized even if the queen elevated Alexander, Elsie would still be bound to marry Lord Hathwaite. Such depressing thoughts could not be lifted even by the spectacular sunset over the serene waters of Kings Mill.

She was feeling out of sorts, restless, and extremely unhappy, though she did her best to hide her feelings. She was angry with herself for that insane nighttime walk. What had she been thinking, that she could share another kiss with Alexander and be unaffected by it? She knew, she knew, she knew and yet she'd done it because she was impetuous and just a little bit in love.

She'd ruined everything with that foolish bit of flirtation. It had started out so innocently, so delightfully, until she felt the full effect of his searing kiss. They hadn't even touched, and yet she'd known she would never feel that way with another man. Would she? Would she melt when Lord Hathwaite kissed her? Would her body burn, would she feel as if she wanted him to touch her in places that no one had touched? Would she yearn for things she didn't even truly understand yet?

Alexander had come to the ballroom each night since that ill-fated kiss. And yet, the man she knew, who made her heart so full it felt as if it might burst, was gone. Certainly, she could not share with her aunt that her heart was breaking because the man she was quite certain she loved had turned into a man she no longer recognized. Each night, Elsie told herself she would no longer subject herself to Alexander's frosty demeanor, and every night she walked into the ballroom, her heart singing at the sight of him. She'd even embarrassed herself by pleading with him to tell her why he was being so cold, but he'd pretended ignorance, making her feel foolish. Was this the same man she'd laughed with at the piano, the same who had kissed her so passionately beneath the mistletoe? He was pushing her away and he was right to do so, but still, it hurt so much.

As the carriage approached the rather impressive estate, the western sky held only a hint of daylight and the grand manor house was well-lit, showing off a long queue of fine carriages and coaches in front of the grand entry hall.

"I fear my dress will be quite wrinkled," Elsie said, pulling at the light sea-green silk. Beneath her skirt and petticoats, fabric clung wetly and uncomfortably to her legs. The two women had long ago mastered the notion of sitting wearing the hoops required for the bell-shaped silhouette fashion required, but such a style meant inevitable wrinkles along the back.

"Nonsense. It's as lovely as when you put it on," Aunt Diane said, waving a fan in front of her face. It was uncomfortably warm in the carriage, even with the windows open, and Aunt Diane was feeling a tad irritable. "I do hope they have ices," she said, fluttering the fan with even more vigor.

Elsie peeked out the window, her eyes widening at the queue of carriages, including some with large crests upon the doors. This was, after all, Nottinghamshire, and no doubt a party such as this would attract the area's highest ranks. Her stomach sank. "Is the duke expected here tonight?" Elsie asked, knowing she needn't explain which duke.

"I should expect so. I know Lord Browning is a special friend of His Grace. No doubt Lord Hathwaite will also be in attendance."

"How lovely," Elsie said unconvincingly.

Lord Huntington, whom Elsie had thought to be dozing in the corner, lifted his head. "Elsie," he said, with enough censor in his tone to make her feel slightly ashamed of her behavior.

"Why, you'd think you would welcome the chance to spend more time with the man you plan to marry," Aunt Diane said, her voice full of reproach. As an unmarried woman, she simply could not understand Elsie's reticence at marrying the heir to a dukedom. While the older woman was usually very understanding of Elsie's moods, her niece's behavior this night seemed to be trying her patience.

"I think this heat is simply spoiling my mood," Elsie said, knowing that her aunt would commiserate with her on that point.

"It is ungodly, is it not? How much longer is the line?"

Elsie surreptitiously looked out her window, trying not to appear gauche by craning her neck out like some country bumpkin. "Seven more," she grumbled.

"My goodness, half of Nottinghamshire must be here."

An uneasy feeling gripped Elsie, who prayed her future father-in-law was not among the guests. There was something about him that frightened her, although the duke had never been anything but polite and charming. She thought, perhaps, it was because even when the duke smiled, his eyes were blank, emotionless, as if he were schooling his face to make the proper expression, but felt nothing inside.

The duchess, who rarely attended such events, always stood meekly by her husband's side. She was a lovely woman, with a still-youthful appearance, but she somehow looked cowed standing by her imposing husband, as if in a perpetual flinch.

"I wonder if the duchess has accompanied His Grace," Aunt Diane said, as if reading Elsie's thoughts. "I do hope the duke hasn't subjected her to such a crowd. Poor woman."

Elsie looked to her aunt in surprise. "Why do you say that?"

"We were debutantes together and she was painfully shy," Aunt Diane said. "She had few friends, but the sweetest disposition. Some of the girls thought she was a terrible snob, but I knew her better than most. Kingston is the very last man I would have paired her with. But I doubt she had any choice in the matter. It was an arranged marriage."

"Not all arranged marriages are tragedies," her father said, sounding put out by the entire conversation.

"I was not referring to Elizabeth, who as far as I can tell, will be the luckiest girl in attendance here," Aunt Diane said, looking pointedly at Elsie.

"I think Lord Hathwaite is more like his mother than his father," Elsie said. "For that, I am grateful."

"Yours and hers are entirely different situations," her aunt said, putting on a tone she used for lecturing on Proper Behavior. "You see, Kingston arranged the marriage himself. He picked her because he thought her pretty and for no other reason. An ornament to display on his sleeve."

"How dreadful."

Lord Huntington let out an impatient sigh, putting an end to their gossip.

When their carriage reached the grand entrance of Hartley Hall, Elsie welcomed the cool air that touched her face and shoulders the moment the footman opened the door. Getting out of a carriage with full hoops was not a task for the faint-hearted, but Elsie managed well enough, exposing only a bit of ankle on her descent.

Once inside the grand hall, Elsie looked around, dreading that she'd see the duke. Indeed, they'd only been in the home a few moments before she spotted Lord Hathwaite chatting with some friends.

Elsie tried not to catch his eye, but when he did look up, she smiled a greeting, feeling rather ashamed when he gave her a smile back.

Lord Hathwaite made his way to them and gave the ladies a bow. "You look a bit fearful," he said rather charmingly, making Elsie laugh.

"I must confess I was wondering if His Grace is in attendance."

Lord Hathwaite gave her the most genuine smile she'd ever seen cross his features. "He changed his plans at the last moment. That is why you see me in such a buoyant mood, I daresay."

Next to her, Aunt Diane fluttered her fan so vigorously that Lord Hathwaite blinked against the gust.

"The heat, it is quite stifling," Elsie said, giving her aunt an exasperated look as she continued to fan herself.

"Yes," Lord Hathwaite agreed. "We shall have to take a turn 'round the garden later. It's rather nicely lit with hundreds of Japanese lanterns."

"I should like that," Elsie said.

"Have you retrieved your dance card as yet, Miss Elizabeth?"

"No, we were waiting for the line to lessen."

"Make certain you pencil me in for at least two," he said, with a charming smile. Then he winked. "If we really want to set tongues wagging, make it three. Waltzes, if you please. I'm afraid it is too warm for a schottische or redowa."

Elsie smiled, surprised and slightly perplexed that he seemed to be flirting with her. "Oh, I agree.

Three waltzes then. How very daring of you, Lord Hathwaite."

"I am feeling daring this evening." He gave her a cheeky smile, a small bow and went back to his friends, leaving Elsie slightly mystified by his mood.

"He seems rather happy this evening," Aunt Diane remarked.

"Certainly a nice change from the sulking man he usually is," Elsie said, missing the chastising look her aunt gave her.

The two women waited in line for their dance cards, Aunt Diane keeping up the steady motion of her fan. "Aunt, I do believe the energy required to keep that fan going at such a pace is only serving to make you hotter," Elsie said, laughing.

Aunt Diane snapped it closed, but smiled. She was a handsome woman, and Elsie thought she was prettier now than when she was a younger woman. She'd always been thin, which did no service at all to her sharp features, but the recent few pounds she'd added softened her face, making her actually pretty when she smiled.

"You are looking lovely this evening," Elsie said, eying her aunt critically. She had no idea how old Aunt Diane was, knowing only that she was her father's younger sister. Elsie realized that even though she'd assumed the older woman was near her father's age of forty-six years, she had very few lines upon her face and her figure was quite girlish. Her dark blond hair held hardly a gray strand.

"Thank you. I've decided to put myself back on the marriage mart," her aunt said dryly.

"I know you are jesting, Aunt, but you are prettier

now than ever." Her aunt actually blushed, then began to fan her face again.

"Nonsense. I don't even know what I am in line for. I think I shall find some other old spinsters and discuss how ill-mannered today's youth are."

Elsie made a face at her aunt and was about to retort when she realized she was next to receive her dance card. It was a pretty thing, clearly expensive, with thickly embossed paper and silver embellished corners. "Lovely," Elsie said, thinking instead how much nicer were these dance cards than the simple ones she had ordered for her birthday party.

In the ballroom, the orchestra was tuning up and people were beginning to mill about awaiting the Grand March, which started so many of these events. Elsie spied Lord Hathwaite among a group of other young men, looking far livelier than she'd ever seen him before. Goodness, he even let out a laugh and slapped a chum's back. It was then she realized the stifling affect His Grace had on his son.

Alexander stood on the lawn, hidden in the shadows, where he had a perfect vantage of the ballroom and Desmarais. There had been more than one occasion when he'd needed to help the man from a social event before he made a complete ass of himself. He now recognized the signs, the flamboyant gestures, the way he played with his thin mustache in a clumsy way, how he walked. Perhaps few people recognized that he was heavily in his cups on those occasions, but Alexander knew the man had a great capacity for fooling people even when he was nearly falling over drunk.

This was, he realized, one of the more elegant balls he'd witnessed. This was the cream of society, the lords and ladies who were the toast of London, the powerful, the wealthy, and he wondered, fleetingly, if his father was amongst those in attendance.

One of the drivers spied him beneath the tree, and to Alexander's annoyance, made straight for him. He stiffened and tried to stem the sharp pang of anxiety at the man's approach, with minimal success. The driver, wearing bright blue livery, pulled out a small, tarnished case, holding it out to him. "Smoke?"

"Thank you," he said, taking a thin cheroot. He examined it, noting its high quality, and bent while the man lit it for him then lit his own. He took a few experimental puffs, then smiled. "Nice."

"Lord Hansard's right generous with his smokes," he said with his broad Yorkshire accent. "Got these left over from Christmas."

The man looked him over, noting his obvious lack of uniform, as well as the fine cut of his clothes. "Yer not a guest," he said, but with enough question Alexander could tell he was not completely certain.

"No. I'm with Monsieur Desmarais, the muralist. I am his assistant," he said, wishing the man would go away. "Thank you for the smoke. Good evening."

"Good evenin' ta you, as well," the man said, sounding slightly put off that his overtures of friendship were met so coldly.

Alexander didn't relax until the man had disappeared toward the stables, where the other footmen and drivers were no doubt gambling and sneaking drinks from well-hidden flasks. Part of Alexander longed to be the sort of man who could walk up to a stranger and offer him a smoke. He could hear the men's laughter, their obvious camaraderie, but felt nothing but intense unease at the thought of joining them.

Disgusted with himself, he took a long draw of the cheroot, exhaling angrily. He felt like such a coward, like that trembling little boy who couldn't speak to strangers or even his own father. It didn't matter how many times he swore he would change, would be better, would be normal, he simply could not. It was times like this when he realized how ridiculous and pathetic it was to even dream about having someone like Elsie to love. He could never give her what she wanted, could never be the normal man she needed. He prayed to God to give him the sense to walk away from her, before the pain he felt in his heart completely destroyed him. Already, he was consumed by her, by the thought of kissing her, touching her, listening to her talk. In his weaker moments, he let himself dream they were together, alone in a cozy little thatched-roof cottage surrounded by roses, just the two of them, living a comfortable life as man and wife. It was such a simple dream, filled not with riches, but with laughter and music and his Elsie. And perhaps children, with reddish-gold hair and a scattering of freckles.

Alexander swallowed and threw the cheroot down, crushing it beneath his heel. He had better things to do than pine for a woman he could never have and dream impossible dreams.

The Browning ballroom was on the first floor, with guests spilling out onto a large terrace that had an impressive fountain featuring a pod of playful dolphins spewing water from their mouths. A faster crowd would have no doubt made use of that fountain before the evening was done, but it was quite obvious that the people in attendance at this ball wouldn't even consider such vulgar behavior. Staying to the shadows, Alexander looked for Desmarais, knowing that it was more likely his mentor was playing cards in some other room that was not visible from his vantage point.

He searched the room, trying to avoid resting his eyes on any woman wearing green, but found himself arrested by the sight of Elsie standing with her back to him beside an elegantly and expensively-dressed young man. He could see her profile, and watched almost unwillingly, as she talked with him, laughed, even touched his sleeve with her gloved hand. That simple, innocent touch, caused a rush of red-hot jealousy that he didn't even try to suppress. The man was blond and they made a lovely pair, a pair he wanted to drive apart with a fist to the man's face. Alexander realized he was clenching his fists so hard his arms were shaking and he forced himself to relax. He wanted to barge into that ballroom, to crash through the mullioned windows, and tear her away from him, from any man, he realized.

"Ah, hell," he whispered, when his gut clenched painfully at the site of her laughing, her face tilted charmingly up to the man. The music changed, and the man bowed in front of her, holding out his hand for her to take, then sweeping her off into a waltz. The man was touching her, his hand about her small waist, and he leaned forward to whisper something in her ear, something that made her eyes sparkle. Alexander's mind screamed for him to turn away, to stop the torture, but another part of him forced himself to watch, to recognize fully the futility of his love.

Monsieur Desmarais was all but forgotten as he watched the couple dance around the room. To anyone else, they were merely one of a dozen couples dancing. But to Alexander, they were the only couple on the dance floor. Every smile they gave one another, every touch, every step they took in unison, tore at him. Finally, mercifully, the dance ended, but instead of bowing to her and leading her to the side, her partner brought her to the terrace and down the steps. Alexander withdrew deeper into the shadows, his heart pounding, as the cad pulled her, quite willingly it appeared, down a garden path well lit by Japanese lanterns of all shapes and colors.

What a pretty picture they made, he thought, a tight, sickening feeling making his stomach actually hurt and he wondered if he were about to cast up his accounts. He watched with mute horror, as they stopped, as she looked up at her escort, as he bent his head down, as their lips touched. Alexander's entire body was shaking now, as he watched Elsie, *his* Elsie smile up into another's face. The young man looked ridiculously pleased with her rather tepid kiss. Then he kissed her again, this time longer. With a small impotent growl, Alexander took a step toward them, breaking a small twig beneath his boot, and the couple sprang apart guiltily. Alexander quickly stepped back behind the tree, his entire body hot and stiff with rage as his greatest fear was realized. He was simply a diversion, a pathetic nobody who stupidly fell in love with a girl who clearly did not love him.

He stood, his back pressed against the tree, grinding his head painfully into the rough bark, as if he could stop his heart from hurting by doing so. As if he could stop it from breaking.

Diane Stanhope was not a woman given to fanciful thoughts. She prided herself on her ability to be analytical, even with herself. It was a trait that had developed over the years of hope and disappointment. In her twenties, rail thin and with such pointed features young children called her a witch, she had still hoped for a husband and children. She attended balls and soirees and the opera when she was in Town. She paid attention to the latest fashions, practiced conversation, and cultivated friendships that would benefit her.

And then she hit thirty and the realization came that she was and always would be one of those unfortunate women that other women pitied and men ignored. She was a spinster, and suddenly it seemed ridiculous to attend balls wearing the finest fashions, to stand in line for dance cards that would never be filled.

Diane tried not to become bitter, that awful cliché of the unhappy spinster. She developed interests outside the ton, and, in her own circles, she was known as one of the leading experts on England's flora and fauna. If she could not be married, then she would be a bluestocking, which made her unmarried state more understandable for those who bothered to think of her at all.

She had, over the years, become quite invisible. And yet, this evening, as she'd stood in line for her dance card, she'd been unaccountably pleased when her niece had complimented her.

Diane Stanhope was thirty-two years old and realized, much to her growing horror, that all those hopes she'd had in her twenties of hearth and home and children, had not simply disappeared, they'd only been suppressed by her dogged determination and insistence that she had accepted her fate.

How she hated the feeling that came over her at the oddest times, the feeling that perhaps, just perhaps, there was some nice widower out there who would take one look at her and fall to his knees in romantic rapture. No matter how she tried to fight it, it was still there, like an insidious mold that cannot be completely removed no matter how hard you scrub.

Which was why, when the Earl of Braddock approached her, smiling and looking so completely dashing, her heart fluttered like a young girl's, allowing that ridiculous hope to flare once again.

"Miss Stanhope, I wonder if I might have a word with you," Braddock said, giving her that half smile she'd seen him give so many, many women. But he'd never given it to her, so it was quite a novelty.

Unconsciously, she fiddled with her dance card, and Braddock's eyes flickered down. "Would you do me the honor of the next available dance?" he asked.

Diane opened her dance card, knowing that but for her brother, it was completely empty. "It just so happens, my lord, that I have this dance open." She smiled at him and he looked momentarily startled, to the point that Diane wondered if she had something stuck to her teeth.

He led her to the middle of the ballroom and pulled her gracefully into a waltz. No matter how Diane screamed at herself to stop her ridiculous heart from beating madly in her chest, it wouldn't stop. She'd danced with hundreds of men, but never had she felt so foolish as she did at the moment. She could feel her face grow hot beneath his gaze as she stared with great intensity at his neckcloth. For years she had watched Braddock dance with women, listened to gossip about whom he would marry, about who was his mistress. He was, and had been for years, the focus of many marriage-minded mamas. And now, he had asked her to dance. Perhaps Elsie had been right, perhaps she did look lovely that evening.

"I don't know if you are aware, but I have become the ward of a young girl who requires a London Season," Braddock said.

"I was not aware, my lord," Diane said, finally finding the courage to look up. It seemed each time she did, Braddock was taken aback, and Diane, with a deep flash of insecurity, wondered if she were even uglier than she'd realized. With a courage she did not feel, she smiled at him, even as her throat began to ache.

"I am looking for a suitable chaperone for my

niece and it is my understanding that your duties as chaperone to your own niece will be ending about the same time the Season begins."

Oh, of course. He wants the safe old spinster to chaperone his ward. Of course.

"We've made no formal announcement as yet, but that is my understanding as well," she said, feeling foolish and stupid.

"I know it would not be entirely proper, as I am unmarried," Braddock said unnecessarily. No one in their right mind would even bother to raise an eyebrow if she chaperoned his ward.

"I daresay no one would think a single improper thought even should they find me in your bed, my lord," she said with self-deprecation.

Braddock let out a sudden burst of laughter, as if he were completely surprised by her wit, but Diane felt like running from the room and giving in to the tears that burned like acid in her eyes. "Perhaps you are right," he said softly. "But they might be wrong."

Ah, a bone. He pitied her, after all. "I would be more than happy to act as chaperone this coming Season, Lord Braddock. What is the girl's name?"

"Melissa. She is the daughter of my brother, who died a fortnight ago. It is an unusual situation. We have no other suitable women in our family. You do still live in Flintwood, do you not?"

Diane was, frankly, surprised that they were practically neighbors. Indeed, on a fine day, it was possible to walk to Flintwood House from her far more modest home. "Yes, I do."

"Well, then," he said, as if all was agreed upon, which, apparently, it was.

"Of course, my duties couldn't officially begin until after my niece's wedding."

"Of course," he said, and looked slightly relieved that their conversation had ended when the music did. Now, Diane realized, he would not be forced to converse with her any longer. And yet, he lingered.

"I . . ." He looked suddenly uncomfortable.

"Yes, my lord?"

"Would it be too much of an inconvenience for you to spend some time with Melissa before the Season starts?" He gave her a charming, self-effacing smile. "You see, I've no experience with young girls and she has had an unusual upbringing."

"I shall write to you when I return home and perhaps we can arrange something."

The earl let out a sigh of such relief that Diane found herself smiling at him again before she remembered how startling he found her smile. It came again, that strange look, and she immediately frowned.

"Good evening, Miss Stanhope. You have put my mind greatly at ease."

Diane nodded, then made her way over to the side of the room, feeling unsettled, a feeling she didn't much like. No, not at all.

Oscar was so relieved, so completely astonished by his reaction to that rather innocent kiss, he almost wanted to shout out to the world how happy he was. For the first time in his life he felt a glimmer of hope that the coming years wouldn't be a long, tepid journey of responsibility and tedious duty.

His fiancée, it was turning out, was quite charming and rather a flirt. He hadn't expected that, hadn't thought she'd let him kiss her after their last disastrous meeting, and he certainly hadn't expected that he'd have to force himself not to draw her more firmly into his arms. She *moved* him, this beautiful girl he'd known all his life. He'd hardly wanted to relinquish her to her aunt when they returned to the ballroom. *My God*, he thought, *am I falling in love with my future wife?*

It seemed impossible, and he wanted to war against such feelings for they would only give his father satisfaction to see that the choice he'd made for his son had been the right one. Could it be that all this time he'd been fighting the match only to be contrary to his father?

He grabbed a wine glass from a passing waiter and took a thoughtful sip, his eyes seeking out and finding his fiancée. She *was* lovely, he thought, emptying his glass. A wonderful haze of alcohol and love flowed through him. Why hadn't he seen how lovely she was before now? Certainly he'd known she was beautiful, in the same way that a rose is beautiful. It was something pretty to look at for a day or two before the bloom faded. But Elsie, his lovely Elsie, was becoming more lovely. Such soft lips, such a warm touch. She made him feel suddenly alive, suddenly hopeful about a future that had before seemed so bleak. With just two kisses. Imagine, he thought, what bedding her would do.

Nothing. Elsie had felt absolutely nothing when Lord Hathwaite kissed her, and she'd tried her best, even letting him kiss her twice. He had smiled down at her, but she'd felt none of the thrilling heat she'd felt with Alexander. The most exciting part of the kiss was when they'd heard a twig snap and thought they might be discovered.

At the moment, she wasn't certain if that was bad or good. It was bad, of course, that she felt none of the physical attraction toward her future husband that she felt for Alexander. And it was good to know, she supposed, that she was not some wanton who got weak in the knees at every man's kiss.

Lord Hathwaite led her inside and promised to see her for their next waltz. He then left her with Aunt Diane, who looked flushed and hotter than ever.

"Aunt, you look in need of some punch. Shall we go to the refreshment table?"

"I'd like to sit here, if you please. Would you be a darling and get it for me?"

Her aunt truly looked about to collapse from the heat, so Elsie smiled and said she would. As she made her way over to the long table, Monsieur Desmarais saw her and waved her over.

"Madamoiselle Elsie, you are my savior," he said. "I must leave and I'm afraid I, well, I am not feeling well."

"Shall I fetch Father for you?" She looked about the room. "Oh, dear, he might be in playing cards and I do not wish to disturb him. He so rarely spends time with his friends anymore."

"If you could help me find Andre, I will bid you adieu."

"Andre?" Elsie asked, and then realized with a horrible premonition that he was talking about Alexander. "Where?"

"No doubt with the surrey," Monsieur said, sounding quite odd. "I'm afraid I'm not well."

Indeed, his eyes were glassy, his face florid, and he seemed to be swaying a bit on his feet. Elsie realized suddenly that Monsieur Desmarais was quite, quite drunk.

"Sir, I have promised my aunt some refreshment. But if you sit here," she said, leading him to a chair, "I will be with you directly and we shall find Andre for you."

She was back in minutes, which was a good thing, for Monsieur Desmarais was trying to rest his chin on the heel of his hand but it kept sliding off. "Shall we find Andre now?"

"Yes. He's a good boy. A good boy."

Elsie took his arm, but quickly realized he needed a bit of steering. Getting the artist out of the Browning ball without anyone being the wiser that he was deep in his cups was not such an easy task. The man weighed a great deal more than Elsie, even though they were of a similar height, and steering him in the right direction became more difficult the further they walked. Fortunately, as they were approaching the stairs that had seemed so easy to navigate on the way up but which now appeared impossibly steep, Alexander appeared.

"Not feeling well, mon fils," Monsieur slurred.

Elsie looked at Alexander, trying to gauge his mood, but his eyes, full of concern, were on the artist. She stood there near the bottom step, unsure whether to follow them or return to the ball, until Alexander jerked his head, commanding her to follow. There was absolutely no warmth in his gaze, but Elsie followed, praying he had not seen her with Lord Hathwaite but fearing that he had. Why else would he look so angry? As she walked behind him, noting how gentle he was with the inebriated man, she wondered what she should tell him. *The truth,* her conscience told her, even as her heart warred against such a command.

Somehow, Alexander managed to practically lift the portly man into the surrey. It seemed impossible, but as soon as the artist sat upon the cushion, he slumped and was snoring loudly.

Alexander came to her, looming over her, his eyes cold with fury, his jaw clenched so tightly the muscles in his jaw bulged. "When you return, come to the ballroom." *Oh, God, he did see.*

He turned abruptly without waiting for her answer, jumped lithely into the surrey and snapped the reins.

But as horrifying as was the thought that Alexander had seen her kissing Lord Hathwaite, Elsie still found enough indignation to be affronted by his imperious tone. "You cannot tell me what to do," she shouted with false bravado, and nearly bolted when he heaved onto the reins and stopped the horse's progress.

He jumped down from the surrey and gave her

a mocking bow and a smile that did not touch his eyes. "My pardon. If you please, Miss Elizabeth, I should like to discuss a matter of great importance with you." Then he let out a small laugh that held no humor. "Actually, I'm sure it is of no importance to you whatsoever, but I humbly request an audience at any rate."

Elsie still did not answer him. Her throat was too thick with unshed tears. But she nodded and watched as he climbed aboard the surrey and drove away without another look.

It was nearly four in the morning before the Huntington carriage pulled up in front of Mansfield Hall carrying three exhausted ball-goers. Elsie looked worriedly at the house, half expecting an angry Alexander to be waiting on the doorstep for her.

"I'm for bed, as I expect are you ladies," Elsie's father said, still groggy from his short nap in the carriage.

Aunt Diane wrestled angrily with her skirts for a moment before stepping down onto the graveled driveway. The ball, she said, had not gone well. For a good part of the way home, she actually sulked in the corner, something that was quite uncharacteristic of her.

"Is something wrong, Aunt?"

She stared at the steps as if they were an insurmountable mountain. "I've just had a dose of reality this evening, that is all." Then she turned to Elsie, her eyes unusually bright, and Elsie had the sudden feeling that her aunt might actually be holding back tears. "I want you to know how very lucky you are, Elizabeth."

Elsie wanted to argue, but that fleeting look of despair in her aunt's eyes stopped her. What, after all, did she really know of her aunt? Elizabeth actually thought she was content with her life, had envied her the freedom she had as an older woman with the means to live independently. But perhaps, as her mother used to say whenever Elsie envied someone, "You don't truly know what's in their heart."

"I know I'm lucky," she said. "And I'm sorry if I've seemed ungrateful for all that I have. I suppose it's human nature to want more."

"Yes," Diane said thoughtfully, as if Elsie had just said the most profound thing.

The two women walked into the house together and up the main staircase to the second floor, where they went in opposite directions.

"Good night, my dear."

"Good night, Aunt," Elsie said, and walked toward her room, only to stop once she heard her aunt's door clicking closed. She waited but a moment before tip-toeing back down the stairs, her heart hammering in her chest, a feeling of dread making her almost ill. She must tell Alexander about her upcoming wedding. She should have told him weeks ago, which made this confession all the more difficult.

Elsie pushed open the ballroom door and immediately saw Alexander's silhouette as he stood looking out into the garden. Although it was nearly daybreak, he was only a dark shadow against the early morning gloom. A fine mist fell outside, enshrouding the garden in gray and giving the impression that nothing existed beyond this room. He didn't turn when she entered but Elsie knew he must have heard her. She walked as far as the sofa, then braced a hand there, feeling suddenly weak and unbearably tired.

"Alexander?"

He remained absolutely still, reminding Elsie of the first night she'd entered the ballroom to find him working by lamplight.

"Who is he to you?" he said, not turning to her, his words unusually clipped.

Elsie suddenly found it difficult to breathe, never mind answer his question. Her hand clutched the sofa hard, as she felt for the first time in her life that she might faint.

"Who is he to you?" he repeated, annunciating each word, as if he were restraining his anger only with the greatest effort.

"We are to be married in May." Elsie waited for some reaction, but saw only an imperceptible nod of his head.

"I see."

"No, I don't think you do. Our fathers signed a marriage contract when I was still a baby. I don't love him." Her eyes stung suddenly from unshed tears. Oh, how she hated this, how she wished everything were different.

"We must honor the wedding contract," she said in a rush. "There was a great deal of money involved. If I do not marry, then my father will be ruined. We'll lose this house and Mary's future will be uncertain at best. It all had to do with a vote His Grace needed."

At that, Alexander's head snapped up and Elsie took an involuntary step backward. "His Grace?" he asked, with lethal calm.

"I'm to marry Lord Hathwaite and will one day be the Duchess of Kingston."

Alexander stood at the window and stared at her, his expression one of complete horrified disbelief. "Kingston," he repeated. "You're to be . . . Kingston." And then he started to laugh, great chest-heaving guffaws that suddenly seemed tinged with bitterness. "Kingston," he repeated, wiping his eyes, and giving into another bout of uncontrollable laughter.

"I fail to see what is so amusing," Elsie said, completely taken aback by his reaction.

"Oh, God, Elsie. I'm a bloody idiot, did you know that?"

"I don't understand."

He walked up to her and for the first time she realized his eyes seemed almost feverish, as if he were tinged with madness. He then gave a most proper bow. "Allow me to introduce myself. I am Alexander Wilkinson, the son of Edgar Wilkinson, Duke of Kingston. And you, my dear," he said, "are about to marry my brother. My *younger* brother."

Chapter 11

Alexander felt as if his entire world had just collapsed in on itself and reformed here, in this ballroom, where he stood before the only woman he'd ever loved, knowing with a certainty he would never possess her.

He stepped back from her, back from her confusion, back from what he knew would be the inevitable conclusion in her very intelligent mind. Ah yes, he thought, as he saw her face move from confusion to something close to happy, here it comes.

"If that is the case, I am engaged to marry you," she said, and gave him a smile that would have melted the heart of another man, a man who wasn't painfully aware of the futility of those words.

"No," he said with a clear note of finality. "You are not. And that's the rub, you know. That's the true cruelty of this. My God, it's almost as if someone is having a grand joke with my life. First, let's make him mentally deficient. Then, kill his brother, have him sent to an institution, and then for a sick twist, let's have him fall in love with his brother's fiancée."

He knew his voice held a hard, maniacal bent, but he didn't care . . . until he saw her tears, and his heart broke, truly broke. "Please, Elsie, don't cry."

"You're frightening me."

"I know," he said, drawing her against him.

"Are you truly Kingston's son?" she asked, looking up at him.

"I am, but I have no way to prove it. No one knows who I am. I left Warbeck Abbey when I was ten years old and no one has seen me since. Monsieur does not know who I am—only I do."

"But surely your father would not deny his own son."

He tugged her closer. "When I was twenty years old, Monsieur and I returned from Italy. One of the first things I did was go to Warbeck Abbey, to see my brother Henry's grave. There was another gravestone there, as well. It was mine. A headstone carved with my name, my date of birth, and the date of my death. He let everyone believe I had died. I don't even think my mother knows I live."

"He is evil," Elsie said, shaking her head. "Someone should expose him. The world should know what he has done to you."

"No one would believe it. He is a very powerful man and I am no one."

"You are his heir," she said with such ferocity, Alexander kissed her forehead. She believed him, without question, and he loved her all the more for it. "This is horrible. Horrible, Alexander. Oh, I wish I didn't know. It makes it all so much worse, to know I should have married you. Oh, God. How can you stand it? How can you sit by and let him do this to you?" She pushed away, her expression fierce. "If you love me as you say, we'll find a way. Hire a solicitor, prove you are who you say you are. It's not impossible. I will tell them the truth."

"I could be lying to you," he pointed out, and immediately saw a flicker of doubt that she quickly tried to hide. "Do you see how easy it is to instill doubt?" he asked gently. "My situation is impossible and we must accept it."

"You must not give up. You have no choice."

Anger hit him with unexpected force. "I do have a choice and I choose not to be the next Duke of Kingston. Just the thought of that title being attached to me makes me sick. Do you think I could stomach going to that man and begging for him to recognize me? Do you think I could go before the House of Lords and eloquently state my case when I can hardly order an ale in a taproom? It is beyond my capabilities. And beyond my concern."

Elsie lifted her chin. "And what of me? Am I to be beyond your concern?"

"You must be."

"Oh, you are maddening," she said, and began to pace wildly in front of him, chewing on her thumb. "If you will not pursue this, then I will."

"And become a laughingstock by claiming the mute assistant of your muralist is actually the heir to a duchy?"

Elsie stood in front of him, her small fists straight at her sides, looking like an avenging angel. "We can make them believe," she said.

"How?" he demanded, then shook his head in frustration. "My love, please. Don't you think I have thought of this for years? And I have come to the same conclusion each time I torture myself with such thoughts. It is impossible. I am no one. I don't even exist." She started to speak but he held up a hand to stop her. "Even if I could prove it, I wouldn't."

She paled and took a step back as if he'd physically pushed her away. "You don't mean that."

"I do. I could never perform my duties as a duke. I could not take my seat in the House of Lords. I cannot manage the estates, the business interests, the employees, the tenants. My brother has been trained to do that since the day Henry died. It is his right, not mine, *his* duty, not mine. I am incapable of taking up the responsibilities required of the title. For that reason alone, I could have the title stripped from me."

"You could do it, I know you could," Elsie cried.

He gave her a small smile, gratified that she had such blind faith in him. But she didn't know what it was like, what he was like, and God willing, she would never know, never see him shaking, never see him vomit because the thought of speaking to someone was so overwhelming. She would think him such a coward, a failure. And she would be right.

"I am not whole," he said with painful honesty.

"You should have more faith in yourself, Alexander. I will be there. I will help."

He looked at her bleakly. "Before or after you marry my brother?"

"What do you mean?"

"Even if I was able to gather the proof of my identity, which could take months, I still would need to file a petition with the Queen. Then the House of

Lords would need to hear it and make a decision. Surely you will have been married by then. Even if the title is put into abeyance, you will be married to my brother. So, I ask you. Would you still try to help me obtain the title after you are my brother's marchioness?"

"I would still help you."

"Would you? How altruistic of you, my love."

Elsie wrapped her arms around herself. "Please don't speak to me that way. I don't like it."

"One of us has to be a realist. Is that not what you once told me? Now it is my turn. I will never be the Duke of Kingston. And, therefore, you will never be my bride." He walked from the room, ignoring her when she called to him, because he didn't much care for the thought of Elsie seeing him cry.

Elsie stemmed the urge to chase after him. She was so tired, and now heartbroken beyond what she'd thought was possible. It hurt, physically hurt, to think of how cruel fate was to have her fall in love with a man she was meant to marry but now never would.

He'd said he loved her, and usually such a declaration would make a girl's heart sing with happiness. But that knowledge only made this entire situation more maddening, more impossible. He was the Earl of Hathwaite and she was legally contracted to marry him. And yet, she couldn't. It was as cruel as holding out a morsel of food to a starving man and then yanking it away each time he opened his mouth for it.

But beyond the heartbreak, she was angry, with the duke, of course, but also with Alexander. For if he loved her, if he truly wanted to marry her, wouldn't he fight for them? Wouldn't he do everything in his power to make her his? Wouldn't he face the very devil himself if it meant they could be together? He said he loved her, but clearly he didn't love her enough.

And what of her? Was she willing to put her father and sister, her very home, in jeopardy by marrying a man who was not heir to the duchy? Was she so very different from him? Elsie always tried to be fair, but she felt that her decision was not selfish and his was. She was marrying Hathwaite because to renege would put the people she loved most in harm's way. He refused to seek his title for purely selfish reasons, even though obtaining his title meant they could be married.

By the time Elsie reached her room, she was far more angry than heartbroken. How dare he claim to love her when he was completely unwilling to sacrifice anything to be with her? She would talk to him tomorrow after he'd had a chance to think things over. She knew he would come 'round. Alexander said he loved her, and if he did, he would present himself before his father and claim the title.

Elsie walked in her room to find Missy fast asleep on her bed, apparently waiting for her mistress to come home so she could assist her. She was snoring softly, her brown hair in a loose braid peeking beneath a nightcap.

"Missy," she said, giving her maid a good shake. "Missy, I'm sorry, but I need your help."

Missy opened her eyes and scowled. "I was havin' myself such a lovely dream, miss. I was in a field o' pretty flowers an' there was a party goin' on and I was just about to have myself some food when you shook me awake."

Elsie smiled. "Sorry. But it's practically morning and I need to get out of my gown."

Missy sat up and looked toward the window, seeing the glow of dawn in the crack left by the heavy drapes. "Goodness, I should be gettin' up now anyway. You must be plum tired, yourself, Miss."

"I am," Elsie said. "I think I'm even tired enough to fall asleep on my bed." She was, indeed, suddenly overwhelmingly tired. It almost felt as if she'd been drugged, so sleepy was she.

"I'll believe that when I see it," Missy grumbled, as she started to attack the long row of buttons down Elsie's back.

Missy had her mistress undressed down to her shift in no time, then left to fetch her nightgown from her large wardrobe. After draping the ball gown across a chair, she turned, then stopped in midstride, holding the nightgown in her hand and stared at Miss Elizabeth. For the first time in more years than Missy could count, Miss Elsie was on her own bed, sound asleep.

Chapter 12

Alexander got a late start the next day, for Monsieur suffered from an aching headache and sick stomach from too much drinking the night before. He was in an unusually foul mood, which did nothing to help Alexander's own temper. At the moment, all he wanted to do was to finish this mural as quickly as possible, leave Mansfield Hall and never return. He wanted to wipe it from his brain, forget about Elsie and her smile and the way she looked when she was sound asleep.

Nothing had changed. He'd never allowed himself to be foolish enough to think he could have her as his wife, not really. If the thought had come, it was put away like so many other unattainable dreams of home and family. He used to dream that his father loved him, too, but he knew that would never happen either.

Which was why he didn't understand this feeling of impotent rage he felt at the unfairness of his fate. It was almost as if he'd actually thought he could have her as his wife, could wake up beside her every day of his life, as if that silly little cottage of his imagination had a chance in hell of being real.

The day his father had put him in that asylum, he hadn't felt anger, but a piercing yearning for a life that never existed. He wanted a father who loved him, a mother who would not allow him to be thrown away. He'd never suffered from the loss of what was rightfully his, simply because he'd never wanted it before. And perhaps, he'd believe on some primal level, that he didn't deserve it, wasn't worthy of the title and all that came with it.

He would go on, he always did. He would love Elsie, yes, for the rest of his life, but he would not allow himself to dwell on this pain, this nearly unendurable ache in the pit of his stomach. In time, it would fade. All the other pain he'd suffered had faded. Eventually. He would not dwell on the fact that if he'd been a whole man, she would be his wife.

He would not dwell. He would not.

Monsieur sat at the small table, a cup of strong coffee between his hands, looking blearily out the window where the wind caused the branches to move madly about. "The day, it fits my mood," he said.

Alexander had had enough of sitting about, waiting. He got Monsieur's attention, then jerked his thumb, telling him he was going to work.

"Okay, okay. I will come later, oui? When this stomach of mine stops rolling. And be careful, mon fils."

Alexander nodded, knowing that the older man still feared discovery. Walking across the lawn toward the house, he prayed Elsie was still asleep somewhere other than the ballroom where he had left her the night before. There had been more than one occasion when he'd come to work and found her there, asleep on the couch. More than once, when it was empty, he'd thought about that night they'd fallen asleep in one another's arms and he allowed himself to dream of a time they could do that every night.

It was not to be, as he'd known even when he'd been foolish enough to indulge such fancy.

Alexander was not a man who fell into bouts of self-pity, but he was a man who frequently allowed himself a good bit of self-loathing. For he knew Elsie was right. If he loved her enough, he would go to the ends of the earth to find a way for them to be together. It was fear, nothing more, that stopped him. And that recognition made him feel as if he were falling into an all-too-familiar black abyss.

He had on more than one occasion in his life contemplated the beautiful release that death would bring. When he became so tired of living with the pain that scraped him raw, it seemed to be the perfect answer. The day he'd stood at the foot of his own false grave, knowing his father had ordered someone to carve the stone, had perhaps even pretended grief, had pushed Alexander close to the end of his endurance. As a boy, Alexander had dreamed constantly of coming home, of being well, of showing his father that he could be good and be all that was expected of him. He dreamed of standing before his father and talking to him, talking and talking and talking. As he'd stood before that tombstone set above an empty coffin, that grave became a metaphor for his life. He was dead. Alexander Wilkinson was dead to everyone he'd ever loved. Why not make it the truth?

He'd foolishly cried standing there, mourning for his brother and also for the other little boy, whom his father had killed without compunction. That betrayal had scorched him, and deadened him for a long while afterward.

The only thing that had stopped him from suicide was knowing the grief his death would bring Monsieur. And the only thing that had brought him out of that dark place was the knowledge that Monsieur was suffering for him. "You are well, mon fils?" he would ask worriedly, and Alexander would always nod his head until finally it was the truth.

Now, he could feel himself standing at the edge of the kind of despair that killed men. "Coward," he said softly to himself as he stared at the mural, at the two boys who played so full of joy by that lake. "You goddamned coward."

In a frenzy, he began mixing paint usually used for a mural's base, the sharp scent of solvent making his nostrils flare. Perhaps he would suffer this pain for the rest of his life, but he would not allow his mother to suffer it. He knew that when his father announced Oscar's engagement at Elsie's birthday ball, it was almost a certainty that his mother would be there. Taking up his largest brush, he began slashing at the scene, once, twice, before stopping to look once more at his beloved brother's face.

He reached up and touched him, as if he were touching flesh and bone instead of the cold paint and plaster. That day, up until the moment of his brother's death, had been the happiest of Alexander's life. Any day spent frolicking about with Henry was a happy day, but this one in particular, had been marvelously joyous.

The two boys, ages twelve and ten, swam in the lake within site of Warbeck Abbey, the principal residence of their father, His Grace, the Duke of Kingston. They were not supposed to be in the lake, not at that time of the morning, when Henry was supposed to have been in the classroom with their frazzled tutor Mr. Thoresby. And this secret made swimming in the cold water all that much more enticing.

The idea to swim had been Henry's, of course, for Alexander tried with all his being never to do anything that would cause him to be the center of attention. He lived in paralyzing fear of being called before their father, for it always ended the same way. Henry would charm his father and Alexander would enrage him, which resulted in a severe beating handed out by His Grace's poor beleaguered secretary, Mr. Farnsworth. The only time he saw his father, other than rare glimpses through his office door, was when one of them did something wrong—and it was usually Alexander who bore the brunt of their punishment simply because he could not argue his case with the eloquence of his older brother.

Henry always defended him, raising him to heroic levels in Alexander's eyes, but it did nothing to save the younger boy from his father's scathing wrath. Inevitably, His Grace would demand to hear Alexander's side of things, and that was when the trouble would start. For Alexander could not speak in front of his father, could not utter a word, no matter how hard he tried, no matter the consequences, which only enraged his father all the more.

He'd stand there, feeling his throat fill with something thick and dark, while he trembled with the effort to answer his father's shouted question. And then, for his stubbornness and insubordination, for having the audacity to refuse to answer his father's questions, he would receive a beating. Worse, though, was receiving his father's look of pure disgust.

But spending time with Henry was almost worth having to go before his father and suffer in silence as his father spat venom at him while he shook and gasped for breath, trying with all his might to say one word, just one, that his father wanted him to say.

"Race me to the rock," Alexander shouted, running into the lake, his pale backside naked for all to see. Henry gave his brother the head start he needed to make a race of it, then ran full tilt, water splashing about, laughing with abandon, before he dove into the water and started swimming to his younger brother.

The boys reached the rock at about the same time, scrambling up its slippery surface. More of the rock was showing this time of year, for the area had suffered a minor drought, which made climbing to the top all the more difficult.

"Thoresby will see us if we stay on top," Alexander said, slightly out of breath from the swim and the climb. He held his hand out to Henry and heaved him up, even though Henry could easily make the climb himself.

"I don't care," Henry said bravely, though he did

sneak a look toward the grand house to see if Thoresby was running toward the lake. "I'm off to school in a week, so I deserve a break."

Alexander scowled, not liking the reminder that his brother would be leaving for school in a matter of days. He'd be left here with their younger brother, Oscar, who at three years old was nothing more than a baby to pester him. He could not go to school with Henry. He had tried, but could not speak to the professors. Thoresby had been with the boys since they were small, and Alexander had no trouble speaking to him, which only proved to his father that his inability to talk to his new professors was pure obstinacy.

"I wish I could go with you," Alexander said, not for the first time.

Henry wiped his wet hair from his face and grinned. "You're not missing anything, but you could go if you wanted to."

Alexander felt that familiar burning in his gut whenever anyone mentioned his defect. No one understood, least of all him, why he could only speak to some people, why he would stand in front of others like an idiot and open his mouth futilely, looking like some sort of imbecile. He hated it, hated himself, hated every human in England.

"I can't," he said, turning away from his brother.

"I'll give you a million pounds."

"You don't have a million pounds," Alexander said, and found himself smiling.

"I will some day. When I'm the duke." Henry stood up and shook himself like a dog, droplets of water falling on Alexander's face like cool rain. "Race you to the gazebo," he said, right before diving in.

Alexander stood and jumped in. He didn't like diving from so high, something Henry had teased him about more than once. The cold water covered his head, his ears filled with the rush of water and bubbles, and he burst to the surface, ready to follow his brother to the distant shore, where the white-washed gazebo sat a few yards from the beach.

Except Henry was not there, swimming strongly ahead of him. The water was calm. Silent. Alexander wasn't immediately worried, for Henry had played this game before, rushing to the surface just as Alexander was beginning to think that no one, not even Henry, could stay under for so long. He waited, treading the surface, telling himself Henry was fine, that he'd pop up laughing, spitting lake water onto him.

And he waited.

Until the panic set in, until he knew that not even Henry could stay under as long as this. He dove under, his eyes wide open, straining to see anything in the clear water. He rose to the surface, gasping for breath, and called out Henry's name, before diving down again. On the third try, he saw his brother's pale form on the bottom of the lake near an underwater rock outcropping. Grabbing his hair, he pulled up, swimming frantically toward the rock, crying, screaming, his lungs burning, his throat raw. His hand grasped the rock and he pulled up with all his might so that Henry's head would be above the surface.

Thoresby was on shore, shucking his shoes, swimming toward him, taking Henry from him, swimming to shore, dragging his brother behind. Alexander stayed at the rock, staring at Thoresby as he dragged Henry onto the beach and shook him, pleading with his brother to awaken, crying. As Alexander clutched the rock, shivering, it seemed as if the entire house emptied of all occupants, and among them, his mother. And his father.

He swam to shore slowly, unnoticed, until he stepped up, dripping and naked, next to the now-covered, still body of his brother.

"Not Henry," his father said, his voice harsh. "By God, not *him*." And then his father raised his eyes and looked at his second son with such pure loathing, Alexander fell to his knees, shaking his head as if denying his brother's death, his father's hatred.

"What happened?" his father shouted, stepping toward his son. "What happened?"

Alexander had covered his ears, still shaking his head, but he could hear his father shouting, shouting, shouting and his own silence screaming in his head.

A few more deft strokes of the brush, and the scene was gone, those two smiling boys obliterated forever. The ballroom door opened and he heard his mentor gasp.

"What have you done, mon fils? The mademoiselle, she will be angry, non?"

Alexander stared bleakly at the mess he'd made, feeling hollow and so very tired.

"It is all right. It is still the most beautiful mural," Monsieur said, his tone soothing, like it was when he'd awaken from a nightmare as a boy. "You can fix it and it will be beautiful. Perhaps a swan or two? A big frog, eh?"

Alexander forced a smile and gave Monsieur what he needed, a small nod.

"You are well, non?"

Alexander felt his eyes burn and he swallowed, turning his head abruptly away from his friend. He felt a strong hand rest on his shoulder and heard the words he wished were true repeated. "You are well, mon fils."

Chapter 13

Elsie awoke slowly and stretched, her muscles quivering, and stared up at her crimson canopy smiling. With a deep breath, she realized that for the first time since her sister had died, she had slept well and soundly in her bed.

"Good afternoon, Miss," Missy said cheerfully, coming into her room with a stack of fresh laundry.

"Afternoon?" Elsie said, laughing. "Isn't that something, Missy. What time is it?"

"Just after noon. Seeing as how you were up 'til dawn, we all thought we should let you sleep."

"And in my own bed," Elsie said, as if she'd just accomplished something grand. The sun was shining brightly, and a breeze pushed the curtains away from the window. It was a glorious day, and she refused to allow thoughts of how stubborn Alexander had been last night to ruin it. She chose, instead, to think about how wonderful it was that he'd told her he loved her. And how very much she loved him.

Two people in love could move mountains if they wanted to. It was almost as if the previous night and all its terrible implications had never happened at all. Elsie was strangely, almost frenetically, happy. She didn't know how, but she knew she and Alexander would triumph. After the bleakness of the night before, she knew Alexander would have awakened much as she had—ready to face the world with the person he loved. Certainly, there were obstacles to their love. Anything truly worth having did not come easily.

"I'm ravenous," Elsie said, whipping off the covers and leaping from bed and walking to her washstand. Splashing her face with water and giving the rest of herself a quick wash, she changed into her simplest gown, a pretty butter-yellow muslin. It was the sort of dress a duchess would never wear, which was perhaps the reason she loved it so.

"My, you're just a bubble of joy this afternoon, Miss, if I may say," Missy commented as she gave Elsie her slippers.

"You may say anything you like today, within reason," Elsie said, smiling as she put her hair up into a simple bun. She felt an odd twinge of trepidation and she stoutly ignored it. "Do you know where Mary is?"

"In the garden, Miss."

That only made Elsie smile all the more. She dashed down to the kitchen, where cook clucked over her for not eating a more substantial meal than a buttery roll and two juicy plums. "Oh, heaven," Elsie said, a bit of juice running down her chin.

"Now I'll not have enough for my plum cake," cook grumbled.

"I'll fetch you more from the garden," Elsie said,

waving back at the woman as she hurried to find Mary. They could go on an adventure, the two of them, hunting for the plumpest plums.

A squeal of little girl laughter gave away Mary's location, where she sat on a soft blanket in the shade having what appeared to be a tea party with imaginary everything. Not a tea cup or pot to be found. Hating to disturb Mary's fun, she simply watched for a while, until her nanny announced it was time to clean up their mess. Elsie giggled, and approached the pair.

"What a delightful tea party," she said to the blushing nanny.

"Mary decided to have a tea party and we both thought it'd be a bit easier than running back into the house for her set, Miss Elizabeth."

"Very imaginative. I wonder if I might borrow my sister and go hunting," Elsie said with a mischievous grin.

"Hunting," Mary gasped. "For what?"

"Why the Plum Fairy. She hides behind the biggest, plumpest plum in the tree. And if we find that plum, we just might find the fairy."

Mary clapped her hands together, an endearing copy of what Elsie herself did when she was extraordinarily pleased. "Where shall we go?" Mary asked, her blue eyes wide.

"Why to the orchard, of course."

Elsie spent the next two hours searching for the plum fairy and eating more than a couple of small fruits with Mary, whose chin was turning a bit purple. The little girl was getting tired, and it was clearly time for her afternoon nap.

After giving Mary back to Miss Lawton, Elsie spent the rest of the afternoon writing invitations for her birthday ball. She felt on the edge of a strange hysteria, for shouldn't she be crying into her pillow rather than planning the ball at which her doomed engagement to Lord Hathwaite would be announced? It was to take place in a matter of three weeks. Three weeks to come up with some sort of plan that would convince Alexander to claim his title or convince her father that being transported to Australia as a debtor was a viable option. Her stomach was suddenly filled with butterflies, not the nice sort that one felt in anticipation of something wonderful, but the ones that battered one's stomach until it lost its contents.

Elsie put her pen down and stared blankly at the last of the invitations. What if Alexander did not love her enough to seek his title? What if he tried to attain his title but was put back in an asylum by his powerful father? What if he were discarded as a fraud?

What if he simply left?

She needed to see him, to speak to him. It would be hours until she could safely go into the ballroom so they could talk to one another. But what if he stayed away? Should she simply take that as a sign that he wanted to forget her? They'd both been so tired last evening, and shocked and upset by what they'd learned about each other. The glow of optimism that had made her feel almost giddy had seeped away slowly throughout the day, leaving Elsie nearly bereft. Alexander couldn't have been more clear. He did not mean to seek his title. He would not.

And she would not leave her father open to scandal or worse and her sister to a life of poverty. She had no doubt, none at all, that His Grace would make her father suffer if the wedding were called off. Elsie shivered.

I will never be the Duke of Kingston. And, therefore, you will never be my bride.

Really, what was there to talk over?

Elsie steeled herself against the tears that threatened. She would not cry, not until all hope was lost, not until she spoke to Alexander. Surely, if he loved her at all, he would seek her out this evening. He knew she would go to the ballroom as she had been nearly every night since that fateful evening she'd wandered down and seen his light. He would be there. He would.

But that night, and the four nights after, Alexander did not make an appearance and it was driving Elsie slowly mad. Had she imagined that he'd told her he loved her? Was it simply a game to him, to try to seduce the daughters of the households he visited?

No. He was suffering and no doubt felt he was doing the noble thing by staying away from her. It was maddening to know that he was in the ballroom painting, working hard to finish the mural, but was completely out of reach to her. She couldn't barge into the ballroom and demand to see him. Not only would she give up Monsieur's secret, she would also be giving up Alexander's and she loved him too much for that.

She tortured herself by watching them approach the house from her room, willing Alexander to look up, but he never did. The entrance to the ballroom was directly below her window. How could he not see her? She felt as if she were losing her mind. She could not be this girl who pined for a man who clearly did not give a damn for her. But she was, oh, God, she was.

On the fifth night, her father remarked that she looked a bit peaked. "Are you unwell, my dear?"

"Just a small headache," Elsie lied, finding it remarkably difficult to talk past the lump that had taken up residence in her throat. She felt as if she were on the verge of tears constantly. She stared down at her book, the words swimming before her, and prayed her father did not say something kind, for that would be her undoing.

"Elsie."

She looked up, trying to put a normal, happy expression on her face. "Yes, Father?"

"I wish you were happier," he said after a long moment.

"I am happy, Father. Please don't worry about me." But even as she said those words, two tears slipped from her eyes.

"Happy tears, then?"

Elsie closed her eyes briefly, then lowered her head and shook it. "I'm just being a ninny, that's all. I shall miss you and Mary and each day my wedding draws closer, I sense the loss more." She looked up, hoping he believed her explanation. It was the truth, in part.

"Warbeck Abbey is not so far, you know."

Elsie smiled. "I know. I told you I was being a ninny." She forced a laugh, one that made her father relax and smile.

That night, Elsie did not go to the ballroom. She

cried herself to sleep, her face buried in her pillow so Missy would not awaken. She knew one thing: If Alexander loved her, truly loved her, he would do anything so they could be together. He did not love her. He did not. It was a litany in her head, a heart-breaking, soul-shattering realization. She went from anger at herself for her foolishness, to anger at Alexander for his cowardice, to heartbreak and back to anger. He didn't even have the decency to say good-bye. How dare he treat her so shabbily? How dare he claim to love her and then torture her so?

By morning, she was frazzled and tired and ready to make a complete and total fool of herself in front of the entire household. Once she was dressed, she marched down the stairs and went directly to the ballroom, rapping on the door loudly.

"Yes, Mademoiselle?"

"Monsieur Desmarais," she said, looking past him and seeing Alexander standing at the mural, his back to her, stiff and unmoving. Her heart wrenched, which only fueled her anger more.

"We are having a small dinner party this evening, just the vicar and his wife and their two grown daughters. And I would like you and your assistant to attend," she said.

"That sounds a fine time. But Andre, he is not one for the company, so I regret he cannot come."

She let out a brittle laugh. "But surely he eats. We don't stand on formality in this house, sir, if that is your concern."

Monsieur Desmarais looked back at Alexander, who still stood like a statue staring at the mural. "I don't think Andre . . ."

"I absolutely insist," Elsie said, her voice uncharacteristically shrill.

Monsieur gave her a little bow. "Of course, Mademoiselle. We shall be delighted."

Monsieur closed the door softly and looked worriedly over to the younger man, who stood so rigid before him. He had not been himself these last days and Monsieur worried that Andre was slipping away from him. Never had he been so withdrawn in all the time he had known the boy. Even those days after he'd taken him from that asylum, he had never been so *silent.* Andre might not speak, but his expressions spoke volumes. Lately, his face was stone, a blank slate of misery, and Monsieur had no idea how to help him because Andre couldn't say what was wrong and he refused to write it down.

He knew his boy was getting little sleep, for the weariness was etched on his face and his eyes were red-rimmed.

"You heard the Mademoiselle?"

He watched worriedly as Andre nodded bleakly.

"I can say you have taken ill. She does not understand what she asks of you. She does not know."

It was a warm evening, and so Elsie had her windows opened as she prepared for the small dinner party, feeling more than troubled about forcing Alexander to join them. But what was she to do? Go to the artist's cottage at night and demand to see his assistant? Drag him from the ballroom so he could tell her . . . something, anything to take away this burgeoning hurt. The worst was knowing that he was right to stay away from her. It was useless, completely so, for her to pine for a man she could never have. Yet this madness would not leave her. She had no idea what she hoped to accomplish by inviting him to dinner. He could not speak, not in front of Monsieur, and she had no hope of taking him aside to talk. He was little more than a servant, and yet she had demanded he attend a dinner party. Even her father had raised his brows at the news.

She simply wanted to see him, so that he could give her some indication that he was suffering as much as she. Yes, that was it. *No, it was not.* She wanted him to declare his love and tell her he would seek his title, he would do anything, so they could be together. She wanted him to get on his knees and beg for her hand and tell her over and over that he loved her and nothing could keep them apart. That's what she wanted. She might as well believe in plum fairies.

A male voice outside drew her to the window and she watched, her heart slamming in her breast, as the two men made their way across the lawn. Alexander looked so handsome wearing a formal suit and cravat, and it took little imagination to envision him as the lord he truly was. Monsieur was talking rapidly in French, and though Elsie spoke nearly fluently, it was difficult for her to keep up. What she could tell, however, was that Monsieur was attempting to comfort Alexander. Monsieur had one hand on his back and was looking up at him, worry etched on his face.

When they were nearly below her window, Alexander bent over, his hands on his knees.

"Breathe, my son, breathe," Monsieur said in French. "It will pass. It always passes. I don't know why the mademoiselle insisted that you come. I will tell her you are ill," he said angrily. "It is too much for you. She does not understand, for if she did, she never would have asked this of you."

Alexander shook his head, and even from this distance, Elsie could see his face was bathed in sweat.

"Are you going to be sick?" Monsieur asked, stepping back just as Alexander vomited, a wrenching horrible sound that made Elsie nearly cry out. What was wrong with him? Was he truly ill? Perhaps that was why he'd stayed away from her all those nights.

She could hear Alexander's shaking breaths as he tried to regain control of his stomach.

"Are you done?" Monsieur asked, more than mere concern in his question.

Alexander shook his head and held a shaking hand up to stop Monsieur from coming closer, just as he retched again.

"I told her you did not like the company," Monsieur said fiercely, as Alexander retched again.

Elsie stepped back from the window, stunned. Nerves. It was nerves making Alexander so ill. The mere thought of sitting in a room with people he did not know was nearly debilitating for him. She put her hands over her mouth, feeling wretched. She knew he was shy, she knew he'd suffered as a boy, but she had no idea he was so afflicted. But hadn't he told her? Hadn't he said it was impossible for him to attend public functions? She hadn't understood. No wonder he thought it so impossible to claim his title, to go before the House of Lords and state his case, to carry on the duties of duke. If the thought of sitting down to an ordinary dinner could make him physically ill, what would the thought of speaking before a roomful of peers do?

Missy entered the room, carrying a pair of silk gloves in her hand. "We got that stain out, Miss Elizabeth," she said, holding up the pair of gloves triumphantly.

"Marvelous," Elsie said, pulling them on quickly. She wanted to intercept Monsieur and Alexander and let them know that it was not necessary for Alexander to attend. But as she descended the stairs, a carriage pulled up carrying the Picket family, and Elsie was forced into hostess duties.

Her father and Nelson Picket were long-time friends, and the two had become especially close when her mother died. The vicar had been one of the few people her father had leaned on in his terrible grief, and the Pickets were one of the few families to visit the manor since the death of her mother.

Their daughters, both seemingly happily unmarried, were an innocuous pair. Frances and Martha were plain girls with absolutely no sense of adventure and even less sense of humor. They both took words at face value, but Elsie liked them well enough, even if she did deem them too serious. Though they were three years apart, they dressed almost identically, in plain, light gray dresses that would have suited a very proper governess. Their hair, though a slightly different shade of brown, was parted sharply in the middle, and pulled into an unrelenting bun with nary a hair out of place. But despite their stern appearance, they were pleasant girls. Elsie always had the idea, one that she rather liked actually, that they thought her slightly improper and bold. Of course, they were rather isolated from society and hadn't any experience with the truly bold girls of the ton.

"It's so wonderful to see you," Elsie said. "I do believe the weather cleared just for your drive."

Martha smiled. "Do you think so?"

Elsie, who refused to believe Martha was being purposefully obtuse, said, "Of course. The heavens would not dare rain on our guests."

The sisters smiled uncertainly, as they always did when someone didn't speak completely plainly.

Elsie led the family into the large drawing room, where her father was already talking to Monsieur Desmarais. Alexander stood with them, stiff and silent, his hands thrust behind his back. When they entered the room, he looked at her with such intensity, Elsie's knees went momentarily weak. Then he looked away, and Elsie didn't have time to interpret that look.

"May I introduce you to Monsieur Desmarais, who has done us the great honor of agreeing to paint a mural on our ballroom wall," Elsie said. "These are our neighbors, the Pickets and their daughters, Miss Martha and Miss Frances. Mr. Picket is the local vicar. The entire family was a great comfort to us when my mother died."

"A pleasure," Monsieur said with a small bow.

The group looked curiously at Alexander, who continued to stand stiffly by Monsieur's side, like some powerful guardian. Someone who did not know him might have interpreted his cold countenance as arrogance, but Elsie knew better. His features were taut, his body almost painfully erect, his jaw clenched tightly. Elsie couldn't get the sound of his retching from her mind as she looked at him, trying to silently communicate how sorry she was to have forced this on him. But he refused to meet her eyes.

"This is his assistant, Andre," Elsie said, glad that she didn't slip and call him Alexander.

He nodded, a sharp jerk of his head.

"When will we be able to see this masterpiece, sir?" the vicar asked.

"Unfortunately, not this evening," Elsie said with forced cheer. "He has demanded that the unveiling be a surprise. The anticipation is quite maddening and I have had to force myself not to take a peek."

"The effect would be ruined," Monsieur said, smiling.

Elsie led the Pickets away on the pretense of discussing her birthday ball and quickly explained that "Andre" was a mute who did not speak.

"Oh," Martha said, her eyes filled with sympathy. "The poor man. How good of you to include him, though, Elsie."

"I fear he would rather not be here," Elsie admitted, daring another quick look at Alexander who looked stoic, as if enduring a great discomfort. "I think I might excuse him before dinner. I rather believe my invitation to him is frightfully thoughtless."

"But uninviting him might be even more devastating," Mrs. Picket said. "I think it was all kindness to include him. He seems clean enough and well behaved."

"Why ever might he not be clean?" Elsie asked, feeling her skin burn from the older woman's unintended slight. Alexander was not a stray pet, he was a brilliant artist and heir to a duchy.

"My dear girl, as a vicar's wife I am often called on to care for such people. Often they cannot be taught to wash or care for themselves in even the simplest way. It can be quite disconcerting, indeed."

"The Hayworth boy," Mr. Picket said, shaking his head. "Sad, sad case. But the Lord has a special place in His heart for such creatures."

Elsie knew of whom they spoke. The poor lad could only grunt, and his parents were quite unable to care for him.

"Al . . . Andre is not an idiot. He simply cannot speak," Elsie said, trying to rein in her temper. Even though she knew the Pickets meant nothing critical or unkind, she wanted to throttle them both. Hearing them gave Elsie new insight into what Alexander had no doubt suffered.

"Yes, there are varying degrees of affliction, I daresay," Mrs. Picket said soothingly.

"Still, it was all kindness," Martha said.

Never had Elsie intended the inclusion of Alexander to be something cruel. She hadn't thought of how difficult this evening would be for him. She'd only thought of herself and how she yearned to see him. Any anger she'd felt was gone. He might have been wrong to avoid her, but the knowledge did not make Elsie feel any better about what was happening at this moment.

Their butler announced dinner and the group made its way to the little-used formal dining room. When her mother had been alive, they'd had dinner parties at least once a week. It had been a house filled with guests and gaiety, and these small, solemn dinners only made Elsie miss her mother all the more.

Elsie's father sat at the head of the table, and Elsie took a seat to his right. Across from her sat Monsieur, then the Pickets and their daughters, and sitting at the end like a forgotten extra piece, Alexander. His sitting without a companion across from him made his attendance even more glaringly incorrect.

Even though she knew he was extremely uncomfortable, Elsie couldn't help drinking in the sight of him sitting with her at the table. They'd spent every moment together in the dim light of a gaslight or a lamp. Now she could see his true beauty, the sharp line of his jaw, the soft waves of his too-long chocolate hair. He did not look her way, but kept his eyes on the table in front of him. Still. Silent. *Angry.*

Yes, he was angry. She saw that now. Elsie bit her bottom lip as the footmen began to serve the first course. She joined in the inane conversation, and even laughed a time or two, but she was ever aware of the man sitting at the end of the table, his eyes burning, his hands shaking when he dared take a drink, his mouth pressed tight.

"How ever did you find Andre?" Mrs. Picket said, and Elsie saw Alexander give a nearly imperceptible jerk at the mention of his name.

"He was orphaned and I took him in when he was just a lad. He is like a son to me," Monsieur said, looking pointedly down the table to where Alexander sat. Anyone else would have looked at Monsieur and smiled, but Alexander simply sat staring at the table as if transfixed. "A good and loyal son."

"How lovely," Mrs. Picket said. "You are a good man to take on such a burden."

"He's not a burden," Elsie blurted out before thinking.

"No," Monsieur said, looking at Elsie thoughtfully. "He is not. He is a great help to me and good company. The life of an artist can be a lonely one."

Elsie squeezed her hands together on her lap. She wanted to stand up and scream that Alexander was a wonderful man, the true genius behind Monsieur's murals, and a man she loved with all her heart. But, like Alexander, she remained silent.

"I sometimes wish I had a silent companion," Frances said. Then, as if realizing she'd just made a joke, she covered her mouth so that Martha could not see her smiling.

"That, my dear, was a terrible thing to say," Mrs. Picket said sternly.

Frances bowed her head, but Elsie could see she was still trying not to smile.

Finally, a dessert of peach cobbler was served. Alexander seemed slightly more relaxed, slightly less enraged, perhaps. It was, beyond a doubt, the worst dinner of Elsie's life. She'd spent the entire time worrying about Alexander, and wondering how she could put things right.

Soon after the meal was ended, the Pickets left for the evening and Alexander disappeared back to the small cottage he shared with Monsieur. Her father, who'd had a bit more port than usual, was engaged in a lively discussion with Monsieur about, of all things, lichen. To his credit, the artist seemed actually interested, and expressed enthusiasm when her father suggested he show the artist his drawings.

"They're not nearly as fine as what you do, but perhaps you could appreciate my crude attempts, sir."

"If you don't mind, Father, I think I shall retire," Elsie said. Her father nodded absently, completely distracted by having someone finally share his love of the beautiful fungus.

Elsie had no intention of going to her rooms. Instead, she slipped out of the house and began walking directly across the lawn in the direction of the cottage and Alexander.

Chapter 14

Alexander returned to the cottage, threw off his jacket and yanked off the cravat that felt like a noose around his neck. This night had, perhaps, been one of the most humiliating of his life. To have the woman he loved see him like that was torturous. He hadn't thought her a vindictive person, but why else would she force him to be the night's entertainment? Had she enjoyed his discomfort? Was this the punishment she had exacted for being ignored? It seemed so unlike Elsie that his heart rejected what his mind was telling him.

He took a deep, ragged breath, trying to force himself to relax, his entire body was so taut, his muscles had begun to ache. A knock on the door made him wince. He didn't want to face anyone, not even a helpful footman. But when he opened the door, it wasn't the young servant who'd been attending them; it was Elsie, tears streaming down her face.

She threw herself into his arms on a sob, wrapping her arms around his torso and pressing her wet face against his chest. "I'm so sorry, Alexander. Please forgive me," came her muffled words.

Slowly, Alexander brought his arms around her and buried his face in her neck, like a small child seeking comfort after a terrible hurt. He let out a sound that sounded humiliatingly like a sob and he brought her closer against him.

Elsie lifted her face and looked beseechingly at him. "I didn't know. I couldn't. But you refused to see me and I was going mad. I had to see you. I had to know that what you told me wasn't a lie, that you do love me. Tell me you do."

Alexander swallowed down the misery that gripped his throat. "It does no good whether I love you or not, but if you must know, then yes. I love you. I will always love you."

"Then why did you stay away?"

"It is because I love you." He let out a short breath. "I thought it would be easier, for both of us, if we stayed apart."

Elsie shook her head, looking adorably sad. "It wasn't at all easy."

"I do know that now," Alexander said on a small laugh. "I don't know what I shall do when you are lost to me forever."

"Let's not think of it," Elsie said, gripping him even tighter and laying her head against his chest. "I can hear your heartbeat," she whispered.

Alexander kissed her hair, breathing in slowly so that he might remember her warm scent.

"I don't think I can bear being with another man."

"Don't speak of it. Please don't."

She lifted her head again, her eyes filled with anguish. "I want to know what it's like to be with a man I love. I want to carry the memory of it with me. If I only have that, I can bear it. I can close my eyes and think of you."

"God, Elsie," he said, pushing her away. "Stop."

"I cannot help it. I want to make love to you, Alexander."

He looked down at her earnest face and was sorely tempted to drag her into the cottage and do as she asked. But he feared loving her would only make their parting even more unbearable, not to mention it was simply wrong.

"Do you really think I'm the sort of man who would cuckold his own brother?" he asked gently, tipping her chin up with his forefinger.

She dropped her gaze and bit her lower lip. And when she looked back up at him, he saw a glimmer of mischievousness in her gaze. "I *was* hoping."

He couldn't stop the chuckle that erupted from his throat. "It would be wrong."

"It would be wonderful," she said, and he could not argue. "I love you Alexander, and I want to show you in every way. Please."

She grabbed his hand and started tugging him from the door. "You mean now?"

"Absolutely. If I give you a chance to get away, you'll surely come to your senses."

"I've already come to my senses," he said, even as he let her lead him away. He was no saint, and the woman he loved, who would soon be lost to him forever, wanted to make love. He could not and would not say no.

The two hurried across the dew-filled grass, two

shadows beneath a sky lit dimly by a half moon. She brought him into the ballroom and secreted him up a set of stairs, to the second floor of the manor.

She stopped outside one door and turned to him. "It's a guest room and hasn't been used since before my mother died. No one shall discover us." With that, she slipped into the room, and, God help him, he followed.

"Are you certain of this?" he asked.

"Yes." No hesitation, no uncertainty. "Are you?"

"No," he said with a tinge of exasperation. "I fear I shall regret this. I fear *we* shall regret this. I fear . . ." He stopped and swallowed. "I fear. I fear everything."

She smiled at him, as if a smile could wipe away the sort of man he was. "Then stop."

"Stop?" he asked, bewildered.

"Stop and kiss me."

If there was a glimmer of resolve left in him, at that moment it was swept away. How could he not kiss her, with her face uptilted, her mouth slightly open, her eyes beseeching him? And so he kissed her, feeling the softness of her lips against his, her sigh of pure joy. He moved his mouth, slanting his head, and she matched him with unpracticed enthusiasm, letting out a sound that went straight to his groin. God, he wanted this, he wanted to feel her against him, he wanted to sink into her slick heat, he wanted to taste her skin, to make her moan, to make her come. He thrust his tongue into her mouth, loving her taste, the way she matched his strokes, the way she pressed against him and moaned when she felt his erection.

"I think we should undress," she said, backing

away. The window let in little light, only the cold gray of a half moon that left a weak rectangle of light on the carpeted floor. She turned her back and looked over her shoulder. "You need to unbutton me," she said so matter-of-factly, he laughed.

"As you wish, Mademoiselle." His fingers shook as he undid them one by one, revealing more of her to him. When he reached past her small waist, he pulled the gown down over her shoulders and placed his mouth on that perfect spot where her neck gently curved to her shoulder. She let out a sound of pleasure and he brought his hands to her front, cupping her breasts, his knees nearly buckling beneath him.

"So soft," he murmured, kissing her exposed skin.

Elsie turned around and pulled off her dress and well-starched petticoats, the great mass of material falling to the floor with a rather loud rustling sound that made her giggle. In a matter of minutes, she'd loosened her corset laces and stood standing before Alexander wearing only her chemise, silk stockings, and pantalets.

"I am always amazed at how many layers of clothing women insist on wearing even in the middle of summer," Alexander said. She looked delectable, the white of her underclothes seeming to glow even in the dim moonlight. She looked down, shy and awkward, as if, along with stripping her clothing she'd also stripped away any confidence she'd had. "I think I can handle the rest," he said, his voice low.

Elsie looked back at the large bed behind her, a thrill going through her stomach. She felt strangely alive, her body sensitive to the barest touch. Even his breath upon her skin made her shiver with anticipation. This was right, she told herself. And even if it wasn't, she refused to care. All her life she'd done what was expected of her, and now, for this brief moment of time, she was being utterly selfish. She would spend the rest of her life with a man she didn't love to protect her family. For this one time in her life, she would do something just for herself.

Behind her she could hear Alexander removing his clothes—the thump of his boots, the sound of his braces snapping off his shoulders, the starched collar and cuffs being put aside, his trousers being pulled down. She closed her eyes and smiled. The man she loved was undressing and they were about to make love. Her eyes suddenly burned with unshed tears, and she shook her head at her silly emotions.

She turned suddenly, and stared. He was completely nude, and her quick turn startled him into stillness. He was gloriously masculine, and even in the moonlight she could tell he had a fine form. "You're naked," she said unnecessarily.

"And you are not."

She giggled nervously. She never giggled and here she was doing it again and again. She must stop, for it was annoying even to her own ears. That thought made her giggle again. "I'm quite nervous," she admitted, and turned toward the bed.

This was a little used guest room. The furniture was shrouded with covers to protect it from dust and to make preparing the room for unexpected guests a simple job for the servants. Alexander walked to the bed and removed the protective covering, revealing a rich, embroidered satin coverlet whose color was impossible to discern in the dim light. He neatly folded the cover and pulled back the coverlet, laying the folded cloth neatly on the bed, before letting out an audible sigh.

"What is wrong?"

"I have never been with an innocent girl," he said. "I have heard there is blood. And pain." He let out another breath. "I don't want to hurt you."

"It hurts?" she let out on a squeak. Her mother had died before she'd been able to talk to Elsie about what happens in the marriage bed, and she'd assumed her aunt would give her "the talk" before she got married to Lord Hathwaite.

"Well, you won't die of it. I don't think," Alexander said, clearly teasing. "Come here."

Elsie walked to him, her shyness growing with each step. He was, after all, completely nude, while she still had on a considerable amount of clothing.

"Give me your hand."

She held her hand up and he grasped it, his own large and warm and immensely comforting. Then he laid her hand on his chest and she could feel his heart beating madly in his chest. Elsie smiled up at him, her love expanding so suddenly, it was all she could do to stay firmly on the ground and not fly up to the moon in complete joy. He let out a shaky breath, and pulled her hand down so she could feel the taut ridges of his torso, and then, the completely foreign appendage that made him so completely male.

"Oh," she said, and pulled her hand back. He gently placed her hand around him, thick and hard and hot, and he hissed out a breath. How odd, she thought, letting her hand explore the velvety length. She'd never given much thought to a man's parts, what it felt like, what would happen should she touch it. Certainly, she'd never thought the men around her were hiding such large things in their pants. That thought almost made her giggle again. Now, she was overcome with curiosity, and she let her fingers move along his length, not realizing that he'd stopped breathing, that his fists were clenched by his sides as if he were in agony.

"It's hard. And rather larger than I imagined," she said thoughtfully.

"It is not usually so hard. This is what happens to a man when he desires a woman," he said through gritted teeth.

"And you like it when a woman touches you?"

"When *you* touch me it is exquisite torture," he said, then nudged her hand away with a groan. He pulled her up for a long, drugging kiss, his hands on her round bottom, pressing her up and against his hard member. She could feel heat and liquid pool between her legs, and the beginning of what she knew was sharp arousal. Unknowingly, she began moving her hips and discovered unexpected pleasure in the movement. Her hands lay against his lightly-furred chest, then snaked up behind his neck to pull him close. She could not get enough, no matter how deeply she kissed him, no matter how she moved against him. She needed something more, something she instinctively knew Alexander could give her.

Suddenly, he lifted her and placed her on the bed, never breaking their kisses, never stopping his caresses. He pulled back only long enough to tug at the ribbon on her chemise, pushing it down to reveal her breasts to his burning gaze. With a low, soft sound, he kissed one nipple, already pebbling in the cool night air. And then, he sucked, gently, sending such an expected shard of pleasure between her legs, she cried out. With a male sound of satisfaction, he moved to the other breast, laving his tongue against her taut flesh, drawing her into his mouth, making her hips move of their own accord. She could feel him move against her, pushing his arousal against her hip in a provocative rhythm that instinctively matched her own movements.

He pulled back, his breath harsh, and she let out a small sound of dismay. She never wanted this to end. Never.

"You are a miracle," he said, kissing her mouth again and again, as if she were a drug and he could not get enough.

"And you, sir, are very practiced," Elsie said with mock anger.

She could tell he smiled down at her as if pleased with her comment instead of shamed by it.

"I want to please you, Elsie," he said with endearing earnestness.

"You do please me."

"No. I want to make you feel intense pleasure, but you must trust me."

Elsie grew alarmed at his seriousness. "Trust you with what?"

"Your body." He moved his hand to her pantalets and found the slit and her most private place. Elsie stiffened, but he kissed her and stilled his hand.

And when he moved it again, he let out a groan of satisfaction that Elsie didn't understand. "You are so wet, my love."

"That's good?" she gasped as one finger slipped slightly inside her. He kissed her and began moving his finger in time to the subtle shifts of her hips, in and out, in such a primitive, carnal way she found herself letting out small sounds of pleasure.

And then he did something purely wonderful. He touched the spot where all the pleasure seemed to pool, a place she hadn't known could evoke such intense feelings. She shifted on the bed, digging her heels into the soft blankets, flexing her hands on his shoulders, not knowing what to do, what was coming, only knowing that never in her life had she felt so wonderfully, beautifully out of control of her own body. He moved his hand against her, making her throb, making her jerk her hips against his, making her nearly scream out with the pleasure of it. And then it came, an intense wave that radiated from between her thighs to her toes to her breasts, leaving her mind blank and her body at the mercy of the man she loved. Her hips jerked uncontrollably as he held her against him, murmuring that he loved her over and over as she relished the feeling of her body contracting, throbbing in her release.

When she finally came back to the guest bedroom, where she lay nearly naked with the man she loved, Elsie laughed. "That was lovely," she said. "Truly."

He kissed her and she could tell he was smiling. He ought to be rather proud of himself, she thought, after what he'd done to her. She could never forget this, never forget how his hand touching her could send her to heaven and back.

Alexander had never in his life felt such intense joy as he did watching his beloved in the throes of passion. She was as responsive as she was innocent, and that somehow only made his feeling more powerful. He would not think that another man might bring her such pleasure, he shut his mind down and simply felt her beneath him, all warm feminine softness. His Elsie.

With deft movements, he tugged at her pantalets and pulled them down over her still-stockinged legs. Then he slowly untied her garters and rolled the stockings down, kissing the exposed flesh as he went. She let out a contented, well-sated sigh, and he smiled down at her. Now she was truly naked and his only wish was that they'd had a candle or lamp to light so that he might see her completely.

"I'm going to put myself inside you, love," he said, positioning himself between her legs. He gently pushed her legs apart, caressing her briefly with his fingers before easing himself into her slick, tight entrance. He gasped at the feel of her against him, hot and wet, and he pushed as slowly as he could even as his body screamed at him to enter her completely.

"It's all right," she said, looking up at him, her gaze direct.

She felt so good and it was all he could do not to thrust inside her, to feel her tight heat, to move again and again until he found his release. She moved her hips, driving him closer to her maidenhead, and he groaned.

"Kiss me, Alexander," she said, and when he moved down, she thrust her hips up, making it impossible not to match her movement. He buried himself inside her, taking her sharp sound of pain in his kiss. He stayed like that for a long moment, his eyes pressed closed, his breathing harsh, as he felt her muscles contract around him.

"Don't move," he said, kissing her jaw, her mouth, her chin. "It is too much. Too good." He hardly recognized his own pleas. He would not spill his seed inside her, but he might if she moved even the smallest bit. When he'd gained control of himself, he began to move, slowly, in and out of her, making her gasp.

"I'm hurting you," he said, his voice raw.

"No. No, you're not. It feels rather wonderful now."

He kissed her again, moving faster, losing his tenuous grasp on control, thrusting in a quick frenzy of movement that she met by raising her hips to meet his. With a final groan, Alexander pulled out, spilling himself on the sheet he'd folded beneath them before collapsing on top of Elsie.

"I love you," he said against her neck, tasting her salty skin. He moved to the side, dragging her with him, holding her tightly, still fighting the panicked knowledge that she would someday be another's. He pushed away the sudden and almost painful rush of self-loathing.

Elsie let out a contented sigh, snuggling down until her head rested in the crook of his arm, her soft hair caressing his chest and shoulder. "I am officially a fallen woman," she said, sounding entirely happy. Her words only made Alexander wince. At the moment, he was fighting fierce regret.

"Have you ever been in love before, Alexander?" she asked, kissing his jaw.

"No."

"But you seem to be, well, knowledgeable. Or perhaps all men are as skilled?" He heard the teasing note in her voice but ignored it. She got up on one elbow and took his jaw in her hand, forcing him to look at her even though it was far too dark in the room for them to see each other's expressions clearly. "I'm jealous."

"Do not be. The others were meaningless."

"Others?" she asked, emphasizing the plurality of the word. "Do tell."

"Women of the aristocracy have few morals," he said, then realized, too late, that he was in bed with one of those women who clearly shouldn't be in bed with him. "I didn't mean you," he added quickly.

"Well, I am one of them," she said, sounding far too cheerful for a ruined woman. "How many meaningless women were there?"

"Enough."

She giggled. "Who was your favorite?"

"You."

Elsie gave him a playful swat on the arm. "Other than me, of course. I had no idea you were such a rogue."

Abruptly, he sat up. He didn't want to talk about other women when he was in bed with the only one he'd ever loved. "The other women were nothing, as I said," he said angrily.

She was silent for a long moment, then said quietly. "I was teasing you. And I *am* curious."

He let out a long and beleaguered sigh. "The Countess von Zinnen. She was very young and married to a very old man. I met her when I was sixteen in Italy."

"Did she love you?" Elsie asked.

He let out a short laugh. "No, she loved what happened in the bed, but not me. I realized this fairly quickly."

Elsie wrapped her arms around his torso, pressing her soft breasts against his back, and he let out another laugh because his male parts were getting extremely attentive to her every movement. "Did you speak to her?"

He lay back down, and she returned to her position in the crook of his arm, as if it were the most natural thing in the world to do. "Yes. She was quite disappointed. I was like a little pet to her, I think. A novelty. And when I spoke, she was angry. I believe now that she thought I could tell her husband or someone else what she was doing. I imagine she thought she'd found the perfect lover, someone who could satisfy her needs and never be able to talk about it."

"That's terrible."

It was a pattern that had repeated itself more than once before he'd learned to keep his mouth shut. "Yes, it was at the time."

Elsie tightened her hold on him. "You haven't had enough happiness in your life, Alexander."

He was silent.

"I wish . . ."

"Don't," he said.

"But I do wish, just the same."

And then, so quietly he wasn't even certain she heard, he said, "As do I."

Chapter 15

For the next three days, Elsie lived a double life. In the daytime, she was a devoted daughter planning for her birthday ball at which the Duke of Kingston would announce her engagement to Lord Hathwaite. She played with Mary, ran the household, solved the little day-to-day problems that arose. A maid discovered a large hornet's nest in the attic, another maid spent hours polishing the wrong service for the ball, then burst into tears when Mrs. Whitehouse informed her of the mistake (Elsie calmed her down by insisting on using the polished set even though the pattern was quite old-fashioned). And through it all she floated about the manor as if on a cloud, filled with love and pushing aside with brutal determination any thought that threatened to ruin her mood. The very smell of paint and turpentine that permeated the air outside the ballroom made her think of Alexander and sent a warm frisson of happiness through her.

Her nights were spent in Alexander's arms. She'd wait for him, her knees tucked under her chin, then leap from the bed and throw herself into his arms the moment he softly clicked the door shut. They made love with a frenzy that left them both laughing and out of breath, only to make love all over again. They talked and laughed and made love as if nothing would ever change. They didn't talk about the mural, which was nearly completed, the ball, which would end their idyll, or anything that touched upon the reality of their situation. Each knew, of course, that what they were doing would only end in heartache, that reality marched on outside that guest room door, but they silently and firmly shut out that reality when that door snicked closed each night.

On the fourth night, Elsie ate her supper early, foraging in the kitchen for anything that would fill her stomach so that she could spend an entire evening with Alexander. That's where her father found her, swinging her legs on the tall stool that was usually tucked beneath cook's large preparation table, munching on a slab of ham and warm, buttered bread.

"You won't have an appetite for supper tonight if you eat all that," her father said, eying the large portion of ham in front of her.

"This is my supper," she said after hurriedly swallowing.

"You've forgotten, then." At Elsie's blank stare, he added, "Sir William's ball. When we received the invitation you were beside yourself."

Elsie pulled a face. "I'd completely forgotten." She had, though she didn't know how that was possible. When they'd received the invitation to Sir William's masquerade a month ago, she'd talked of nothing else. The annual event was always fun and the only masquerade she'd been allowed to attend, for the guests were a small, select group of people whom she'd known for years. It was always great fun trying to determine whom everyone depicted. Masks were discouraged, as that was considered a bit scandalous, but a few more daring people—usually the gentlemen—continued to wear them. This year was most important because it was the first fancy dress ball her father was attending since her mother's death three years before. Elsie, out of mourning, had attended the last ball wearing a deep lavender gown, decorated with fall flowers, going as Autumn. This year she'd planned to go as Luna, wearing a luminescent gown of satin and silk that shimmered as she moved.

"You're going as Robin Hood again?"

Her father gave her a sheepish grin. "It's the only costume I have and your mother always said I looked quite dashing in it."

"So you do," Elsie said, her heart contracting a bit at the mention of her mother. She noticed lately that her father had been able to bring her mother into a conversation without his eyes taking on that dark look of despair.

"I'm going as Luna, but I fear I haven't time for the elaborate coiffure I'd planned," she said with an easy shrug. Her father gave her a strange look, and Elsie felt a flush grow on her cheeks. Normally, planning for a ball was her only concern, and the fact she wasn't running about planning every last detail was highly unusual. "I think it's planning my own ball that has distracted me so," she said, her cheeks growing even more red with her lie. The truth was that nearly every waking moment had been consumed with thoughts of Alexander, of the time they spent together. It was almost as if she'd shut her mind away from all else, including their inevitable separation. "What time is it?"

"We must be leaving in two hours if we're to arrive before nine o'clock. Will that give you enough time to prepare?"

"Oh, goodness," Elsie said, leaping up. "That is a sharp challenge. I'll go fetch Missy."

Elsie hurried away, but instead headed toward the ballroom, knocking lightly on the door and praying it was Alexander who answered, not Monsieur Desmarais. Fortunately, Alexander appeared in the door's crack.

"Meet me in our room," she whispered, and hurried off.

In minutes, Elsie was in Alexander's arms, kissing him and wishing she had nowhere else to go that night. She pulled away with real regret, for she wanted nothing more than to lie with him talking, making love, holding one another. Any feelings of guilt or shame were firmly pushed aside. She simply refused to think about them and ignored the persistent sick feeling in her stomach that hit her occasionally, the one that reminded her she was lying with a man she was not married to, one she knew she would likely never marry. That she was engaged, even if not formally so, and was conducting herself shamefully. No, she would not think of these things; she would only think about how much she loved Alexander and how he loved her.

"I fear I cannot be with you tonight," Elsie said. "I'm forced to attend a masquerade."

"Horrors," Alexander said, giving her a mock shiver.

"It is not so bad as that," Elsie said, smiling up at his horrified expression. "I would look forward to it, except I don't want to miss a night with you. We have so few left."

"No," he said, kissing her lightly. "Go to your ball and come to me afterwards."

"I do wish you could go, too. Masquerades are such fun." At his look of disbelief, she said, "They are. You can be anyone you want. It's a lovely sort of freedom. Not that I am shy, as you well know. But I've actually seen the Picket sisters dancing with men who would never have noticed them if not for their costumes. I'm very sorry to say that I absolutely adore balls and dancing and seeing friends. It's quite isolating here, you know, especially since my mother died. I feel a bit guilty enjoying myself sometimes, but I know my mother would want me to have fun. It's hard to understand someone who doesn't like to dance."

"I like to dance, I just don't like to dance with people about," Alexander said.

"That quite would put a damper on any ball, then," she said, letting out a laugh. "It would be just yourself, dancing with a ghost partner."

"No. With you."

Elsie smiled. "We could hire an orchestra and

they would play only waltzes and we would dance all night."

"Now that sounds like a ball I could enjoy."

It did sound lovely, but also quite lonely, and something in her eyes must have given her thoughts away.

Alexander's expression turned serious. "You really would like me to go?"

"Oh, no. I would never ask that of you. I know how difficult it would be for you."

Alexander's expression became set, almost angry. "It would be difficult. It shouldn't be. I'm a man grown. I should be able to attend a party or ball without becoming physically ill."

"Perhaps," Elsie said, keeping her tone light, "but you are that rare male who dislikes balls." Elsie laughed. "I think the secret is that all males feel very much like you do. Except, perhaps my father. He enjoys balls and masquerades. At least he did before my mother died. I think he is starting to miss socializing."

Alexander pulled her to him and tucked her head beneath his chin. "I wish I were not so afflicted. I wish I could make you happy."

"You do, silly man. Happier than I can express. I love you."

She felt him heave a sigh and kiss the top of her head. "You may go," he said imperiously. "And you may dance. But I do not want you to enjoy dancing with anyone under the age of, say, sixty."

Elsie pulled back and lifted one eyebrow. "My own father is only forty-six. Am I not allowed to dance with him?"

"Relations are the exception." Suddenly, he pulled

her to him and kissed her fiercely. "In truth, I cannot stomach the thought of you in another's arms, even for a dance."

Three hours later, Alexander stood outside the very crowded ballroom of Sir William Fenton's manor house, a sturdy-looking house located just a thirty minute ride from Mansfield Hall. In one gloved hand he held his mask. The other hand was occupied holding the contents of his stomach in or alternately wiping the sweat from his glistening forehead.

He stood in the shadows trying to gather the courage to go into the ballroom and ask the woman he loved for a dance. Just one. One dance to prove to himself and to her that he was a normal man, that he could dance at a ball, that he could conquer this thing that had slowly destroyed his life.

Elsie had been easy to spot, for her hair fairly glowed in the ballroom's soft gaslight. In fact, the entire manor was illuminated, a bright and cheerful sight in the black night surrounding him. He could stay there, watch from afar, wish it were he holding Elsie in his arms. He could pretend he was with her and perhaps that would be enough. But he'd come all this way, ridden a horse even though he hadn't been in the saddle for years, wearing a ridiculous costume he'd thrown together. He was Michelangelo, sans beard, wearing a simple black mask, flowing black overcoat and holding a paint-smattered pallet. He felt as ridiculous as he felt ill.

He could clearly hear the music, clearly see Elsie

dance again and again. It was no less torturous than the last time he'd watched her—perhaps even more. For now he knew she loved him and he loved her and still they were separated by his great and childish fear. What was wrong with him? What was it that made him physically ill at the thought of walking into a room of strangers. Good Christ above, sometimes he hated himself.

He watched her walk to a table laden with small treats and punch, watched as a footman handed her a glass, which she took with a brilliant smile. The footman grinned at something she said, and Alexander realized he would have given anything to have heard what it was. She had a way of making everyone around her relaxed and happy, an effervescent quality that could not be practiced or faked.

Taking a deep breath and swallowing down the bile in his throat, Alexander walked up the stairs to the balcony outside the ballroom and entered the doors, acting for all the world like he belonged. A stranger looking at him would see only a stiffly-held, tall man, looking slightly bored, as he strolled toward the refreshment table, black coat billowing out behind him. They would have no idea he was trying his utmost not to flee, not to vomit on his finely polished shoes.

"Beg pardon, Miss. Would you honor me with the next waltz?"

Elsie turned quickly, her eyes flashing in recognition and unadulterated joy.

"Careful, my love, you do not know me and have

no reason to look so overjoyed," he said, his voice low and full of warning.

"Oh, Alexander, how did you . . . why . . . oh, you are the most wonderful man on earth. You truly are the bravest man I know."

Alexander was embarrassed beyond words. He had done nothing more remarkable than attend a masquerade uninvited and ask the woman he loved to dance. And yet she was treating him like some returning war hero.

"Is there another waltz?" he asked, ignoring her reaction.

She grew serious, but her lips twitched suspiciously. "I'm afraid we haven't been formally introduced," she said in her haughtiest voice. And then, her eyes flew open again as she glanced over her shoulder. "Aunt Diane," she hissed. "Oh, goodness. You are Lord Firth of Lancashire. Your father knew my father at Eton. We met five summers ago at the Bellingham house party." She turned, smiling brightly. "Aunt Diane," she gushed. "You remember Lord Firth? We met his family at Bellingham's."

The aunt hardly spared him a glance. "Yes, of course. Elizabeth, I need to speak to your father. It seems that I may be forced to leave for Bamburgh, of all places. Of course I'll be back in time for your wedding, but I did promise Lord Braddock to chaperone his niece and a minor problem has developed."

"Oh?"

"The girl refuses to leave her home, even though it's been sold right out from under her. It's quite a tragedy, as I understand it, and she needs a woman's firm hand. Lord Braddock is beside himself and now must travel all that way himself. It's practically in Scotland!"

"Poor Aunt Diane. And, poor girl. She must be very frightened," Elsie said. "I'm sorry, Aunt, but I haven't seen Father in a while. Did you check the library? I understand several of the gentlemen are there playing faro."

Diane nodded. "I did. Oh, there he is. On the dance floor," she said with some surprise. "He's dancing with Mrs. Goodall." Her surprise was slowly replaced by a smile. "I do like her," she said.

Elsie frowned heavily. "Just because he's dancing with her doesn't mean he's going to marry her."

Diane simply nodded and smiled again, leaving Elsie frowning adorably.

"It's far too soon to talk of remarrying, don't you think?" Elsie said after Diane had left.

"I wouldn't know."

Elsie gave Alexander a dark look, not liking his neutral tone at all. She wanted him to be as outraged as she was. "Well, it is." She scowled at the dancing pair, her mood lightening greatly when she saw the look on her father's face. He seemed almost . . . happy. She might not like the idea of her father remarrying, but seeing him smile like that almost made such a thought palatable.

"The waltz?"

Elsie looked up at Alexander, hearing an almost desperate tone in his voice. A fine sheen of sweat covered his forehead and his beautiful mouth was set, his jaw bunched as if he were clenching his teeth to ward off some great pain.

"There is one next," she said, worriedly searching the eyes behind the dark mask. "You don't have to do this, you know. In fact, it makes me feel horrible knowing that this is so torturous for you."

Suddenly, he smiled, taking her breath away. "My dear, if dancing with you is torture, then please torture me to death. Please, Elsie, I am fine. I do not like being here, I will not lie. But any discomfort I feel is worth it to have you in my arms."

The orchestra began a Strauss waltz and Alexander laid down his pallet on a nearby chair, gave Elsie an elegant bow, and led her to the dance floor. She would never forget this dance, feeling as if she were the center of his world, the only thing on earth that mattered. He gazed at her with such intensity, Elsie had to physically stop herself from drawing him down so she could kiss him. It was torture to pretend he was a mere acquaintance when she wanted to dance close, feel his body against her. But he kept them apart, and danced like a man used to balls and waltzes.

"You're a wonderful dancer, Lord Firth."

"Grueling lessons as a boy. Obviously, one does not forget. My last dance partner was my mother," he said, with the smallest of smiles. "It truly was my favorite part of the day, because I could be with her. My father would only allow her time with us when it was absolutely necessary. Although, sometimes she would sneak up to our rooms and tell us stories. She would make them up, and make us the characters."

His story made her long for her own mother, and wonder what it had been like for him, a young boy, kept apart from his one loving parent. "I have always felt sorry for your mother. I suppose because she was married to your father."

Alexander laughed, and pulled her a bit closer than propriety allowed. He bent his head by her ear. "I do love you, you know."

Elsie looked up at him, her eyes shining with emotion, and nodded. It was the most wonderful dance she'd ever danced, and she prayed this moment would stay with her forever. She wished she could capture it, put it in her heart to take out whenever her life turned ugly. *Remember this,* she told herself. *Remember this moment.*

The dance was over far too soon, and it was clear that Alexander wanted—even needed—to leave. She walked him to the terrace doors, and he bowed to her, holding her gloved hand in his a bit too long before departing. He was still descending the stairs, Elsie watching him go, when one of her dear friends came up to her.

"Who was that?" Charlene Bennet gushed. "I didn't recognize him at all."

"I don't really know," Elsie said.

"He came here just for that one dance. Surely you must know who he is."

A deep sadness swept over Elsie. She couldn't claim him, couldn't tell her friend who he really was, that she was in love with him. She could never be seen with him again, or they would cause gossip and questions she wouldn't be able to answer. He was a phantom.

"It doesn't matter who he is, does it?"

"Maybe not to you, but to everyone else. Come now, who was he?"

"No one."

Charlene gave Elsie a look of pure exasperation. "Perhaps he was beyond ugly under that mask. Horribly scarred or had a mashed nose." Her friend was obviously baiting her, trying to glean some information.

"I really wouldn't know," she said mysteriously, then giggled.

"You already have a marquess and now you have a man of mystery. You should share a bit, you know, Elsie." Charlene gave her a look of mock anger. "Speaking of your marquess, is he here tonight?"

"No. He usually doesn't attend the squire's events."

"Too far beneath his notice?"

Elsie shrugged. "Perhaps. Personally, it's my favorite ball of the year and I shall insist we attend after we are married."

Charlene moved closer and whispered, "Have you a date set?"

"May tenth." It seemed as if that were her date of sentencing, not her wedding date.

"Are you nervous? I would ever be so nervous. When are you announcing it?"

"At my birthday ball."

Charlene grinned. "I received my invitation. It's lovely. Fit for a marchioness."

Elsie shot her a look of exasperation. "Stop. I

really want to stay Miss Stanhope. I cannot think of myself as a marchioness, certainly not a duchess. It actually makes me a bit queasy."

"I suppose you'll get used to it."

"I suppose I'll have to."

"Good morning, all," Elsie said, entering cook's sunny kitchen on the morning after the masquerade. She'd begged her father to return early, and spent the night in Alexander's arms, which made her world all brightness and light. The staff, having completed their morning chores, sat drinking their tea at a little table near the back door. It was a cozy spot, and Elsie had spent many hours sitting there watching the staff work and helping when they'd allow it. "Mary and I are planning a little picnic this afternoon and I wondered if I might have a small basket made up."

"Of course, Miss Elizabeth. We've got some nice cold chicken and an apple beet salad I made with the first of the apples. The apples are a little tart, if you don't mind."

"Oh, no, I love tart apples. And beets," Elsie said, grinning. She walked over to the table and fished one of the beets out of the jar, popping it into her mouth with a grin. She didn't know why something so tasteless as beets tasted so good to her, but she'd always loved them and this day, they made her smile even more. She was always smiling it seemed. She loved tart apples and wormy apples and rotten apples and bland beets. She loved everything, she thought, and tried not to giggle out loud.

"Don't you be putting your fingers in the food," cook said good-naturedly.

Elsie laughed and walked from the kitchen to search for her little sister, inhaling deeply the smell of paint and Alexander as she passed by the ballroom.

Elsie found her little sister in the nursery playing with her old wooden blocks, the painted letters faded and chipped. Miss Lawton sat nearby darning one of Mary's little socks, putting her sewing aside when Elsie came into the room.

"Miss Elizabeth," she said, standing.

"May I borrow Mary for a picnic today, Miss Lawton?"

The older woman smiled, no doubt appreciating the fact that her charge had an older sister who was always "borrowing" Mary. "Of course," she said. "You'd like a picnic with your sister, wouldn't you, Mary?"

"Picnic. I love picnics," Mary shouted, jumping up and down.

Elsie held out her hand, loving how her little sister automatically put her soft little hand in hers. "Shall we hunt for bunnies today? I saw some this morning eating sweet clovers."

"You saw a bunny, Elsie? Really? Can we bring it in the house? Do you think Papa would mind? I don't think he would," she ended thoughtfully.

It was amazing to Elsie how quickly her little sister was mastering the art of good conversation. It seemed only yesterday that she was babbling nonsensically, and here she was sounding quite grown up.

The two had a wonderful picnic, even though there were no rabbits in sight. Elsie ate every bit of apple and beet salad, unable to convince Mary that, even though it looked "horrid" it was really quite good. Instead, Mary filled up on a small apple tart and more chicken than Elsie thought she could eat.

Afterwards, Mary climbed up on Elsie's lap to listen to the story of *Little Red Riding Hood.* Mary was delighted with her gruesome descriptions of the wolf's appetite for grandmas and little girls. Soon after, Mary got drowsy, her soft, downy head getting heavier and heavier, until she was sound asleep. Elsie, looking down at her brown curls, felt the sharp prick of tears, and squeezed her eyes shut against the pain. No matter what, Mary would always need her, always be a part of her life. Even marchionesses loved their little sisters. Even duchesses. Perhaps she could convince Lord Hathwaite to have Mary live with them.

At the thought of Lord Hathwaite, that hidden little bit of ice in her stomach grew. *No,* she told herself, *I will not think of it. I will not.*

Elsie pressed a kiss onto Mary's head and took a bracing breath, desperate to push back the tears that threatened. For she knew if she let them flow, she might never stop crying. And that would never do.

"The mural is nearly done."

Elsie ignored him, kissing him instead. They had just finished making love and he was stroking her hair, his eyes on the dark ceiling above them. He was miserable and she was pretending that their time together wasn't at an end. He swallowed down his misery, kissing her again, closing his eyes as if that would somehow sear his brain with this memory.

"Did you hear me?"

"I don't like it. The mural, that is. I think you should start over," Elsie said, teasing.

"I have some small touch-ups. Two days at the most. And then we'll be leaving. Monsieur says we are to travel to Bristol. The marquess there has commissioned a mural for his dining room." Bristol seemed like the other side of the world, and it might as well be.

"I don't want to speak of it," Elsie said, as if that would stop him from leaving.

"We must. You must. Elsie, I am leaving. We have one or two nights together, and I . . ."

She turned around and put her hands over her ears like a child, but he gently removed them and kissed one ear.

"I just thought if I pretended hard enough, it wouldn't happen," she said, her voice watery. "I don't want you to leave. I don't want to marry Hathwaite. I want to run away with you and never come back." A small sob escaped her throat. "But I cannot."

"Please, don't cry," he said, feeling helpless.

"Don't cry. Don't smile. Don't pretend. How else am I supposed to cope with what is happening?" she whispered harshly, and he knew had they been elsewhere, those words would have been shouted. "I love you, but sometimes I hate you." The moment after she said it, her eyes widened in horror and she clamped a hand over her mouth.

Alexander looked away, unable to bear seeing her

so hurt. "I deserve your hate," he said with utmost sincerity.

Elsie stared miserably at him, then lay back down, her hand seeking his and holding on tight. "Being star-crossed lovers isn't nearly as romantic as I'd imagined. It simply hurts." She sniffed loudly and dashed the tears away with her free hand. "Two days?"

"Three if Monsieur doesn't lose too much patience with me. It's done, actually. I could leave tomorrow. But, there are things I can add. Change. I will insist and he will let me." He sighed, bringing her hand up and kissing her palm. "I don't think . . ." *I can bear to lose you.* He stopped, knowing that to complete his thoughts would only hurt her more.

"You don't think what?"

"I don't think I can stay longer than that." Suddenly, he brought her against him, kissing her deeply, trying to capture her essence with his mouth, his hands. She arched against him, moving her hands to his back, moving her hips upward. He growled, low and hard, entering her, relishing her gasp, the way she lifted her hips to meet him. He turned so that she straddled him, giving him access to her center. He loved looking up at her, at her drowsy eyes, her hair touching his chest, her thighs smooth and taut beside him. He loved watching her become aroused as he touched her between her legs, the way her mouth opened, the way she moved against him, the intoxicating sounds she made. She moved up, bringing her breasts to his greedy mouth, and he groaned at the sensation, the slick friction on his arousal. She moved frantically against his hand, seeking her release, knowing it was coming. He guided her, he watched her come, that beautiful moment of complete and utter bliss, when everything was erased but the pure pleasure of the present. He loved feeling her muscles clench around him, the spasms that squeezed him, that made it near impossible not to simply thrust into her and find his own release.

But he would not take the chance that he would leave his child inside her. What he was doing was bad enough, God knew, he could not, would not make her pregnant. Staying inside her, he turned them again, thrusting deep and hard, letting the sensations take over his mind, erasing all other thoughts. He pulled out, giving a guttural sound, his seed spilling harmlessly onto yet another furniture cover.

Lethargy hit him, and he hardly summoned the energy to take the soiled sheet and toss it on the floor, before gathering Elsie to him and falling asleep, where his thoughts could no longer torment him. He awoke when she kissed him, slipping silently from the room like a ghost. He stared at the closed door for a long moment, his thoughts warring with his heart. Fear washed over him in such a wave he became nauseous with it. Sweat bathed his body as if he were physically ill. And, truth be told, he was. Desperately, terribly ill.

Because he knew, lying there, his hand on her pillow still feeling the lingering warmth of her body, that he could not let her go. And the only way to keep her was to claim his rights as Kingston's heir.

* * *

Elsie made her way to her room just as dawn was touching the sky. Like every other night since she and Alexander had become lovers, she climbed into her bed, slipped beneath the covers and fell asleep for another two hours. The novelty of finding Miss Elizabeth in her bed asleep had begun to wear off on Missy.

But this morning, Elsie felt rather ill. She'd kissed Alexander good-bye, her face feeling strangely numb, as if she'd been out in the cold. Her stomach roiled uncomfortably, making her reconsider before getting under the covers. She'd woken up feeling vaguely nauseous, but hadn't given the feeling much thought. But now, just the sight of her pretty chamber pot made her stomach ache, and she barely made it to the porcelain pot in time. The room swirled around her as she felt her stomach convulse again.

"Missy," she called, realizing that she'd actually called out "mishy." Her tongue felt strange, she thought, just as another wave of nausea hit.

"Oh, my word, Miss Elsie, are you all right?" Missy's hand was on her back, stroking as she again felt her stomach heave.

"I feel sick," she said, realizing to her horror that her tongue and mouth were no longer working properly. "Wash hap'nin'" she asked, the room spinning crazily around her.

"Are you done castin' up yer stomach?" Missy asked, her eyes filled with concern.

"I thin' so," she managed. Never in her life had

she gotten so sick so quickly. She'd been fine just a few hours ago, and now was perhaps sicker than she'd ever been in her life.

She clutched her stomach as another cramp assailed her, and swallowed heavily. It felt as if someone had stuck a large cotton ball down her throat. So strange. It was almost impossible for her to walk to her bed, and the thought of climbing in was almost like climbing the tallest tree in the garden. Missy heaved her onto the bed, pulling up the covers.

"I'm going to wake your father," she said.

Elsie nodded, even her neck feeling strange, as if she couldn't really control her movements. "Thirshy," she said, trying to swallow past the growing cottony lump in her throat. But Missy had hurried from the room just as another cramp had her crying out in pain.

Elsie tried to look at the door, but saw two entries, two doors, moving about each other. It was as if she'd been spinning about for a minute and was now trying to focus. She closed her eyes against the wave of dizziness and nausea that followed. Her father, still wearing his nightcap, rushed into the room.

"Elsie, Missy says you're not feeling well. I've sent Carl to get Dr. Peters."

"I'm thirshy," Elsie said, feeling frightened by her own slurred speech. Her father's face swam before her, two foggy images swirling in front of her. It was almost as if someone had given her a powerful drug, one that was slowly paralyzing her. "I'm frightened, Father," she said, and saw that he was, too. "I wan'—" She tried to say Alexander's name but it was too much effort. "I wan' 'im."

"The doctor's coming, Elsie. He's coming."

An hour later, Dr. Peters emerged from her room, his face grim. Lord Huntington was frantic with worry. Now dressed, he'd paced in front of Elsie's room growing more and more agitated every moment, stopping his frenetic movements only when the doctor came out of his daughter's room. Dr. Peters looked uncertain and worried, and he thought he might scream in frustration.

"I'm not certain what is wrong, Michael," the doctor said. "It may be a brain fever of some sort. Is anyone else in the house ill?"

Michael shook his head. "No one," he said, his voice raw. "She'll get better. She'll be fine."

Dr. Peters looked to the floor, and Michael's heart nearly stopped. The last time the doctor had looked at him that way it was to tell him his wife was dying, that there was nothing he could do, that he should go and pray. They had become friends in those terrible two weeks and yet had not spoken since his wife's funeral. He remembered praying so hard his head had hurt, and nothing had come of it. If the doctor told him to pray this time, he'd likely strike the man, friend or not.

"She's having difficulty breathing. It's a kind of paralysis, perhaps from Kerner's disease. But if no one else is suffering the effects, I just don't know."

"Kerner's?"

"It's caused by eating tainted food. But if no one

else is suffering from the same symptoms, I doubt very much that this is the cause. Let's pray it is not."

Michael sat down heavily. "She's dying."

"It is not always fatal. People survive, but the recovery can be long. I wish I could do more. If her breathing improves, then she'll be out of the woods. That's the danger, you see. It's a sort of paralysis that moves throughout the body and can attack the lungs. If her breathing improves, she will live and fully recover."

Michael looked up at the doctor, his eyes bleak. "And if it doesn't?"

"Let's just pray it does."

Michael clenched his fist, but struck his thigh instead of the doctor's concerned face. Pray. He could not pray again for the life of someone he loved. He stood and went to his daughter's room, shocked at how she looked, and let out a small sound of despair. How could this be the same girl he'd dined with the night before? Her eyes were drooping, her features slack.

"Oh, my lord, she's been asking for someone, all frantic like," Missy said, her face brightening when he entered the room. "But I can't make it out. She seems glad to see you, though. Perhaps she was asking for you."

Elsie seemed almost completely devoid of expression. She mumbled something, moving her arm awkwardly, and Michael bent and pressed a kiss on her cheek. "The doctor says you'll be fine," he said.

"What's wrong, my lord?" Missy asked, her eyes filled with tears.

"He doesn't know."

Dr. Peters entered the room, bending over Elsie to listen to her breathing. The doctor saw his questioning look and shook his head. Just then, his daughter made another sound that tore at his heart.

"See? It sounds like gander or dander. But that can't be right, can it, sir?" Missy asked miserably.

A sob escaped Elsie's throat, and Michael bent and gathered her into his arms. "It will be all right, Elsie, darling. Don't you worry. You're going to be fine." But Elsie continued to cry until Michael thought he'd go mad from hearing her. Hugging her once more, he left the room, frantic to do something, anything to help his daughter.

"She's dying, damn it," he said, pulling the doctor down the hall. "Do something, John. Bleed her, anything. You can't just sit around and let her die as you did my wife." Michael let out a harsh breath when he saw the doctor's stricken look. "I'm sorry. It's just that I cannot lose Elsie. She is my heart." He pressed the heels of his hands against his eyes to stop the tears that threatened.

Dr. Peters laid a strong hand on his shoulder. "It is times like these that I wish I had chosen a different profession. Your daughter is young and strong and if it is some sort of food poisoning, she should recover. I have seen this sort of thing before and cannot say with certainty the outcome. I should not like to give you hope where there is none, nor tell you there is no hope when there is some. The truth is, sir, I just do not know."

Michael nodded his head. "I understand."

"Send for me if there is any change."

Michael swallowed, and glanced down the hall toward his daughter's door. "I will."

After the physician left, he wandered about the house aimlessly, wishing he could do more. The smell of paint made him smile faintly. Elsie was so excited about the mural, if not about the ball that would mark her engagement. With a sense of deep weariness he realized that it was likely he would have to postpone the ball, unless Elsie had a miraculous recovery. His heart aching, he thought of the mural that she might never see. If she should die, he would have it painted over. He did not care. He would not want the mural there to remind him of his daughter and of how she'd never gotten a chance to see it.

Michael walked to the ballroom and opened the door, ignoring the stifled gasp of outrage from Monsieur Desmarais. Michael sank down onto the couch and stared at the mural, his heart swelling painfully in his chest. It was stunning, magical. It was just as his Elsie had asked for, and she might never see it. The beautiful image blurred before him as tears flooded his eyes.

"My lord, what is wrong?" Monsieur Desmarais asked, moving toward him.

"My daughter is dying," he said, his throat raw. Dimly, he was aware of something crashing to the ground. "And I thought I would come see the mural so I might describe it to her. But, my God, no words can capture this. Elsie should see it. Before she dies."

Michael buried his face in his hands and began to sob, not caring that he was humiliating himself in front of the artist. A commotion at the door made him raise his head, only to see Elsie's little maid rushing to him.

"Miss Elizabeth's been askin' for someone an' I couldn't understand what she was sayin'. But sir, it's Alexander. She said it real slow-like, clear as day, and it just about wore her out," Missy said, filled with excitement. "The only thing is, sir, no one knows an Alexander or Alexandra if that's what it is. Do you have any idea who she could be askin' for? Sir?"

Michael stood and stared at Missy, feeling helpless. He'd didn't know of any Alexander of note, and shook his head as the muralist's mute assistant stepped in front of him.

"Sir," the young man said, his voice strong, clear, and cultured. "My name is Alexander Wilkinson. I am the eldest son of the Duke of Kingston. And, sir, I am desperately in love with your daughter. May I go to her? Please."

Michael's stunned gaze went from the young man to the artist, who shook his head helplessly, raising his hands in supplication. "Kingston, you say?" he asked, even as his eyes took in the incredible likeness the boy had to the duke. It took only a few moments for him to realize that it was possible this boy spoke the truth. Memories assailed him of another son, one who had supposedly died not long after the first. He remembered thinking how tragic it was that a duke would lose two sons the same year. He looked into the young man's anguished expression, knowing even if he were not Kingston's heir, this young man loved his daughter.

"Go, then." He watched the man run from the room, listened as his footsteps pounded up the stairs.

"My lord, I assure you I had no idea he could speak. Nor any knowledge of his parentage. If he is telling the truth . . ." The artist broke off, an expression of pure puzzled amazement on his features.

"If he is telling the truth," Michael said, "then he has every right to be with my daughter."

Chapter 16

Alexander ran up the stairs, taking two at a time, his heart pounding in his chest. It was not true. How could Elsie be dying when not more than a dozen hours ago they had been making love? How could she be dying when he'd just realized that he could never lose her?

He was dimly aware of reaching the top of the stairs, of looking down two halls, of the frustration of not knowing which door was hers, when the tap-tapping of steps came up behind him.

"This way, my lord," a maid said, rushing by him and leading him to the right. She opened the door and he stopped at the entrance, suddenly afraid of what he might see. What did a dying person look like?

He walked silently over to Elsie, painfully aware of her labored breathing, the sharp, short intakes of a person who cannot get enough air. He knelt on the floor and grabbed her limp hand, pressing it to his mouth. "Elsie, I'm here."

She turned her head, her eyelids drooping, her face slack, but he could see that she was glad to see him. Tears filled her eyes and fell down her cheeks.

"Don't cry," he said, even as his own tears filled his eyes. She uttered a sound and he pressed her hand against his cheek, closing his eyes. "I have some wonderful news. I've decided to claim the title, to claim you."

"No," she said, quite clearly.

"Are you saying you don't love me?" he teased.

Her eyes softened. "No," she said. "I do." Her words were muffled, as if her mouth was full of cotton and she was attempting to talk around it.

"It's actually quite inconsiderate of you to become so ill when I was planning to propose." She laughed, her eyes filling again with tears. "I'm not entirely certain I can do it, but I will try, Elsie. I cannot live without you and I cannot allow another to have you, so it seems I have no choice but to marry you myself." He kissed the back of her hand. "Miss Elizabeth Stanhope, will you do me the honor of becoming my wife?"

"I will," she managed. "Sure?"

"I've never been more sure of anything in my life. But, I daresay, you must get a bit better before the wedding. I do wish you'd hurry up with that."

Elsie, her breath coming in short little gasps, stared at him as bleakness filled her eyes, and he felt her slip away from him.

"Elsie. You must get better," he said, squeezing her hand tightly even as he watched her struggle to breathe become more difficult.

Her father entered the room, his eyes only on his daughter. "Her breathing is worse," Lord Huntington said.

"No," Alexander said, even though in the short time he'd been in the room he'd noticed a marked deterioration. He stared at her chest, willing her breathing to become more normal.

"Elsie, the doctor thinks this might be from something you ate," the baron said. Elsie turned her head to her father. "Did you eat anything unusual yesterday? Perhaps something no one else ate?"

She let out a small sob. "What, darling?" Alexander asked.

"Salad. Mary almost ate. Didn't. Tried to get her to."

"Mary didn't eat it?" Lord Huntington asked, frantic.

"No."

"Thank God." The baron called for Missy and directed her to go to the kitchen and tell the cook about the salad. "Tell her to discard any remains."

"Yes, my lord," Missy said, bobbing a quick curtsy.

"Did the salad taste off?"

"No. Tired."

Lord Huntington let out a shaky breath and patted his daughter's free hand. He noted with a bit of annoyance that Desmarais's assistant had a strong grip on the other.

"I would like to speak to you. Alexander is it?"

A small, clear voice came from the bed. "Lord Hathwaite."

"Yes, well, I need to borrow this man for a moment, whatever his name is."

"Lord Hathwaite," she whispered.

"I'd like to stay here, if you don't mind, sir," Alexander said.

"I do mind, as a matter of fact," the baron said, then softened his voice. "Certainly you would agree your announcement is a bit of a surprise to me."

Alexander let his gaze linger on Elsie for a moment before standing and following Lord Huntington out the door and to a private study down another hall. He hated leaving Elsie, but knew he could not put off this confrontation with her father.

Lord Huntington entered and sat behind a desk, motioning for Alexander to sit. For a moment, he was a child being summoned by his father. The baron's small study was far different from his father's imposing room, but he still remembered vividly the feeling of fear that overcame him when he'd been summoned by His Grace. Perhaps it was the smell of beeswax or the leather upholstery, or the way the sun cast milky white rectangles on the dark wood floor. Whatever the reason, he felt his throat thicken.

"Now," the baron said, his tone hard. "Who the hell are you?"

Alexander swallowed down the hard knot in his throat and lifted his chin, refusing to be beaten by his fear. He should have known that Elsie's father would not take his word for it. Why should he? It was a rather fantastical story, even if it was the truth.

"I am who I claim to be. My father is the Duke of Kingston."

"Are you a byblow, then, conspiring to obtain the title through illicit means? And bringing an innocent girl into your schemes?"

"No, sir," Alexander said, trying to cool his anger. "I am the duke's second son. Henry, the eldest, died in a drowning accident when he was twelve years old. Soon after, my father sent me to an idiot asylum, where he no doubt believes me still. Or not. I do not know. I do know that he has told everyone I died, though I don't know the cause of my supposed death."

"This is information anyone could have. Do you have any proof?"

Alexander shook his head. "No, sir. And I'm not fool enough to believe anyone, including Kingston, will believe who I am without it."

Lord Huntington let out a heavy breath. "If memory serves, the duke's second son was sent away to school soon after the death of his brother. He died there in some sort of an accident."

"I did not die," Alexander said levelly.

"For me to believe you are Kingston's son, I would have to believe that he lied to everyone, including his own wife. I attended that funeral and I can tell you Her Grace was not pretending grief. She was inconsolable. To lie in such a way to one's wife would require the coldest of hearts. And, frankly, I don't believe even Kingston could be that cruel. Your claim also begs the question of why Kingston would go to such lengths."

"He hated me. He thought I was flawed, weak, and unfit for the title. Perhaps he is right. But I also believe he blamed me for Henry's death. After Henry died, he put me in an idiot asylum, and he had no intention of ever letting me out. Rather than suffer the shame of having an idiot child, he killed me."

Lord Huntington shook his head. "What you are saying is diabolical."

"Yes, it is."

The baron shook his head, clearly trying to comprehend how such evil could exist. "You have put me in an untenable situation. If you are, indeed, who you say you are, I am quite certain Kingston will fight you and you will lose. He is a powerful man with resources neither of us can imagine. If Elsie does not marry Lord Hathwaite, the consequences will be devastating."

"Your daughter has apprised me of the situation, which is partly why I was so reluctant to come forward. But I love your daughter and am willing to do anything to be with her."

"Even put her very future in jeopardy?"

"I shall be successful," he said with more assurance than he felt.

Lord Huntington stood and began pacing the room. "And if you are not successful . . . ? Do you realize what will happen should you fail? Elsie shall be ruined, we all shall be. We shall lose everything, our homes, our lands. Is that what you want?"

"If I cannot prove that I am heir, Elsie will be free to marry Lord Hathwaite," Alexander said softly. "It is a chance I am willing to take."

"Are you telling me you would be willing to put Elsie aside if you cannot prove your claim? Is she so integral to your plans? Kingston will not put any credence in her support of your claim, none at all, if that is your belief."

Alexander flinched at his words. "You misunderstand. I would *not* be willing to let her go, not at all. But I will do whatever is necessary to make her happy and make the people she loves safe. And if that means letting Elsie marry another, I shall do it. She would not be happy knowing that she had ruined you and put Mary's future in jeopardy. If Kingston cannot be convinced, if my petition fails, I will let her go."

Lord Huntington stared at the floor for a long moment. "Does my daughter love you?"

"I believe she does. I know she does."

The baron closed his eyes as if bracing for some pain, and then he asked, "Did you compromise her?" He opened his eyes and stared at Alexander the way only a father can stare at the man who has ruined his daughter.

Alexander thought, briefly, that he should lie. What good, after all, would telling this man the truth do?

"To my great shame, yes."

Lord Huntington sat down as if pushed, his eyes closed, as if this was just too, too much to bear. "I should have you shot," he said wearily and without conviction.

"I would gladly take a bullet if I thought it would be better to do so."

"Under my roof. I allowed this to happen under my very roof," the baron said with disgust.

"We're in love," Alexander said. "And we knew the situation was desperate. We knew."

"Yes, I'm certain you did," Lord Huntington said softly. "I suppose you thought each other star-crossed lovers and convinced yourselves that all would be fine, all would work out, like a fairy tale." He let out a bitter laugh.

"I am sorry to have caused you further distress," Alexander said sincerely.

"God help me for a fool, but I'm inclined to believe you—in that alone." The baron sighed and shook his head. "But I cannot help you. I cannot give you one ounce of support publicly. Now, before I have you removed from my home, convince me of who you are. Tell me your story, Alexander Wilkinson, if that is your true name."

When Alexander left the study, Lord Huntington remained sitting behind his desk looking weary and unconvinced. Alexander realized that his story proved nothing. He could be an imposter who'd gleaned this information from the true heir at school. He could have schemed and planned and seduced the intended wife of Lord Hathwaite. He tried to see the situation from Huntington's point of view. How utterly fantastical that the true heir to Kingston would show up as a painter's mute assistant, fall in love with Hathwaite's fiancée, and then claim the title. It sounded like a melodramatic play, a bit of nonsense conjured up by an imaginative mind. That it was true gave Alexander little comfort. He needed to prove who he was, not only to his father, but to the authorities. If he wanted to claim the title, he would need indisputable proof, and he was beginning to doubt he would find it.

His head ached and he was completely exhausted when he finally went back to Elsie's room, his spirits lifting only when he realized she hadn't worsened in the hour he was apart from her.

"Hello."

She smiled weakly, her eyes still drooping as if she were too tired to open them. "Does my father believe you?"

"No. Not entirely. I shall need proof and that will not be easily obtained." He had no funds to hire a solicitor or private investigator, and would have to try to find out whatever he could alone.

"You will triumph," she said.

Alexander took up her hand and pressed it against his mouth. "If I do not, you must marry Hathwaite."

Elsie shook her head and let out a sound of anguish.

"You must, Elsie. You know you must."

"You will succeed. Don't talk so."

Alexander leaned over and kissed her soft cheek, flushed and dry from her illness. "As soon as you are better, I will go."

"Where?"

"To the asylum. I can only hope they have records that will prove Alexander Wilkinson was placed there, that he ran away, that the Duke of Kingston paid for my internment. Without that, I'm afraid all hope will be lost."

"Mother . . ."

Alexander shook his head. "My mother believes

I am dead. And her belief in my story would do nothing but make Kingston angry with her. He would ridicule her, call her insane. I need proof."

"Monsieur?" Elsie asked. Each time she spoke, it was as if she was at the limit of her endurance. She took short breaths before and after each slurred word.

"He does not know who I am. He knew only that I was the son of a peer, and was told my name was Alexander. He changed it to Andre to protect me and himself. He knows nothing of my past, of my family. He didn't know I could speak, even."

Elsie started to respond, but the effort was apparently too much, and she closed her eyes, her breathing far too shallow. Laying a finger on her lips, Alexander whispered, "No more talk. Go to sleep and get well. I'll not leave until you are better."

She nodded without even opening her eyes, and Alexander stood, bending to kiss her on the forehead. "I love you," he said, and saw the faintest stirring of a smile on her lips.

Elsie knew she was dying. Knew it in her bones, knew it as her breathing became more and more difficult, and thought: This is a terrible way to die.

After Alexander left her, she squeezed her eyes shut because having them opened only revealed to her how sick she truly was. She could not see anything but a blur of objects, as if she were looking through a very old pane of glass. The only thing she could be positive about was that the nausea and stomach pain were nearly gone. But now, each breath, each swallow, was becoming agonizing. She feared if she fell asleep, she would not awaken.

Elsie knew from the look on the doctor's face that she was going to die and wished someone would simply tell her. She was going to die and see her sister. That made Elsie nearly smile, and she wondered if Christine was still a little girl in heaven or would she be grown like her? Or when she died, would she become a little girl? Would she see her mother?

Or would there be nothing. Just blackness. Just fear and then nothing?

She didn't want to die to find out. She wanted to live forever with Alexander and have his children and go away to some cottage where he would paint masterpieces and they could be alone. Once a year, they would all go to London. Perhaps during the Season. And he would display his artwork in the Royal Academy of Arts, where he would receive accolades and be forgiven for not taking up the duties of his title with vigor.

Elsie struggled for breath, trying to calm herself, trying to stem the panic that was building in her breast. *I can't breathe, I can't breathe, I can't breathe.* But one gasp at a time, one inhale, one exhale, she kept breathing, kept pushing air into her lungs. Tears seeped from her eyes and her hands weakly clutched the blanket. *I can't breathe.*

Missy entered the room, her eyes filled with concern. "Having a tough time of it, are you, miss?"

Elsie nodded, her head feeling as if it were stuffed with cotton.

"You'll get better," she pronounced. "I had a

dream and you were visiting, a married woman you were. A duchess. Did I ever tell you about my dreams?"

"No," Elsie gasped.

"They're not always right, you know, but the important ones is. I dreamed I had a nice big piece of roast beef but that night cook served us all boiled chicken." She wrinkled her nose. "Tasteless, that. But when I was younger, I had a purely awful dream. You were just a little girl, then, and I dreamed that you were playing alone and very sad. Two days later, little Christine passed on. Scared me to death, it did. But then, I dreamed of little Mary being born and it seemed to me that was a good thing, even if the lady did slip away those weeks later. So you see, Miss, you're going to get better."

Elsie struggled for breath, wondering if she had the energy to ask the most important question. "Who was the duke?"

Missy looked at her as if she'd asked the most ridiculous question. "You know, now that you mention it, he wasn't in my dream. But you did seem happy, Miss."

Elsie closed her eyes. "Thank you, Missy."

Her maid touched her arm. "You're welcome, Miss."

For three torturous days, Elsie struggled to breathe, lapsing in and out of consciousness at her worst, which was, quite frankly, a relief to whoever was watching over her. For to see Elsie fight for each bit of air, to wonder if the breath you heard would be her last, was torture in itself. More often than not, it was Alexander, counting her breaths, feeling sick inside when she reached the pitiable number of six breaths in a minute. Six breaths. Then five.

He prayed, even though he hadn't spoken to God in years, even though he wasn't even certain God listened to ordinary people. It was all he could do, so he did it fervently and constantly, whispering into hands folded and pressed against his mouth. He lost track of day and night, falling asleep where he sat, waiting.

"How is she?" Lord Huntington asked on the third night, his eyes red-rimmed and filled with anguish.

"The same," Alexander said, though in his heart he felt as if she were far worse. She would open her eyes and look at him, but she hadn't the strength to speak or even to move her hands to hold his.

"If I have a doubt of who you are, you should know that I have no doubt you love my daughter," her father said, his eyes filling with tears.

"Thank you, sir."

"Elsie? It's Papa," Lord Huntington said, and smiled when Elsie's eyes opened. "You seem better. Your color is better."

Her eyes drifted closed as she struggled to breathe, and the two men looked at each other with hopeless misery.

"The doctor will be here in the morning. Perhaps he'll be able to do something to ease her . . ."

"She will live," Alexander said softly.

Lord Huntington dropped his head and nodded, unable to meet his eyes. "Yes. I daresay she will."

All that night, Alexander held her hand, drifting in and out of slumber, awakening in a panic when he couldn't immediately tell if she lived, during those long periods between breaths. Each time he awoke, he would count—one, two, three, four, five breaths—as he looked at his pocket watch. She was so pale, so incredibly fragile looking, that he could hardly look at her without crying. How could the woman who'd loved him so passionately be this invalid struggling to live?

"Elsie, come back to me. I need you, my heart," he said. "Who shall I play Chopin for if you remain sick?"

Toward dawn, Alexander drifted off again, awaking only when Elsie's maid poked her head into the room. "She should be gettin' better today, then," she said with an odd assurance that made him unaccountably angry.

Indeed, Elsie did seem to have better color, and it seemed as if her breathing wasn't quite so labored. He took out his watch and flipped it open, counting a miraculous eight breaths before the minute was up. That was nearly normal.

"Elsie," he said, rather more loudly than he intended, and Elsie startled before opening her eyes.

"Good morning, sir," she said softly, and smiled. Really, truly smiled, for the first time in days.

"You are better."

"I am a bit," she said with wonder. She swallowed

and smiled again. "May I have a drink of water? I'm quite thirsty."

Missy was there, glass in hand, and helped Elsie to drink the cool water. A blissful smile crossed her face. "Not nearly so difficult to swallow," she said. "And I don't sound like I've been drinking whiskey quite so much."

Alexander laughed. Her speech was still a bit slurred, but far more understandable than before. "Only a glass or two," he said, smiling down at her, completely un-self-conscious of the tears in his eyes.

"Did I frighten you so much?" she asked worriedly. "I'm sorry."

"No, in a way, it is a good thing. Now your father knows who I am. Or at least who I claim to be. And I know that I cannot possibly live without you."

"Did I have to nearly die to make my point?"

Alexander knew she was jesting, but he couldn't bring himself to smile at that moment. "No, I knew before then. I knew."

Laurent Desmarais, once the greatest muralist in Britain, knew he would never paint another mural again. Perhaps, he thought, he would turn his attention to a smaller canvas, one that did not strain his poor fingers so much. Or perhaps, he would give art classes to wealthy children. Or simply buy a town house in London or live out his days wandering the world.

The betrayal he felt warred with his joy that Alexander could speak and was, perhaps, heir to one of the greatest titles in the kingdom. It seemed impossible, but then he remembered the solemn, serious boy Alexander had been, his intelligence, his natural grace. All those years, all those endless lonely, silent days, wasted. Lost conversations, lost time. If he'd known Alexander could speak, he could have fostered his talent even more, he would have . . . No. He would have seen Alexander as a rival, an upstart, a usurper. He would have stopped working long ago, when he lost the ability to hold a paintbrush for more than a single hour. He would have likely lost himself in a sea of fine French brandy. He would have lost his boy far, far sooner had he known. Perhaps that was why Alexander had kept his secret. Perhaps the young man liked their life together as much as he did.

But now he might never know. He could not stay at Mansfield Hall indefinitely, a paid guest. He had written a letter to the Earl of Bristol, explaining that he was unable to work because of a physical infirmity. Now he had only to decide what to do with the rest of his life.

"You're all packed up, sir," a footman said, nodding. His black lacquered wagon stood outside, a young driver awaiting him patiently. How many miles had he traveled with Alexander on that wagon, him sitting back and Alexander acting as his driver?

"Merci," Desmarais said distractedly. He looked about the small cottage he'd shared with the man he considered his son and felt himself unwilling to leave without at least hearing Alexander's explanation. There had to be a reason he'd lied to him. Had to be.

Short of dragging him from the bedside of his beloved, Desmarais could do nothing but leave and hope that one day he would get an explanation from Alexander.

A shadow crossed the door and Desmarais lifted his head, scowling when he saw it was Alexander, even as his heart filled with pride and love. "How is the mademoiselle?" he asked gruffly in French.

"I would prefer to speak in English," Alexander said. "I have not spoken in French before, you see. Only listened." He gave a self-deprecating smile, and Desmarais instantly forgave him.

"A nice baritone, your voice. It would have been very pleasant to have listened to it now and again over the past twenty years, no?"

Alexander dipped his head, but it gave Desmarais little satisfaction to see his shame. When he lifted his head, Alexander's eyes spoke volumes about how sorry he was. "Miss Elsie is doing much better. She will live."

"Very nice. And now I must go," the artist said, with absolutely no intention of leaving before he'd sorted everything out with his foster son.

"When you first took me in"—Alexander began—"I could not speak to strangers. No matter how I tried, I could not. And then, when I grew comfortable with you and realized I could speak, it somehow seemed cruel to let you know." He shook his head as if he, himself, didn't understand his reasons. "I didn't want anything to change. I liked being with you, the smell of the paint, the beauty of what we were doing in Italy. I was afraid that you would send me away. And when I grew old enough to know better, it was too late. I didn't want to hurt you. You are a father to me, more than my own father ever was. I was afraid I would lose you."

"Oh, mon fils," he said, opening up his arms to his son. Alexander embraced him, and Desmarais's eyes filled with tears as he realized he still had a son. Embarrassed by his display of emotion, the artist stepped back, rubbing his eyes dry. "I suppose I must now call you by your English name."

Alexander smiled. "Only if you wish."

"Andre seems to fit you better," he said stubbornly. He searched the younger man's face. "Are you truly a peer?"

Alexander nodded. "My father is the Duke of Kingston. He put me in that asylum after my brother died. And now I must prove who I am. Do you know anything that could help me?"

"Only that Dr. Stelton of the Wickshire Asylum said you needed a home. He did not even give me your full name, but said discretion was of utmost importance. You were such a skinny boy, and so frightened. I had lost my family just two years before. I could not say no."

"Your family?"

"My wife and son died of influenza two years before you came to me. I was so sad that I could not paint. That is why I agreed to do the work in Italy. I had lost my ability to create art and could only repair it. You saved my life, as much as I saved yours."

He held up his ruined hands. "And then you saved me again."

"I think we saved each other, sir," Alexander said. "I do not know what will happen, but you should know that I have loved you as a father and will insist you remain so. No matter what happens, I will continue my art and will need a teacher."

"Bah," Desmarais said, feeling more than pleased. "You could teach me."

Alexander looked out the opened door and toward the main house, where the young lady still struggled. "I plan to marry her," he said, and Desmarais's heart broke for him. Even he knew how difficult a path it would be to prove his lineage. "I may ask you to testify for me, if it comes to that."

"I would be willing to say *I* am the Duke of Kingston if that would help you."

Alexander laughed. "Where can I find you, then, should the need arise?"

"London," Desmarais said, with sudden certainty. "I shall rent a town house and charge exorbitant fees for members of the ton to learn to paint." He walked out the door and toward the wagon in which they'd spent so much time together. Inside, the wagon was packed with the tools of his trade, the brushes, the solvents, and also two narrow built-in cots where they'd slept during their journeys. "I can say I will not miss this monstrosity," he said, even as his throat closed up at the thought of selling it. He would not. He would store it somewhere. "Good luck, mon fils," he said, clearing his throat lest he break into unmanly sobs.

"Good luck, mon pere," Alexander said, and

hearing those words was Desmarais's undoing. He let out a sob and pulled his son into a quick embrace before scrambling up awkwardly to sit by the driver. "Au revoir," he called, then nodded to the driver, who slapped the reins and began the next phase of the old artist's life.

Chapter 17

After the departure of Monsieur Desmarais, Alexander returned to the main house only to find himself confronted by the butler, who stood, arms folded, like a sentinel guarding a palace.

"I've been instructed to tell you to leave this property," the butler said.

"That's not possible," Alexander said, puzzled as to why he was being barred entrance. "Let me pass."

Alexander started to walk by this bothersome guard, but stopped when the older man shifted like a dancer to prevent him from going further into the house, his finely polished shoes tapping on the marble floor. A bit flabbergasted, Alexander said, "Let me pass, sir. I must see Miss Elizabeth."

"I'm sorry, but I cannot allow it." The man didn't look sorry one bit.

"I do understand your need to follow orders, so please do not take my actions as a personal attack upon you, but rather on the orders which you are trying so valiantly to obey."

The butler, who stood perhaps an inch over five

feet, widened his eyes when Alexander approached, grabbed his upper arms, and physically lifted the man out of the way.

"How dare you, sir?" the butler sputtered. "Unhand me." And then: "Lord Huntington! I am being accosted."

"Physically attacking my servants will not put you in my good graces, *Mr.* Wilkinson." The baron stood three steps up on the sweeping staircase glowering down at Alexander. "You may go, Mr. Cobbs, and please accept my apologies for this man's ill-mannered behavior."

Mr. Cobbs gave Alexander a dark look, dramatically straightening his coat as if he'd just been in a major scuffle. A part of Alexander knew he would take a small bit of satisfaction when he returned to Mansfield Manor as Lord Hathwaite and this same man bowed to him.

When the little butler was gone, Lord Huntington stepped down the remaining stairs. "I thought I saw Monsieur Desmarais's wagon leaving," he said, his tone cold.

"Yes, sir. But as I am no longer under his employ and as I consider myself engaged to your daughter, I thought I would return to see her."

Lord Huntington let out a heavy sigh. "You must understand my position. I've no wish to keep you from my daughter in the long term if what you've told me is true."

"It is."

"Even if it is," he said in a tone that told Alexander he did not appreciate the interruption, "I cannot act on your claim unless you can prove it. In the meantime, it is in my daughter's best interests and mine as well, to treat you as a pretender. To welcome you into our home, to allow you to pursue my daughter, could be disastrous for us all."

As much as he wanted to rail against what the man said, Alexander knew it was true. "I understand."

"Do you? I think not. You cannot understand what is at stake." Lord Huntington shook his head. "I do not wish to be cruel, to you or to Elizabeth. And I do believe you love her. But I must be practical. We all must be. Your chances of proving to Kingston and the House of Lords that you are his heir is remote at best. Whereas if he has a death certificate with your name on it, he will have the proof he needs."

"But if he has such a document, it is fraudulent," Alexander said, feeling his frustration grow.

"Young man, what you fail to understand is that it doesn't matter if it is fraudulent. No one is going to believe the word of a nobody over the word of a duke."

Alexander lowered his head, feeling overwhelmed by the odds he was facing. "I know," he said finally. "But I have to try. I promised Elsie." He searched the baron's face for some understanding. "The crazy thing is, I've started to want it for myself. It is my due. My right. And he stole it from me. For so long, I did not care, I hated him and turned that hatred toward the title. He stole my boyhood, but he will not steal my entire life. I will not let him."

The baron gave him a look that bordered on pity. "You may have to let him, young man. I fear it is a battle you will not win."

"I give you my word I will leave, but I need to say good-bye to Elizabeth. I will not go until I do."

Lord Huntington wiped a weary hand across his brow. "Very well. But I pray you do not upset her. She is still very weak."

Alexander nodded and started up the stairs.

Elsie took a sip of water and grimaced. It was still difficult to drink, her vision was still blurred, and she felt uncommonly tired even though all she'd been doing the past three days was sleeping. She hardly had the strength to hold the glass so Missy held it for her. It was the strangest sensation to grow unaccountably weary holding a glass of water.

"Is Mary well?"

"Fit as a fiddle," Missy said.

Elsie smiled. "And Alexander? He's well? I haven't seen him in ages."

"Oh, it's been all of two hours, Miss." Missy winked at her employer. "How did you manage to fall in love with such a strapper with no one in the house the wiser?"

"He is strapping, isn't he," Elsie said, pointedly ignoring the question.

"Here's yer lad now," the maid said, taking the glass and scurrying out the door, but not before giving Elsie a cheeky smile.

"Alexander." Even with her blurred vision, she could tell he looked tired, but he'd changed his shirt and his hair was still wet from a bath. Never had he looked as handsome, his face cleanly shaven, his skin glowing from a recent scrubbing.

He strode to her bed, and gently drew her to him again, holding her silently for a long moment, his hand moving along her back in an almost hypnotic rhythm. "I missed you," she said, her voice muffled against the soft cambric of his shirt. She could feel the rumble of his laughter.

"I fear you are going to have to miss me more. I am leaving today."

"No," she said, holding him as tightly as her weakened state would allow.

"I must. Father's orders." She pulled back ready to argue, but he stopped her. "He is right. I should not be here, not until I can prove who I am. And I should begin my search."

Elizabeth lay down, exhausted and slightly out of breath, her eyes filling with tears. "I cannot see you."

"What do you mean, sweet?"

"You're all a-blur. My eyesight is ruined and I cannot see you. I want to see you before you go."

"You know what I look like," he said, and she frowned at his smile.

"What if . . ." She could not continue because her throat closed up entirely and it had little to do with her illness. She swallowed heavily. "What if you do not come back? What if you cannot prove who you really are?"

He picked up her hand and held it against his lips, then put it to his heart. "Then you shall marry my brother. You must do what you need to for the sake of your family. You know this. It may not be my right, but I would have you give me a promise."

"Anything."

"Wait for me. Wait until I give you word that all is lost. Will you do that?"

"I promise with my soul, with my life."

Alexander smiled down at her. "No need for that. A simple promise will do."

Elsie nodded. "A simple promise, then."

"And if all is lost, I will come to you to say goodbye and you will marry Hathwaite. You must."

Elsie sniffed and nodded, even though she knew in her heart she could never marry anyone other than Alexander. They would have to think of something else, some other way to appease the duke. Surely, it was not so much money they could not raise it some way. She kept silent, though, not wanting to start an argument with Alexander right before he left.

"But I will tell you this—I will not give up easily. I will make my father's life a living hell. I will use every resource, every bit of information I have against him if he refuses me. It is my title. My legacy."

Elizabeth widened her eyes. She'd never seen this fierce side of Alexander, certainly not when he was speaking of the title. "Then you want it."

"Yes. I do."

Elizabeth smiled and felt vastly relieved. "Good. I would not have wanted you to suffer only on my behalf. I should have felt terribly guilty."

"Oh, God, I do love you," he said, laying gentle kisses on her cheek, her jaw line, her forehead, and finally her smiling lips.

"Come back to me a marquess, sir, so that I may be your marchioness," Elizabeth said grandly.

"And some day my duchess."

He said it with such conviction, such pride, that at that moment, Elsie had no doubt, none whatsoever, that they would someday be together.

Chapter 18

Alexander stood outside the gates of the place where he'd been brought more than twenty years earlier, feeling nothing but a sense of overwhelming sadness. He still remembered being led by Farnsworth, his father's secretary, toward what had seemed at the time a foreboding and dangerous place.

"It's not so bad, Mr. Alexander," Farnsworth had said. Even though Alexander was now Lord Hathwaite, the secretary had been given strict orders to not use his title. At the time, Alexander hadn't cared. How could he be Hathwaite when that title was his brother's? Farnsworth's face, despite his reassurances, was etched with worry as he gazed at the building, a large stone structure with tall, narrow windows. It looked, Alexander had thought, like a prison. Indeed, that's what he'd thought it was, believing his father was putting him away for killing his brother. He remembered an overwhelming feeling of panic that he would never see his beloved mother again, that he would never know what it was like to lay his head on his own pillow and stare out his mullioned window at the moon.

Alexander should have hated Farnsworth, but he knew instinctively that the secretary disliked the duke and stayed only because the salary was good. Even then, at ten years old, Alexander knew him to be a weak man, not a wicked one.

Now, he stood, a man grown, staring at a building that held more charm than danger, and he smiled slightly at the remembered fear. Alexander pushed through the gates, for they were not barred, and walked on a graveled drive to the large entrance, nerves boiling like acid in his stomach as they did every time he knew he would have to speak to a stranger. He swallowed down his disgust and took a deep and shaky breath, telling himself to relax, be calm. Still, his hand shook as he reached for the bell and gave it a hard twist.

The door opened, revealing a small middle-aged woman, whose fine clothes told him she was not a servant. "My name is Alexander Wilkinson. I'm here to see Dr. Stelton."

"Is he expecting you?" she asked, her tone soothing, her expression merely curious.

"No."

She stood looking up at him as if she expected him to say something more, but Alexander, already uncomfortable, remained silent. "What is your business, sir?" she asked.

He could feel his cheeks redden. "I was an inmate here when I was a boy," he said, and watched as her gaze went from curious to surprised. Then she let out a gasp.

"Alexander Wilkinson," she said, as if the name suddenly meant something to her. "Oh, goodness. Yes. I'll go get the doctor immediately." She turned to go, clearly flustered, then turned around. "I think it would be better for you to come along." She beamed a smile at him and Alexander smiled back uncertainly.

"Doctor," she said, walking into the doctor's office without even knocking. "You will never believe who I have out here. In the flesh."

"The queen," came a dry reply.

"Better. Alexander Wilkinson." Then she turned so that the doctor could see him, her hands clutched in front of her as if she could barely contain her excitement.

The doctor stood immediately, pushing back his chair, his eyes on Alexander, his mouth opened in surprise. "My God," he muttered. "Is it you?"

Alexander actually backed up a step. "I believe so," he said uncertainly.

The doctor stared at him another beat, then said with enthusiasm. "Well, come in, my boy. Come in." Dr. Stelton stared at him as if trying to see the boy inside the man he'd become. "It is you."

Alexander let out a low chuckle. "In the flesh."

The doctor indicated he should take a seat, then turned his attention to the woman who hovered in the doorway. "My wife, Cecelia."

He gave her a slight bow. "Mrs. Stelton."

"I'll fill you in later, my dear," the doctor said with a teasing smile, as if he knew she was dying of curiosity. With a slight scowl, she closed the door, and he called out: "Away from the door, darling." Then they both heard the sounds of her heels tapping away down the hall.

"What brings you to Wickshire?" Dr. Stelton asked as Alexander took his seat across from the desk.

"I've come to find proof of my identity and I believe you may be the only person on earth who knows who I am and who my father is."

Dr. Stelton sat back in his chair, looking steadily at Alexander, a smile slowly spreading on his face. "It's about damn time," he said, then burst from his seat and walked over to a cabinet, pulling out a leather portfolio after a brief search. He slapped it on his desk and said, "What do you need to know?"

A small thrill went through Alexander as he looked at that portfolio, which just might contain everything he would need to prove his identity and prove his father's misdeeds.

"Do you have a record of who placed me here?"

"Yes. And a record of who has been paying for your care for the past twenty years. Edgar Wilkinson, His Grace, the Duke of Kingston."

"I beg pardon? He is *still* paying?"

Dr. Stelton's face flushed with anger. "No one has ever inquired about your well being," he said, his voice laced with disgust. "Not one letter, not one visit. Just a quarterly check made out to this institution for your care. You've been gone more than twenty years," he said, pounding one fist upon the portfolio. "I will do whatever it takes to prove your identity, even if it means testifying before Queen Victoria herself."

"I sincerely hope it does not come to that," Alexander said. Alexander stared at the floor, trying not to let the news that his father thought him still institutionalized seep into his brain. He'd been completely, thoroughly abandoned. My God, a man selling a horse to a breeder would have had more care for that beast than his father had had for him. He didn't want the realization to hurt, but it did, an unexpected pain in his heart. He'd thought he was incapable of being hurt by his father again, but he'd been wrong.

"I am sorry, sir. It is unconscionable. I do want you to know that each check was deposited in a special account. I prayed this day would come, when you would return and could claim it. No one deserves that money more than you, sir. You have been ill used by a man who no doubt is held in high esteem by most."

Alexander looked up at him, gratified that the doctor was so angry for him, that he'd had such a champion all these years. "Money?"

"Quite a large sum, actually. Four quarters, twenty-two years, with interest." He pulled out a ledger. "Approximately ten thousand pounds."

"Ten thousand . . ." It was a small fortune. "Sir, are you certain you want to . . ."

Dr. Stelton held up his hand. "I've never been more certain of anything in my life. However, I would be remiss if I handed over this amount of money with absolutely no proof whatsoever of your identity. So, tell me what you remember of your time here."

Alexander closed his eyes and pictured his ten-year-old self walking through the halls, crying himself to sleep in his little room. "I was delivered here by my father's secretary, Mr. Farnsworth. I had a room on the second floor. There were two hallways, one went to the right, the other to the left, and my room was first on the left hallway. Downstairs, there is a parlor. It seemed rather large to me then. The other children, the best behaved ones, would gather there in the evening. I hated every moment I spent here until one night you called the children over to sing while you played the piano. Badly, if I recall. I wandered over and you asked if I wanted to play. I think you asked if I wanted to make some noise. And I played Mozart. That night, you came to my room and told me that I didn't belong here. The entire time I was here, I never spoke, for I was very frightened. After that, I was here a bit longer," he said, furrowing his brow. "Perhaps a month or two? And one day, you brought me out and introduced me to Monsieur Desmarais, the great muralist."

Alexander opened his eyes to see the doctor looking at him with raw emotion. "Yes. Exactly." He let out a breath and shook his head. "What father could do that to a son?"

"It does not matter. It was a gift. I have been with Monsieur Desmarais until very recently. I had a good life with a man I came to think of as a father. I was happy."

"What has happened, then, to bring you here after all these years?"

Alexander felt a silly grin spread on his face, but couldn't stop it. "I fell in love with my brother's fiancée. Of course, I didn't know until it was too late."

Dr. Stelton steepled his hands in front of his face. "So, this is for love?"

"That is how it started, but now I want my rightful life back. I was hiding behind my affliction and now I must face it, face who I am."

The doctor smiled. "That is good to hear. But tell me. How is it that you are able to speak so well now? I detect nothing in your speech that would hint of childhood difficulties."

Alexander explained about his difficulties, how even now he found it rather terrifying to walk into a roomful of people he did not know well.

The doctor narrowed his eyes. "Some sort of severe shyness. I daresay I've never heard of such a thing, but I wonder if some of those children whom we believe are rude or afflicted are having the same difficulties you did." He flipped open his pocket watch. "It's too late to get to the bank today, so I beg you to stay with my wife and me. We've a small cottage on the property and I know Cecelia is very curious about you. Many times we have thought about you over the years. I'm so glad you finally decided to come here."

Truth be told, Alexander would rather have traveled to a nearby inn and stayed in his own room, but he could not refuse the doctor's hospitality. These last few days had been agonizing tests. Hiring a horse, walking into taprooms, renting out a room, had all proved to be exceedingly trying. He hated being out among people, without the comfort of Monsieur and his blessedly silent world. "Thank you for the invitation. As I said, you are my one link to my past."

The doctor handed the portfolio over to Alexander. "This is yours now. I hope it can help you."

Alexander clutched the leather case as if it were a lifeline.

That night, Alexander went through the contents of the portfolio, sickened by the regular payments made to the institution. It was as if his father were paying a coal bill. He'd done nothing to hide the source of the checks that arrived with such regularity; even though he was paying for the upkeep of a son he'd told the world was dead. It showed the man's complete arrogance.

Arrogance, not stupidity. Even with such evidence in hand, Alexander knew it would be difficult to prove his claim. He needed help, and now had the funds to get it. Once he had money, he would hire a solicitor and perhaps even an investigator to prove his father's perfidy. If the duke had filed a death certificate, it would be false, obviously. Alexander need only go to the register office and find the name of the informant, or the person who filed the certificate. He hoped his father had had the document certified by a doctor, giving him one more person to question.

Alexander raked a hand through his too-long hair. Twenty years had passed since that grave was dug. What was the likelihood that whoever had supplied the document was even alive? His head ached from thinking about all that he must do before returning to Elsie. He wished he could go now, take her away and leave this all behind.

Alexander stood and looked in the small mirror above a chest in his room. He hardly remembered what his father looked like, so he couldn't know for certain if there was even a resemblance. He prayed not. He knew only that he had his father's gray eyes, eyes that had looked at him so coldly and with such loathing. To think his father's blood ran through his veins made Alexander physically ill.

What would his brother do? Would he have two powerful foes to go against, or would his brother gracefully give up the title. And his mother? What would the news he was alive do to her? His brain went in circles for hours until finally, exhausted, he fell into a fitful sleep, waking just before dawn. Outside a soft mist fell, frosting the grass and branches. A deer grazed in a nearby field, lifting its head and bounding off as a wagon rode by. The entire world was going on as if he wasn't in the midst of this turmoil. People were making fires, preparing for the day, and he stood at the precipice of a cliff that would change his life forever.

More than anything, he wished Elsie were with him, giving him strength with her unwavering faith in him. He tried to imagine himself as duke, Elsie as his duchess, but he couldn't conjure the image. He always ended up in that little cottage of his imagination, that safe cozy place where he lived with his Elsie alone.

Chapter 19

Wallace Champlin had been working in the law offices of Hampton and Crowley for seven years and prided himself on knowing the difference between a gentleman and a pretender. But the man standing before him had him a bit baffled. He had none of the arrogance of an aristocrat, but his clothes were of the finest material and the cut near perfection. If he were not a member of the ton, he was certainly a man of means.

He held himself stock-still, hands thrust behind his back, eyes devoid of emotion. His speech was educated, but had a slight, almost foreign-sounding accent. Most people, he thought, would not hear it, but Wallace was a bit of an expert on dialects. French? Italian? Definitely continental. He was soft spoken and yet commanding, his gaze not quite direct.

"Do you have an appointment, sir?"

The man clenched his jaw as if he'd asked an impertinent question. "No."

"I'm afraid I cannot accommodate you, then."

Wallace made a great show of looking through Mr. Hampton's appointment book, languorously flipping through page after page. "The first opening I have is in five weeks." He looked up expectantly, surprised to see a thunderously angry expression developing on the man's face.

"That is unacceptable."

Wallace gave the man a tight smile. "I'm afraid it's going to have to be."

"I do not think Mr. Hampton will be pleased to know you have put off the future Duke of Kingston. I suggest, sir, that you tell him Lord Hathwaite is here to see him about a long-term arrangement."

Wallace's eyebrows nearly disappeared beneath his stringy bangs, not only from the tone, but the fellow's claim. "You are Lord Hathwaite? But you introduced yourself as *Mr.* Alexander Wilkinson," he said, stressing the common title. "I beg pardon for the mistake." Again, the man clenched his jaw and Wallace thought he detected a slight bunching of his shoulders. Fear sliced through him as he recognized the strength and power of the man—and his obvious anger. There were many things the secretary was, but brawny was not one of them.

Wallace stood abruptly, still uncertain what or whom he was dealing with. The man in front of him was not Lord Hathwaite. He knew Lord Hathwaite. Well, didn't actually *know* him, but had seen him on occasion accompanying his father into their rival's office. Lord Hathwaite was blond and not quite as large as this man. This man looked more like the duke than Lord Hathwaite, actually . . . Now that gave him pause.

Sensing that Mr. Hampton just might be angry if he sent this man away, Wallace knocked on his employer's door and waited to be beckoned into the richly appointed office. "Yes, Mr. Champlin, how can I help you?"

Wallace smiled, glad that he'd decided to send this particular problem to Hampton instead of Crowley, for Hampton was a far more agreeable sort.

Wallace closed the door quietly behind him. "There is a man outside claiming to be Lord Hathwaite but I know for a fact that it is not Lord Hathwaite. But he is also claiming to be Alexander Wilkinson, and I do know that is the surname of the Duke of Kingston."

Hampton smiled as if delighted by this puzzle. "You don't say. Interesting."

"I thought so. I nearly sent him away, for obviously he is not who he says he is. But I thought you might be interested in speaking with him. He does bear a striking resemblance to the duke, sir, if I say so myself."

"I am intrigued," Hampton said, his smile growing. "Do send him in."

Alexander squeezed his hands together and took a deep and shaking breath. He'd nearly vomited in the alley before walking up the stairs just thinking about talking to the attorney. Being in London was nerve-wracking enough; obtaining a room in a fine hotel, making an appointment with a tailor (he'd gotten a recommendation from the hotel's concierge), donning these fine clothes, getting a shave and haircut from the valet the hotel provided. He felt foolish, like the pretender everyone thought he was. And every time he forced himself into a new situation, he had to force himself to act like a normal person, even though inside he was rather petrified.

Now he was to meet with a solicitor, make a case for himself, convince someone else that this impossible quest was possible. He swallowed again when the door opened with a soft *snick.*

"Mr. Hampton will see you now," the secretary said sedately, as if the man hadn't been looking at Alexander moments before as if he were quite mad.

"Thank you."

Alexander walked through the thick paneled door into an office lined with leather-tooled books and richly upholstered furniture. A huge mahogany desk dominated the room, its surface covered with portfolios much like the one he held in his sweating hand. Sitting behind it was a man gone bald, but with eyebrows so bushy one would need a comb to get them in their current uplifted position.

"My secretary informs me that you have an interesting story," he said with a smile that seemed oddly out of place.

"I do, sir." And then Alexander proceeded to tell him his story in precise detail, starting with his youthful affliction and the death of his older brother. The more he told, the further forward the man sat, until he was sitting with one elbow braced on his desk, his chin resting on his thumb. When Alexander was finished, he passed the solicitor the portfolio, which the man perused slowly and thoroughly without uttering one word. Finally he put the leather case aside and gave Alexander a long, hard look, as if he could determine whether or not he told the truth simply by looking at his person.

"We will never win," Hampton said finally, and pushed the leather portfolio back toward Alexander.

Sharp disappointment stabbed at him. From what he had determined, this was one of the finest solicitors in London, second only to his father's firm. He wanted and needed the best if he was to take his father on and claim his rightful place.

"We don't have to win," Alexander said. "We only have to make my father believe we can."

Hampton sat back and pressed his lips together, a glint of admiration in his intelligent brown eyes. "I'd be taking on one of the most powerful men in England and one of the most powerful solicitors as well," he said, as if the prospect of doing so wasn't unappealing. Then he shook his head and sighed. "I don't know if we can take that risk."

"But if you win, this firm will be solicitor for one of the most powerful titles in England."

Hampton smiled slowly. "This is very true. Stay here, young man," he said, having come to some decision, "and let me meet with my partner. I can't make such a large decision without his input. Do you have any other appointments today?"

"No, sir."

Hampton took up a copy of the *Times* that was folded on his desk and handed it to Alexander. "This may take a while."

* * *

Elsie stared at the *Times*, anger filling every bit of her body, even though she knew the duke and her father had insisted on formally announcing her engagement. Yesterday was to have been her birthday ball, and in keeping with their plans, her father had allowed the announcement of her engagement to Lord Hathwaite to run.

She had no way of contacting Alexander to warn him the announcement was going to run and she prayed he did not read the *Times*. How wretched he would feel to read those words. She felt completely helpless, for she had no idea how to reach Alexander or even where he was.

No amount of pleading or tears could convince her father to stop the announcement. It was purely maddening to see that her father, who truly believed Alexander loved her, continue with this false engagement.

"I will not marry Hathwaite no matter what the paper says," she raged, trying to shout but unable to because she was still so out of breath.

"Don't get overly excited," her father said, with such kindness Elsie wanted to scream.

"I am marrying Alexander. On second thought, this announcement is fine, for Alexander *is* Lord Hathwaite." She stared daggers at her father, praying he would say something to contradict her words. She was angry and wanted to be angry, wanted to scream and cry and rant about how hopeless she felt in every way.

"Have you heard from him?" her father asked, even though he obviously knew she had not. And perhaps that was the reason she was most angry.

"No, as well you know," she bit out.

"I'll let you rest," he said, getting up, and a terrible thought came to Elsie.

"Father. You wouldn't keep his correspondence from me, would you?"

"As much as I believe it would be in your best interest, I would not."

Slightly mollified, Elsie watched her father go, a scowl on her face. She hated feeling so helpless, so weak and ill. It was maddening to be stuck in this bed, unable to play with Mary, unable to walk unassisted to the necessary. Poor Missy was being run ragged, even though she never complained.

This illness, whatever it was, was unlike anything Elsie had ever had before. She thought once she started getting better, she would rapidly improve and be up and about in a day or two. But it had been a week since Alexander had left and she still could not walk on her own, her vision was still slightly blurred, and she found it tiring sitting up for too long.

Missy came in and laughed. "You're looking grumpy as usual, Miss," she said, sounding far too happy for Elsie's ill humor. "I've brought the morning post."

That did bring a bit of a smile. Even though she still had trouble reading some of the longer correspondence, she enjoyed going through the missives and get well wishes. Perhaps today, finally, there would be something from Alexander. Flowers had arrived for her nearly daily and her room was filled with the arrangements. The three lovely bouquets she'd had from Lord Hathwaite had been placed outside her room, for they made her feel decidedly uncomfortable.

Elsie flipped through the letters, and paused, finding one with bold handwriting and a small drawing of a fairy on it. "Alexander," she whispered, her eyes filling with tears. She opened the letter, squinting her eyes so that she might read the words better.

My Elsie:

I hope this letter finds you well. I hated to leave you while you were still so ill, but am driven to act so that we may be together always. You are forever in my thoughts, from the moment I awaken, to the moment I close my eyes at night. I will return to you as soon as I have news. I have found some success, but need more time. I am heading to London to hire a solicitor. I will forward you my address when I arrive.

I love you always,
Alexander

Elsie held the letter to her lips, knowing that he had touched this paper, had held it in his hands, had warmed it with his skin. And then, even though it was brief, she read it again, smiling at the words he'd written.

"Why, yes, that handsome man over there painting

a masterpiece and playing Mozart at the same time really is my husband, the Marquess of Hathwaite." She giggled, feeling better than she had in days. He loved her. He would succeed. He would return to her. Truly, all was well in the world.

The Right Honorable Lord Huntington
announces the engagement of his daughter,
The Honorable Elizabeth Stanhope,
to The Most Honorable The Marquess of Hathwaite
and son of His Grace, The Duke of Kingston.

Alexander read the announcement and stopped breathing for perhaps five beats, until he realized that her father had had no choice but to make the announcement. At least he hoped that was the case. Still, seeing those words inflamed the panic already growing in his breast. If Mr. Hampton rejected his case, he would be forced to go to another and another firm until he found someone to hire. No doubt, the less influential, the less likely the solicitor would be to take on such a fight.

What the hell was taking so long? he wondered, throwing the paper back on the attorney's desk. He got up to pace when the door opened and Mr. Hampton, followed by another man, entered the room

"By God," the man said loudly, his bright blue eyes looking at him. "There is a remarkable resemblance." He held the portfolio in his hands and gave Alexander a hearty handshake. "This is a pleasure, sir. A real pleasure." He rubbed his hands together.

"We've got 'em, Hampton. I think this time we really got 'em."

"Your father's firm," Mr. Hampton explained. "Mr. Crowley is not on the best terms with Mr. Tinkerman."

"I see."

"I think you are right, young man. We don't have to have proof, though this is damning on its own," Crowley said, shaking the portfolio. "We only have to make them think we have enough proof and pray they don't call our bluff."

"There is always the grave," Alexander said.

"The grave?" Crowley boomed.

"The grave where my father must have deposited an empty casket. That alone will prove I did not die."

Crowley smiled grimly. "True enough. But it doesn't prove that you are the missing boy, just that His Grace is a bloody scoundrel and lied about his son's death."

"Yes, sir."

Crowley, a stout man with a florid face and shockingly thick white hair, came right up to Alexander and peered up at him as if he were quite far-sighted. "Yes, yes," he muttered. "There is no doubt you have Kingston's blood in you, but we must be prepared that they will claim you are illegitimate. What of your mother? Will she recognize you?"

Alexander shook his head. "I left when I was just ten years old."

Crowley looked at him shrewdly. "And no doubt you'd like to spare her for now, am I right? Yes, then. Yes. We'll find your death certificate, see what it says, try to dispute it. Do you know your cause of death?"

"No, sir, I do not," Alexander said with a mild grin.

"No matter, no matter. We'll find it." Crowley had a habit of repeating himself which Alexander found appealing somehow. "This might take some time. Weeks or months. And then we'll have to present what we have to Kingston's solicitor. I'd like to avoid having to go through an official inquiry. Yes, I'd like to avoid that."

"Do you think we can avoid one?" Mr. Hampton asked.

"You know the House of Lords. They'd vote in favor of Kingston even if they'd witnessed Mr. Wilkinson's birth and watched him grow up. If it comes to that, we have little chance of winning. I want you to be aware of that, Mr. Wilkinson. At best, we win. At worst, you are rejected or the title ends up in abeyance."

Alexander breathed harshly through flared nostrils. It was not uncommon for a title to be held in abeyance for years. Once, a barony title was held in abeyance for more than a century. And yet, testifying before the House of Lords was a terrifying proposition. "I would have difficulty testifying before the House," he said. "I truly don't know if I could manage it. It is possible that I could hurt my case."

Crowley gave him a quick, almost fatherly smile. "Then we'll try our best to avoid that."

"Yes, that would be best," Alexander said, swallowing heavily.

"Now, sir, where are you staying so that we can keep you apprised of the investigation?" Crowley asked.

"I am staying at the Hotel Thornton, but I must travel to Nottinghamshire tomorrow."

"I would recommend against it," Crowley said. "I want to gather up as much evidence as possible before going to Kingston and I'll need you here in town."

"You misunderstand. I will be visiting a Miss Elizabeth Stanhope."

At that, Crowley's eyebrows shot up. "Hathwaite's fiancée?"

"The notice in the *Times* is premature," Alexander said, his voice uncharacteristically hard.

Crowley gave him a look of exasperation. "You have a tendre for the girl?"

"I plan to marry her."

Crowley rubbed a hand across his forehead. "This complicates matters. Indeed it does."

Alexander looked from one man to another. "I don't understand."

"It gives you a more nefarious motive for attempting to attain your title. That you wish not only to obtain the title but to humiliate your brother, who as you know is, as of this moment, Kingston's legal heir."

"I have no wish to humiliate anyone. I love her and wish to marry her. And, because of her father's agreement with His Grace, I must be named heir if we are to be married. It is that simple."

The two solicitors were silent for a long time, until Hampton spoke up. "We could use this in our favor," he said. "Star-crossed lovers, meeting by fate, kept apart by a powerful and malevolent force."

Crowley smiled in understanding. "The duke."

"Go on your trip," Crowley said, "but return here forthwith. No doubt that announcement in the *Times* is motivating this visit?"

Alexander felt his cheeks redden. "Yes, sir." He had to see her, had to touch her, had to hear her tell him she loved him. Seeing that notice had shaken him, more than he cared to admit.

"With any luck, young man, that notice will be valid. You are, after all, the true Lord Hathwaite, eh?"

Crowley gave him a wink, and Alexander forced a smile. Even though things were proceeding far better than he'd hoped, he still could not help feeling that nothing would turn out the way he planned.

Chapter 20

When the Mansfield Hall butler opened the door to Alexander one day later, the only indication that he recognized him was one slightly raised eyebrow. Indeed, Alexander little resembled the man who'd left the estate two weeks prior, the shaggy-haired artist's assistant with his common, sometimes paint-stained garb. The man standing before him was dressed as a gentleman, the cut of his clothes impeccable, if not conservative. His boots were shined, his hair was neatly cut, his jaw freshly shaved. The young man even wore gloves, in which he held an expensively engraved calling card, not one of those pedestrian blank ones in which people penciled in their own names.

Nonetheless, Cobbs took the card, and bade Alexander wait outside while he went in search of the baron.

Alexander stood on the marble landing and gazed back at the estate, a small smile of triumph on his lips. How different he felt now, wearing fine clothes and knowing that his goal of attaining his title, and his bride, were closer than ever. The door momentarily opened, revealing Lord Huntington, scowling at him from the shadows of the house.

"I thought you might come," he said gruffly, and backed into the house, indicating that Alexander should follow him.

"The engagement notice was a bit . . . jarring," Alexander said, "given that I intend to marry your daughter. How is she?"

Huntington grunted and led Alexander to his study. "She's still abed, but improving a bit each day," he said, preceding him into the room.

The baron waited until Alexander and he were seated before continuing on. "I have been put in an extremely difficult situation, and I cannot see a good resolution."

"I understand. I want only to see Elsie before returning to London."

Lord Huntington let out a growl, but his eyes held less malevolence. "What news have you?"

"I have little to report," Alexander said, unwilling to disclose information to a man who very well might be in Kingston's camp. Certainly the news that Alexander had hired a rival firm to represent him—a firm that believed him to be the true Kingston heir—would be information much coveted by his father.

"I am sorry for you, then," Lord Huntington said, seeming to mean it. "I will allow you to see Elsie only because I do believe she would have me murdered if she found out you were here and I sent you away."

Alexander grinned and stood up. "May I go now, sir?"

Lord Huntington smiled indulgently and motioned with his hand, dismissing Alexander.

Alexander certainly hadn't expected a warm greeting, and he was gratified that Lord Huntington was—if not welcoming—at least indulgent. His new boots tapping loudly on the polished floor, Alexander walked hurriedly to the stairs, then took them two at a time, his heart singing.

Elsie was so sick of being sick. Her bum hurt, her head hurt, her eyes hurt. The only consolation she had was that her birthday ball had been suspended and she'd not had to face Lord Hathwaite and accept his proposal in public. How could she when she so loved Alexander? This sickness, as horrible as it was, had at least saved her having to lie and pretend in front of everyone she knew.

Though she had made up her mind not to marry Lord Hathwaite, she was filled with doubts. It was all well and good to want such a thing with your heart, and quite another to condemn your family to a life of humiliation and destitution. At odd moments, a terrible rush of fear would hit her, and her heart would race almost painfully in her chest at the thought of the future and what it would bring.

No matter how she tried, she could not come up with a solution to what she would do if Alexander could not prove himself heir. How could she marry Lord Hathwaite when she loved Alexander so desperately? How could she marry Alexander when it would mean certain ruin for her family?

She stared pensively out the window, wishing she was strong enough to go outside to the garden and breathe fresh air. Missy had refused to open her window, fearing that the cool air would make her worse, and Elsie was hardly strong enough to make the trip to the window, never mind open it. How vexing.

"Would you want to go out to the garden?"

She gasped at the familiar voice, that beloved form, standing at the threshold to her room. "Alexander," she cried, lifting her hands to him. "Oh, I cannot believe you are here."

She was in his arms, his wonderfully strong familiar arms, in a second. She breathed in his familiar scent, then pulled back.

"What have you done to yourself?" she said with mock scorn.

Alexander smiled. "I have made myself quite debonair, don't you think?"

"Quite," she said, running her hands through his shortened hair and frowning. "I hardly recognize you."

With that, he pulled her closer and kissed her gently. "A reminder, then, of who I am."

Elsie pulled him close, unable to let go. "Why did you come? Do you have news?"

"I had to come when I saw that apparently you are planning to marry someone else," he said, his eyes twinkling.

Elsie lifted her head pertly. "I have no idea what you are speaking of."

He kissed the tip of her nose. "It was quite disturbing to see that the woman I love is engaged to another man."

"Nonsense," she said. "You *are* Lord Hathwaite, after all." She watched as his eyes brightened.

"I'm starting to believe that it may happen."

"It will," she said firmly, then pulled him close again, needing to feel his arms around her. Just having him here made her stronger. "Have you heard anything?"

Alexander hesitated and shifted his eyes away briefly. "Nothing concrete, but I am more optimistic than I was when I left. I have hired a solicitor who has promised to investigate my claim."

Elsie smiled uncertainly. "It is more than a claim, Alexander. It is the truth."

"I know that and you know that but I don't want to give you false hope. It could be that I will not be successful and then we shall have to face the consequences."

Elsie shook her head, not wanting to hear any such thing. "But you seem happier, more optimistic."

"Yes. Of course."

Elsie scowled at him, and felt much like a child who wasn't told precisely what she wanted to hear. She frowned fiercely when Alexander laughed at her.

"All right then, you have tortured me with your frown and I fear I must divulge something to you before you throw yourself from a cliff completely despondent."

Elsie clapped her hands, immediately appeased.

"The solicitor I hired is from a very prestigious firm, and though they have been exceedingly cautious about making any promises, they are optimistic we will succeed."

"Really? Oh, Alexander that is wonderful news."

"I haven't told your father because his loyalties are with my father, which I quite understand," he said, when she frowned. "And I didn't want to tell you and put you in the position of lying to your father. But I can see that you will pout my entire visit, so there it is."

Elsie wrinkled her nose at Alexander making him chuckle. "Which firm did you hire?"

"Hampton and Crowley."

"I'm afraid I don't know many solicitors, other than our own. A Mr. Tillings, a very dour man whom I have vowed to make smile once before he dies."

"They are a rival firm of my father's and apparently quite respected."

"However did you afford . . ." She stopped, her cheeks growing pink.

"It is a valid question, and my future wife should be apprised of all my finances. And for that reason, I shall tell you." He kissed her lightly. "For more than twenty years my father has been paying for my room and board at Wickshire. The director has been placing those funds in an account for me on the chance I would one day return. He has also provided documentation proving that my father's secretary brought me to the asylum, as well as an accounting of the payments."

Elsie was stunned. "For twenty *years*? But you've been gone from there since you were ten years old."

"Apparently my father was unaware I had left."

Elsie saw through the nonchalance of his tone to

the pain he tried so desperately to hide. "Do you mean to say His Grace didn't know you had left? All this time?" Alexander shook his head and she thought her heart might break for him all over again. Alexander had been so thoroughly abandoned, the duke hadn't even made a single inquiry in all that time. "Honestly, I could thrash the man."

"What say we get married, instead?" Alexander said, smiling. "I think that will do far more harm to him than a thrashing from you."

Elsie realized that he had changed in the past weeks, seemed more confident, and certainly smiled more easily. If possible, he was even more appealing. He became suddenly serious as his eyes scanned her face, and Elsie felt self-conscious and quite aware of how horrible she must look. Her hair was in a simple braid, her nightgown quite wrinkled.

As if sensing her sudden discomfort, he asked, "How are you feeling, love? Certainly not up to thrashing anyone just yet."

She self-consciously touched her head and her cheeks flushed. "Getting better, but it's taking far too long," she said. "Sometimes I feel as if I will never be as I was."

"You are far better, and far lovelier than the last time I saw you."

"I daresay, anything is an improvement from that," Elsie said, laughing.

Alexander pulled her in for another kiss; it was as if he simply could not stop himself.

"I wish we could make love," she said, her heart aching. "I wish we could start the rest of our lives now. How long can you stay?"

Alexander shook his head regretfully. "I must return to London tomorrow."

"So soon?"

"I wouldn't have come at all if that notice hadn't run."

"I am sorry for that. It must have been terrible to read it."

"Only as bad as a knife to my back, love," he said, teasing.

Elsie wrinkled her nose. "That is not at all amusing."

"Can I play the piano for you to make up for my heartlessness?"

"I don't think I have the strength just yet to go downstairs," she said, frustration welling up in her. She was so tired of feeling helpless.

"Of course not," Alexander said, then swept her up into his arms, kissing her soundly as she laughed in delight. It seemed forever since she'd felt so utterly happy.

He effortlessly brought her down the stairs, her arms wrapped around his neck, and he stole kisses along the way. "What shall I play for you?"

"Something happy."

"And have you seen the mural?"

Elsie shook her head. "My father covered it so that it will be a surprise to me. When I am better, he hopes to unveil it at a ball because my birthday ball was cancelled. It's extremely maddening. I'm dying to see it, even though I saw it when it was nearly complete."

"It's a bit different," Alexander said mysteriously. "I think you'll be pleased."

"How could I not be? It was beautiful even before it was finished. A masterpiece."

"Worthy of kings?" he teased.

"Or at the very least a future duchess."

He sat her on the sofa, then pushed the entire thing across the room so that she was near to the piano. When she was settled, he returned to the piano and pounded out a rousing rendition of the American song, *Old Susannah*, making Elsie laugh. Never had she seen Alexander so animated, so handsome in his confidence. It was as if he were another man entirely.

He stopped and turned, his smile wide, looking so beautiful, Elsie felt her heart nearly stop. "I've missed you so much," she said, her eyes filling with tears. "It's been difficult having you away, wondering where you are and if you are all right. I hate this uncertainty, this unending longing."

Alexander immediately went to her, going to his knees and drawing her close. "Have faith in me, love. Promise me, please. It's all I have."

Elsie wiped her tears, angry with herself for giving in to the doubts that assailed her. "I'm a ninny," she said stoutly. "You know I promise to wait for you. I'm simply growing impatient and maudlin. I wish your father would just accept you so we could marry tomorrow."

Alexander smiled, fortified by her words. Though he would want to die if he could not marry her, at least he knew she loved him, at least he knew she would wait for him until all was lost. That thought would carry him through the next difficult weeks. "How very coincidental that I have the very same wishes."

Elsie gave him a watery smile. "Now. Play me another. A polka, if you please."

Alexander stood and gave her a very gallant bow. "Of course, Mademoiselle."

After a brief concert, Alexander settled onto the couch next to her, pulling her close. Elsie rested her head on his shoulder, feeling completely content. He was here. He loved her. For now, that was all that mattered. They didn't even stir when the door to the ballroom opened and her father stepped into the room.

"Good God, your aunt should be here," he said, frowning down at the pair so cozy on the sofa. "This is hardly proper."

Alexander stood, and Elsie immediately missed his warmth. "My apologies, sir," he said, his hand still holding hers. Her father's eyes drifted to those hands clenched so tightly together, as if he were there to rip them apart.

Suddenly, her father's face changed, almost fell, as if the effort to maintain his stoic manner was just too much. "If not for Mary . . ." he began, then stopped abruptly. "I do not mean to be an ogre, to be a Montague, keeping two people in love apart. I have no choice in the matter."

Elsie felt her eyes burn with unshed tears. "I do understand, Father, even if I dislike it. I wish you could stand up to Kingston."

Her father's face paled slightly. "It has nothing to do with my standing up to him. It has to do with eighty thousand pounds that he gave me in good faith."

Elsie gasped. "Eighty. *Thousand?*"

"And it's all gone. Do you think this house, these grounds, your education, the balls, the town house in London, my stables, would have been possible without such an influx of funds?"

"I knew there was money involved but I never imagined . . ." Elsie felt sick to her stomach. Her father could never hope to pay back such an enormous amount, even if he sold every bit of property he owned. "It must have been an important vote."

"At the time, I was the last hold-out. I am ashamed that my vote was bought, but at the time I thought I could give you and Christine and your mother a better life. A happier life." He hung his head, and Elsie's heart ached for him, but she couldn't help thinking how unfair it was that all hinged upon her marrying someone she'd been engaged to since childhood.

Her father let out a bitter laugh. "The money wasn't enough. It felt dirty, somehow. But then he upped the ante, you see. He promised that one of my daughters would one day be a duchess." He shook his head. "I could not say no."

"Your daughter will still be a duchess, sir, no matter what happens," Alexander said, his tone brooking no argument.

"How can you say such a thing?"

"Because you must, Elsie. It is part of our promise to each other, remember?"

Elsie swallowed down a thick lump in her throat. He was right. No matter what happened with Alexander's quest, she would one day be the Duchess of Kingston. She had promised, after all.

Chapter 21

Wallace Crowley hadn't felt so energized since he'd been in his early thirties. Imagine bringing down a duke and his overpriced lawyers in one fell swoop. It was downright intoxicating.

Crowley was an intelligent and perceptive man. He prided himself on his ability to read people—even those who worked hard to not be read—and he had no doubt the duke would present a bit of a challenge. He loved challenges. He knew, for example, that His Grace had granted his request for an appointment simply out of curiosity. A man such as the Duke of Kingston was forever cloaked in his own sense of security. No one he'd ever met deserved to be brought down as much as Kingston. The more he'd learned about what the duke had done to his son, the more determined he became to set things right. It had become nearly as personal to him as it was to Alexander.

Crowley wore his brown frock coat, his finest boots, his newest pair of gloves. On his head he wore a fine silk top hat that his wife had told him was quite dashing. In one hand he carried an ivory and gold-handled walking stick; in the other hand, he carried proof that the Duke of Kingston was perhaps the coldest bastard in all of Britain. It had been remarkably easy to find proof that His Grace had fabricated his son's death.

Apparently, the young boy had died in a fire that never happened in a school that never existed. Odd that.

What a thrill it had been when Hampton had come into his office, his face flushed with triumph, and slapped the documents on his desk. The death certificate stated clearly that Alexander Wilkinson, ten-year-old son of the Duke of Kingston, had succumbed to a fire at the Billingford School in the town of Fishings.

There was a slight problem with the document. Not only was there no such town as Fishings in all of England, no Billingford School had ever been registered and certainly no fire ever reported. He could not wait to tell the Duke that he had proof his son had never died—at least the way described in the death certificate—and proof that he'd been paying for the room and board at an asylum for that dead son for the past twenty-two years.

It was wonderfully diabolical and Crowley couldn't wait until he presented his evidence to the Duke.

Kingston had a headache, and so he rubbed at his temples and squeezed his eyes shut tightly to relieve the pain. He did not have time to be in pain.

With that thought, he glanced at his secretary, busily scratching away, his thinning hair hanging in unfortunate strands across his bald pate. It looked greasy and unkempt, and Kingston pressed his lips together in distaste.

He would have fired Farnsworth long ago if the man hadn't been so efficient and loyal. And quiet. Yes, quiet. He never spoke unless Kingston asked a question, never inquired about his health or family, never argued about any task given him, including breaking off with Kingston's latest mistress. He hadn't time for that nonsense and Jilly was getting tiresome.

A quiet knock sounded on the door, which Kingston ignored. Farnsworth jumped up from his small desk and went to the door to speak softly to someone on the other side. Kingston was hardly aware of Farnsworth's footsteps as he walked to his desk.

"A Mr. Crowley is here to see you, Your Grace. You have an appointment with him at ten o'clock." Farnsworth snapped open his watch. "It is one minute 'til. Shall I bring him in, Your Grace?"

Kingston sighed, irritated, and nodded. He had no idea why a solicitor who was not his own would care to speak to him. Perhaps it was over some land matter or a business dealing with a client. No doubt someone was trying to get more money out of him than was due, rot them. They wouldn't succeed. They never did.

He frowned over a proposal written by the steward of his property in Weston, a request that a windmill be replaced. Everyone was forever asking for money or favors or time. He put that request in a growing pile for Oscar to handle. Kingston liked to keep his son busy and out of trouble, not like the ne'er-do-wells spawned by so many of the aristocracy. When he died, his son, as inept and slow as he was, would be ready to take over his duties. When Kingston lifted his eyes, standing before him was a well-dressed white-haired man who looked vaguely familiar.

"How can I help you, Mr. Crowley?"

"Your Grace," the man said, bowing with just the proper depth. "I am representing a gentleman by the name of Alexander Wilkinson, who is filing a petition with the House of Lords regarding his rightful claim of title. It is our contention that Mr. Wilkinson is actually the true Marquess of Hathwaite and your heir."

The blood drained from Kingston's head so quickly, he momentarily heard nothing but roaring in his ears and felt as if he actually might keel over. His hand clenched convulsively on his desk as he tried to regain control after hearing the name of his long-dead, not-so-dead son. It took him perhaps two seconds before he'd regained control of himself, and he nodded slightly, congratulating himself on recovering so quickly. Crowley, the fool, appeared not to have noticed his reaction, and was droning on about something. Kingston swallowed.

"I beg pardon, sir, but am I to understand that you are here representing some pretender claiming to be my son? My son died more than—" He paused, quickly calculating the years.

"Twenty-two years ago," the solicitor supplied.

Kingston flushed. "Yes. Twenty-two years ago. How dare you!"

Crowley gave him an almost pitying look, there and gone so quickly, Kingston wasn't even certain he had seen it.

"I do beg pardon, sir. Perhaps you were unaware that your son did not die," Crowley said with maddening patience. "If that is so, you likely have an explanation as to why you've been paying room and board at an idiot asylum—Wickshire Asylum—the same asylum where you—" Crowley stopped, and made a great show of looking at the pages in front of him. "No, not you, your secretary, a Mr. Farnsworth, brought Alexander twenty-two years ago."

"I have made several charitable contributions to many institutions over the years," the duke said imperiously.

"Of course. Quite commendable of you, Your Grace. But please indulge me. Could you explain a death certificate for your son, which claimed he was killed in Fishings at Billingford School?"

Oh, shit. Kingston gave Crowley a look that had sent more powerful men than this solicitor scurrying from his study, but the man simply smiled as if he were touched in the head. "My son's death was exceedingly tragic."

"Perhaps in your grief, you forgot the town where the school was located. And the name of the school itself. For neither has ever existed."

Kingston, like Crowley, was a shrewd man. He knew when he was defeated, so he sat back in his chair as if he hadn't a care in the world. "File your petition," he said. "It should be amusing."

Crowley gave him such a look of triumph that, just for a moment, Kingston felt a frisson of fear go up his spine. Then he remembered who he was, whom he had in his pocket, and knew no matter how true everything Crowley said was, they would never get the votes.

"Your Grace, I do wish you would reconsider, for your sake. This is damning information and would no doubt tarnish your stellar reputation," Crowley said with just the smallest hint of irony. "Regardless of who your friends are now, I will win in the end and your son's rightful place in society will be restored."

"Never."

Crowley gave him an assessing look. "I am curious, sir, as to why you would do such a thing. Your son is a fine young man, quite intelligent and well spoken. I don't know a man in this kingdom who wouldn't be proud to call him son."

"Get out," Kingston growled, and stood up abruptly. "Get out of my house. File your petition. I'll see you in hell before that boy is named my heir. In hell," he said, ending on a shout that even to Kingston's own ears sounded a bit maniacal.

Crowley merely smiled and bowed. "As you wish."

After the solicitor had gone, Kingston sat down in his chair, staring at the door where the man had disappeared, breathing heavily. His eyes flickered to Farnsworth, who sat as still as a statue, pen in hand, eyes wide, skin sickeningly pale.

"Sir?" he asked, his voice shaking even on that single syllable.

"Send for Lord Hathwaite," Kingston snapped. "And then send for my solicitor."

Farnsworth hastened out of the room, and five minutes later, the duke's youngest son appeared before him, looking nervous and uncomfortable, which only made his mood darker. Henry, no matter how he'd scowled, had never feared him.

"I'm afraid we have to move the wedding up," he said, as if discussing a business meeting. "I've just been informed that there is a pretender claiming to be Alexander, which as you can imagine could have grave implications for your future. I'd like to get you married before such gossip does irreparable damage and tarnishes your wedding."

His son stood there, mouth gaping open like a fool. "Did you hear me? Go. Get a license. You'll be wed by the end of the week."

His son turned to go, then stopped. "If it is a pretender, as you say, why must we rush things? Wouldn't that simply lend credence to this man's claim? I would think the last thing we should do is hurry the wedding."

Kingston's eyes shifted away from his son for an instant before hardening with resolve. "Don't think," he sneered. "Just do as I say."

Elsie's cheeks were flushed from the exertion of walking up and down the stairs, but she felt more jubilant than she had in days. Finally, she was getting better, growing stronger. Her vision was nearly perfect, her lungs allowing her to breathe almost normally. Soon, she would go out to the garden by herself and feel the sun on her face once again. By the time Alexander returned, she would very nearly be her old self.

Thoughts of Alexander were never far from her mind. She worried about him, missed him even though she'd seen him only yesterday, but refused to think about what her life would be like should he fail to prove his identity. Nights were long and lonely, days interminable. She wished she could squeeze her eyes closed and make this terrible time pass, until the day of her wedding, when he would stand at the altar smiling at her. The first time she was able to leave her room, she'd walked to the guest room where they had spent so many beautiful hours together. She'd touched the counterpane, pressed the cold pillow beneath her hand, her heart aching.

One of the worst parts was that she had no one to talk to about him. Even now, her father refused to discuss him, and her aunt Diane, who had postponed her trip to Bamburgh when she'd become ill, had no knowledge of him. Her father thought that the fewer people who knew, the better. Just in case.

How she hated this silence, this pretending Alexander wasn't the duke's heir. She knew. That should be enough.

Aunt Diane, oblivious to her mental torment, couldn't understand her complete lack of interest in planning for her wedding. To her aunt's eyes, she was a sullen creature who simply did not appreciate her good fortune. So Elsie did try to show some interest. When her aunt prattled on about Lord Hathwaite, Elsie envisioned Alexander, not Oscar. She refused to believe Alexander would fail in his quest.

Elsie had just finished walking down the stairs for the second time, which turned out to be a mistake. She was nearly shaking with fatigue and her legs felt as if they might crumple beneath her.

"Elsie, there you are." Her aunt, wringing her hands together worriedly, rushed to her side. "His Grace is here," she whispered, "and he has some extremely disturbing news."

Elsie, already winded, suddenly found it near impossible to take a breath.

"Oh, dear," her aunt said, seeing her reaction. "It's not as bad as all that. It's not as if the wedding is called off."

Elsie felt a sudden sense of foreboding. She could count on one hand the number of times His Grace had visited Mansfield Hall, and on those occasions she had been well aware of his visit in advance. "What has happened?"

Her aunt's eyes were stricken, and Elsie's fear only grew. What if he had found out about Alexander? What if he were here to threaten her father? Elsie swallowed and lifted her chin, ready to face whatever it was, knowing she would have to be strong.

Diane led her to her father's study, moving quickly down the dimly lit hall as if the duke were behind them chasing them. Elsie quickly grew out of breath. "Please, Aunt, I cannot keep up."

Diane turned, looking stricken. "I'm so sorry, dear. Take your time."

Elsie leaned one hand on the wall, catching her breath and trying to calm her wildly beating heart, while her aunt hovered nervously next to her.

"Can't you please tell me what has happened?" Elsie asked.

"It is best that His Grace tell you this," she said, and hesitated. "It's about your wedding."

Elsie's eyes grew wide and her fears grew tenfold. Pushing off the wall, she entered her father's study, praying she could face whatever was coming. The last thing she expected was for Kingston to rise and smile kindly at her.

Taken aback, Elsie found herself smiling back and dipping a curtsy. "Your Grace, what a wonderful surprise."

"My dear, dear, Elsie. Please sit."

Elsie looked at her father, who looked quite ill sitting in one of the study's large leather chairs. Elsie knew then, despite the duke's pleasant smile, that something awful had indeed happened.

Elsie sat across from her father and she swallowed down her growing fear. "Has something happened, Your Grace?"

"I'm afraid so, my dear." He looked down at her with fatherly concern and Elsie felt distaste run down her spine. That expression was a lie, she knew it deep in her bones. "I'm afraid we are going to have to move the wedding up to the end of this week. Friday, to be precise."

"I beg pardon?" Elsie asked, feeling suddenly faint and grateful that she was already seated. "That's only four days from now. It's impossible."

"I do realize you are not quite well, but to avoid scandal it has become imperative that you marry my son as quickly as possible. A special license has already been procured, but I thought I would give you at least a few days to prepare."

Elsie looked from her father to Kingston. "I don't understand. What has happened?"

"I came here to tell you that a man has been masquerading as my deceased son, but apparently it is far worse than that. Your father has informed me that he has duped you, taken advantage of your good heart, and convinced you that he is indeed my son and heir to the duchy."

"Alexander," Elsie said, clutching the arms of the chair until her hands shook.

"The claims are ridiculous, of course," Kingston said, examining his fingernails, before bringing his cold, blue eyes back to her. "But you know how petty gossip and innuendo can turn ugly. I want nothing to mar your wedding to my son."

Elsie felt a calm steal over her. So, he knew, and he was denying Alexander, the scoundrel. "Alexander *is* your son," Elsie said, her voice strong. "You abandoned him to an asylum, left him there, didn't even know whether he lived or died and now you are denying him."

"Elsie," her father said harshly, chastising her. "The duke knows all about this man. Let him speak."

"Father, how can you sit there and let him lie about Alexander?"

The duke smiled and Elsie felt her skin crawl. "I am aware of your . . . friendship with this man and I feel very sorry that you were put through this. My dear girl, please do not be embarrassed or ashamed."

"I am neither."

The duke's eyes flickered with unmistakable coldness before he smiled again. "This is not the first time this particular man has perpetrated this scheme. Last year he claimed to be an Italian prince. Two years ago, the long lost son of a viscount. Each time, he has duped well-intended, hopeful people. He preys on the good-hearted, people who are desperate to believe him, and then demands money, among other things."

"That's not true. Alexander is your son," she said, even as horrible doubts assailed her. It wasn't true. It wasn't. It couldn't be. "What could he possibly hope to gain by enlisting my help? Why not go directly to you?"

Again, that sickening smile. "He wouldn't dare try to approach me. And so he went to you, likely hoping for precisely what will happen if you do not marry Hathwaite immediately. Do you realize the scandal that would erupt, the smearing of our good name, if this were to come out? That a future duchess was taken in by a charlatan? What would you pay to save your reputation? What would I pay to save my son such embarrassment?"

Elsie shook her head. "He hasn't made any demands for funds."

The duke stared at her a long while. "Not to you, my dear. Not to you."

Elsie felt her world collapsing around her and fought to draw air into her lungs. Clearly the duke was implying that Alexander had demanded money for his silence.

"Oh, Elsie, please do not distress yourself," the

duke said calmly. "He is a consummate liar, an actor. He's fooled far more sophisticated people than you."

Elsie felt as if she were going to be ill. She recalled suddenly Alexander's fine clothing, his new confidence, his almost aristocratic air when he'd visited. Could it have been only yesterday? Her stomach felt hollow, cold, and her heart as if it might explode in her chest. "No. It's not true. He loves me and I love him. He is your son." A tear slipped down her cheek and the duke handed her his handkerchief. Elsie took it blindly, her eyes unfocused, her breath coming in shortened gasps.

"Oh, my dear," His Grace said, shaking his head sadly. "What are the chances that my long lost son would somehow end up working in your home, and just happen to fall in love with you? He is an opportunist, that is all."

Elsie's mind warred against what he was saying, against what had to be lies. They had to be.

"He knew of the lake," Elsie said, sounding desperate even to her own ears. "The lake hidden by the hedgerow. He painted it just as I remembered. He knew how Henry died, he knew that you blamed him for something that wasn't his fault. He remembered being unable to talk to you because you terrified him so. Your son remembered everything, every detail."

"My son is dead. Good God, must you torture me with this fable as well?" the duke shouted, making Elsie startle and blink rapidly.

"Your Grace, Elsie is still recovering from her illness," her father said, finally coming to her defense.

"Please do not shout at her. She is not to blame for what has happened. That man is."

Elsie dashed a tear away and sniffed. "His name is Alexander Wilkinson," she said defiantly.

"His name is John Parker," the duke spat. "He is well known by the Bow Street Runners and I have little doubt he will be in their custody within the fortnight. That is if he hasn't fled the country already." Kingston turned to her father. "My God, the chit cannot be this obtuse."

"Elsie, please, think of how ridiculous his story is. An artist's mute assistant is truly the heir of a duchy? And he wasn't even a mute, he was lying about that even to the man who gave him a home, who loved him as a son. If he could lie to a man such as Desmarais, do you not think he would lie to you, as well?"

Her father's tone was so kind, so sad, Elsie's face crumpled and she began crying in earnest. How could it be true? How could everything Alexander told her be a lie? It couldn't. "Oh, God," Elsie moaned, as Aunt Diane drew her into an embrace. "It can't be. It can't be."

"Oh, darling, everything will be fine," her aunt murmured. "Thank goodness no one has found out about it. Just thank goodness for that."

Chapter 22

That night, Elsie thought of everything Alexander had told her about himself, fighting the terrible doubts that were assailing her. He'd had an explanation for everything. The grave that he claimed was false, the years away from England, the funds to buy his new clothing. She thought of all those wonderful hours spent with him in the ballroom, hours in which she'd fallen in love with him long before he'd told her his identity. Was that why he'd held off? Waiting for her to fall completely for him, knowing that she couldn't think clearly in the throes of love?

Elsie hugged her knees against herself and rocked back and forth. It couldn't have been all lies. Could a man make love to a woman the way he had if he hadn't loved her? She wasn't that stupid, and Alexander would never do that to her. Never.

But the duke said he'd done it before, duped others into believing he was their child, their long-lost son, a voice nagged in her head. When Alexander had come back, he'd been confident, smiling, wearing new clothes.

How she hated these doubts, this terrible sick feeling in the pit of her stomach, this complete and utter helplessness. She wanted Alexander here, telling her the duke lied, bringing with him the proof of who he was. Should she simply have blind faith? Should she completely disregard her father, her aunt, and a duke of the realm because she'd fallen in love with an artist's assistant? Elsie buried her head against her knees and cried softly, remaining that way even when a soft knock came at her door. She did not answer, but continued to sit, tears soaking her nightgown, as her father stepped quietly into the room.

"Elsie, I'm so sorry."

She lifted her tear-ravaged face and nearly began sobbing anew at the sorrowful look on her father's face.

"He was a very convincing young man," he said, sitting on the edge of the bed. "He very nearly had me convinced, you know."

"But you never believed him entirely."

"I believed that he loved you. And I still believe that, in his own way, he did." He let out a grim laugh. "I must else I would have to kill him, wouldn't I?"

Elsie felt her eyes burn with new tears, but held them back. "I don't know what to believe. It could not have all been lies, it could not have been. He came back to see me, he never demanded money. He wants to marry me."

"Think of this from his perspective. He came back when he saw the notice of your engagement in the newspaper. Perhaps he panicked and thought you'd lost interest, and that would have meant his schemes would end there. It was integral to his plan that you be in love with him when he made his demands."

Elsie shook her head. "He knew so many things. No one could pretend the pain I saw in him, the fear. No one."

"No one in our experience, no. But this sort of thing is not unheard of."

"We are to take Kingston's word on everything? He could be lying about the Bow Street Runners and that John person who he claims is Alexander. He could be lying about everything."

Her father let out a sound of frustration. "Why would His Grace not want to welcome back a long-lost son? Why would this man's appearance incense him so if Alexander wasn't truly dead?"

"Because he hated Alexander. He always blamed him for Henry's death. And because when Alexander was a boy, he was afflicted and could not talk."

"And now he miraculously can."

"He is not entirely cured, but he is far better."

Her father threw up his hands. "No father would keep a child in an asylum for twenty-two years if he didn't belong there."

"Oh, who is naïve now, Father?" Elsie said bitterly.

"I'll grant you that it is possible. Yes. But isn't it far more possible that this mute artist's assistant is precisely what the duke claims he is? An impostor and a schemer?"

"No," Elsie shouted. Then her face cleared as she realized how easily she could prove Alexander was who he claimed to be. "We can write the solicitor he hired. We can ask them."

"And cause even more gossip?"

Elsie glared at her father with mute anger, breathing harshly through her nose. "We can write to them and learn the truth. It was . . . it was . . . Cromley or Crowley . . ." An awful panic hit her as she realized she could not remember the name of the firm. "No. Crowley or Cromley *and* someone. It began with an 'h' I'm certain of it."

"Cromley and Harte?" her father asked dubiously.

"Yes, that must be it." Elsie felt the first surge of hope. "Alexander told me they were a prestigious firm in London."

"They are certainly well-respected enough." That her father was so uncertain Alexander could have hired such a firm only cemented her belief that he had. Now she could have proof that Alexander was who he claimed to be.

"Please, Father. We'll write and send a messenger and then we'll know." She grasped her father's hands tightly and looked pleadingly up at him. Finally, he closed his eyes as if to block out her desperation.

"All right then, I'll send a letter tomorrow."

"Urgently. We need an answer before the wedding and we have only days left."

Finally, her father let out a sigh. "You must know that the answer will not be what you want it to be. Please, Elsie. Use common sense. I know this is hurting you, but some day it will simply be an unfortunate incident, a slight embarrassment."

"If you won't write, I will."

"I told you I would write and I will," he said with a bit of pique. "I would do anything to stop this ridiculous doubt you feel about what we are doing." His gaze softened. "You know that, don't you?"

Elsie's eyes filled with tears. How she loved him. "I know, Father. Even when I don't agree with you, I know you believe in your heart you are doing the right thing. Even when you are very wrong."

"We shan't tell His Grace of this," he said.

Elsie grinned and launched herself into his arms. "I do love you, no matter that you drive me mad sometimes."

Her father chuckled. "If you want to know what mad is, wait until you have a daughter of your own."

Her father kissed her cheek and rose, leaving behind a girl with a smile on her face and reckless hope in her heart.

Elsie awoke the next morning, her eyes swollen and gritty, her head pounding. She lay in bed feeling a cloak of depression settle over her. Last night, the thought of writing to Alexander's solicitor had filled her with exhilaration, but in the cold morning light, the hope that had surged so strong was ebbing quickly. For long minutes, Elsie stared at the thin slice of light behind her heavy draperies that told her she was one day closer to marrying Lord Hathwaite.

Yes, she would marry him and she would pretend that her world wasn't ending, that her heart wasn't shattered. She pushed away the agonizing thought that perhaps everyone was wrong about Alexander, that she was right. But how could it be? How could she be the only person who believed Alexander was the duke's son? Had even Monsieur Desmarais fully believed him? Elsie didn't know and supposed she would likely never find out.

Elsie forced herself to sit up and dragged her feet over the edge of the bed. Mornings were still difficult thanks to her illness, and this morning seemed worse than ever. She stood and shuffled to her wardrobe, opening it and staring at her clothes listlessly. Just then, her door opened and Elsie found herself smiling for the first time in days at the sight of her little sister.

"Oh, Mary, how wonderful for you to visit me," Elsie said, bending over and giving her little sister a large kiss.

Mary pressed one chubby finger against her lips. "Ssshhh. Miss Lawton said I was not to see you. But I missed you," Mary said solemnly. "Are you all better?" Her little sister looked up at her worriedly and Elsie knew she must look a fright.

"I'm far better now that you're here. I daresay I would have been cured long ago if Miss Lawton had let you visit me sooner."

"She said you were taking a nap. A lot of naps," she said, clearly exasperated with the number of naps her big sister had been taking.

"Yes, well, I'm done napping now."

"Can we play hide n' seek, then?" Mary said, her little face filled with hope.

"Your sister isn't quite well enough for that, Miss Mary," her nanny said, her tone slightly chastising. The woman smiled at Mary, because Elsie suspected it was quite difficult to remain stern when Mary looked up with those big blue eyes.

Elsie nodded her head, smiling. "I fear Nanny is correct, Mary. I'm not quite well enough for that yet. But why don't we eat luncheon together today. Wouldn't that be nice? And then I'll read you a story. *Little Red Riding Hood.*"

Mary clapped her hands, delighted, before following Miss Lawton out the door. As soon as the two were gone, Elsie's smile faded, her heart grew heavy once again in her heart. Unless a miracle happened, she was getting married in three days to a man she didn't love. She'd never been quite so miserable in her life.

Alexander was quite certain he'd never been happier in his life.

"This is wonderful news," Crowley said. "In four days, this will all be over. I cannot think of another reason for this meeting between your father's solicitors and us. He's going to acknowledge you, which means we'll avoid a hearing before the House of Lords. You'll be married to your sweetheart before the month is out."

"I cannot believe it," Alexander said, a wide grin splitting his face. "I must tell Elsie."

Crowley held up his hand. "I wouldn't do that just yet. I don't entirely trust His Grace, and their reason for calling this meeting isn't entirely straightforward." Crowley handed over the letter.

Dear sirs:

His Grace, the Duke of Kingston, has requested a meeting with your client on October tenth at 11 a.m. His Grace would like to avoid taking this matter to the House of Lords and is amenable to your petition.

Very truly yours,
Donald Tinkerman, esq.

"While it would appear that His Grace has accepted your claim, it's that word 'amenable' that concerns me. He hasn't accepted your claim, you see. He's merely amenable to it. I'm not quite certain how to interpret that."

"But you believe it is good?" Alexander asked, unable to keep the surge of joy from enveloping him.

"I believe it is very good," Crowley said, moving to a sideboard and taking up two brandy snifters. He took the stopper from a crystal decanter with a flourish and poured Alexander a fingerful and did the same for himself. "To our success, eh, my lord?"

Alexander grinned, feeling almost overwhelmed by the emotions that warred within him, this hope and joy and lingering fear. He turned and looked out the window when he felt tears pressing against his eyes. Crowley came and stood beside him, placing a hand on his shoulder.

"I know, son," he said, giving him a comforting squeeze as he lost his battle with his emotions. "I know."

Chapter 23

Elsie sat in a tiny room off the church's main entrance and stared at her reflection in the same hand-held mirror that her mother had used on her wedding day. No matter how she'd cleaned it, the image had remained foggy.

"You look beautiful," Diane said from the doorway. Elsie turned and gave her aunt an uncertain smile. Aunt Diane was to be her only attendant. Elsie had thought she would have all the time in the world to select her trousseau and name her attendants. She wasn't to have been married for months and months, and so was completely unprepared for this wedding. Even her gown, which should have been white, was a reminder of this hasty ceremony.

"It's happening so quickly," she said, her voice shaking slightly. Already, she was exhausted and it wasn't even ten o'clock yet. She'd gotten little sleep the night before, doubts still nagging at her even though she knew she was a fool. She must be a fool to believe she was somehow betraying Alexander. For if she listened to her heart, she would run from this church, run and run until she found him and begged forgiveness for not believing in him. Alas, she could not listen to her heart anymore, for it was foolish and blind and, dear Lord, held the most treacherously beautiful memories of a love that didn't even exist. And still . . . it was so very difficult to ignore that organ, that beat out again and again that Alexander loved her, that he couldn't have been only using her. She felt torn in two, warring between what her brain told her must be real and what her heart yearned to be real. If only she could talk to him, make him tell her to her face that she meant nothing, that their love meant nothing.

Despite her heartache Elsie was beautiful, pale and delicate as she hadn't been before her illness. Her hair, still vibrant and lush, made the rest of her seem even more fragile somehow. She wore a dress of the palest pink that frothed with lace and a large bell-shaped skirt supported by hoops and four petticoats beneath. It was to have been the dress she wore for her birthday ball, and other than some minor changes to the neckline, it was virtually the same. She hated it. Hated that it reminded her of Alexander, of the mural, of how happy she had been.

The mural. She'd gone to see it that very morning, ripped the cloth that had covered it from its moorings and had herself a good cry when she'd seen what Alexander had painted. The boys were gone, the rock barren. But sitting on the dock, their feet dangling in the water, were two little girls with matching red-gold hair, one telling a secret into the other's ear. Christine and herself much as they had looked that day they'd discovered the lake. It was the most stunning painting she'd ever seen, and she would hate it for the rest of her life.

She realized if she'd never planned that blasted birthday ball, she never would have met Alexander and she wouldn't now want to scream and scream until her voice was too hoarse to say her I do's.

"My dear, this came for your father today," Diane said, handing over a thin envelope with the words Cromley & Harte embossed on it.

Elsie felt the blood drain from her face. She felt nauseous and light-headed, for she could read from her aunt's grim expression what the letter stated. With a shaking hand, she took the letter, holding it a moment as if delaying would change the inevitable. Then, with sharp, quick motions, she withdrew a single sheet of paper from the envelope and opened it.

Dear Right Honorable Lord Huntington:

We regret to inform you that we do not represent Alexander Wilkinson at this firm, nor has he approached this firm regarding representation. We wish you well with your search.

Regards,
Howard Cromley, esq.

"What if it was the wrong firm?" Elsie asked, staring at the damning words.

"Please stop this nonsense," Aunt Diane said. "His Grace told us this morning that the authorities believe the pretender has fled the country, whoever he is."

Elsie's brain seemed to stop. Alexander fled the

country? The man she'd loved, who had loved her, who had made love to her, had fled the country to escape her? It didn't seem real. And yet, here she sat in a church ready to wed another. It had to be real.

"So that is it, then," she said, feeling the hope she'd held in her heart die, leaving nothing behind but a terrible numbness.

"Of course that is it. My word, Elizabeth."

Elsie swallowed and nodded, making a dismal attempt at a smile. "I'm sorry. I didn't want to give up hope. I do that sometimes. I'm perfectly fine," Elsie lied.

"You are to become a marchioness, joining one of the most prestigious families in the entire kingdom. My goodness, just think how horrid this could have turned out."

Elsie forced another smile, but couldn't stop her eyes from filling with tears. "Then why do I still feel as if this is wrong?" she whispered. "In my heart, I know this is wrong but I don't know what to do."

Diane pressed her lips together. "You always were a stubborn child."

"Was I? I don't remember that particular flaw. But I do remember a childhood living in terror that I might die, a childhood without my mother or my sister. A childhood spent alone. The only time I have been happy in the past ten years is when I was with Alexander."

Diane went to her and put two gentle hands on her shoulders. "But it was a lie," she said, not unkindly.

"I know," Elsie said, feeling on the verge of more

tears. "That's what makes it so horrible. I wish . . ." She squeezed her eyes closed.

"I know, darling. I know what you wish."

"If you had been with him. Heard him." Elsie shook her head firmly as if it would rid her of her foolishness. "I'm sorry. How ungrateful I must seem to you. I am a very lucky girl about to marry a wonderful man who truly cares for me."

"Lord Hathwaite adores you."

"And he's been so understanding through this all. He hasn't uttered one disparaging word. He's a veritable saint," Elsie said, letting out a watery laugh.

"There you go," Diane said. "A bride should laugh, not cry on her wedding day." Elsie embraced her aunt, feeling some of the despair that had been gripping her for days begin to melt away, if only a little bit.

"My two favorite ladies," her father boomed from the doorway. "Are we about ready? The church is full to the rafters and His Grace keeps pulling out his watch as if he's got a more important appointment looming."

"We are ready, Father," Elsie said, taking a deep, cleansing breath. Everything would be fine. She liked Oscar, even loved him a bit. After all, they'd known each other for years.

The organist began to play Mendelssohn's "Wedding March" and Elsie had to smile. The duke had insisted on the song simply because Queen Victoria's own daughter had walked down the aisle to it just four years before. Elsie had been slightly surprised when he'd allowed the wedding to be held at the relatively small church in Mansfield. She'd been afraid at first that he would insist the couple be married in London.

Elsie was glad to have her ceremony at home, with familiar faces all around her. Though the wedding had been hastily arranged, there had been little tongue-wagging, as it was common knowledge that Elsie and Lord Hathwaite had been engaged for years despite the recent formal announcement.

She walked down the aisle smiling stiffly at the people she recognized, her stomach full of butterflies, her hands clutching her bouquet as if she were strangling it. She was fine. Absolutely wonderful. Her knees trembled when she stopped at the altar. Reverend Picket gave her a nod, and she felt as if she might faint when her father handed her to her future husband, who looked at her searchingly through the thin veil. But really, she was perfectly composed, as unruffled as her petticoats were ruffled. Elsie had to stop a bit of hysterical laughter at that errant thought. She forged ahead, stepping up and kneeling before the altar, feeling strangely detached from her body.

Reverend Picket hadn't even opened his mouth to greet the congregation, when the front door of the church slammed open with such force, it sounded like a gunshot. As one, the people in the church gasped and turned to see a madman, dirty and sweaty, heaving as if he'd just run ten miles, hair wild and clothes unkempt, standing with clenched fists in the middle of the aisle.

It seemed Alexander hadn't fled the country after all.

Elsie stood and took a step forward, her heart

slamming almost as loudly as the door against the stone church, but Oscar held her back. She looked at his face and saw only irritation at the interruption and perhaps mild curiosity.

"It's Alexander," she breathed, feeling her entire body begin shaking. Oscar's head whipped around to her, and then back to the man standing in the doorway, his eyes narrowing.

"My God," Oscar breathed, staring at the man no more than twenty feet away from him. "He looks just like my father."

With a shaking hand glistening with sweat, Alexander pointed at his father, his burning eyes never straying from the duke. "Why?" he demanded. There was more pain, more emotion in that single word than all the words he'd ever said to Elsie.

"Get that man out of here," the duke barked, but no one made a move. "Where are the footmen? Footmen!"

Alexander stepped further into the church, his eyes fixed on his father with the intensity of a madman. "Why are you doing this, Father? Why?"

The blood drained from the duke's face, and next to him, the duchess let out a small sound of despair. Kingston pushed out of his pew and into the aisle, anger in every movement. "Get out of this church. Someone remove this man. He has no place here."

"I am your son!" Alexander shouted, his voice breaking on the last word. "I am your son," he said more quietly. "And I want to know why you will not acknowledge me as your heir."

Kingston's lips were rimmed with white, so hard

was he pressing them together. "*Henry* was my heir," the duke shouted with such ferocity many in the church gasped.

Oscar stepped forward, in front of Elsie. "Who is this man, Your Grace?" he asked.

Elsie tried to look around his broad shoulders to Alexander, but Reverend Picket laid a restraining hand on her shoulder.

"Stay put, child," he said softly, and something in his eyes, fear or anger, stayed her.

"I must go to him," she said, but the priest merely shook his head and tightened his grasp. "You don't understand. That is Alexander Wilkinson, the duke's son."

The old man's eyes widened but he kept his grip, frustrating Elsie. "This does not concern you," he said, and Elsie was nearly gripped with hysterical laughter.

Kingston turned to Oscar and sneered. "He is no one. Once he is removed we can proceed."

Two burly footmen, both wearing the duke's blue and gold livery, stepped into the church, their eyes on Alexander.

"Remove this man," Kingston shouted, and glared around the room to see if anyone would dare countermand his orders.

"No," Alexander shouted as the two men grabbed his arms and forcefully began dragging him from the church. Elsie struggled fruitlessly against the reverend, surprised by the old man's strength.

Alexander shouted again. "Don't do this thing. Mother, don't let him do this thing." Alexander fought, but he was no match for the two men who were pulling him away. Elsie let out a sound of protest and tried to go to him, but the reverend only tightened his grip.

And then, in a voice filled with despair, Alexander shouted above the fray. "Once upon a time there was a silent boy." His voice, filled with raw emotion, ripped through the congregation, silencing it.

"Stop." The Duchess of Kingston, who had come from behind her husband, stood in the middle of the aisle.

"Sit down, you little fool," His Grace snapped.

But the duchess moved past her husband, her eyes set on Alexander. The people grew almost unnaturally silent, watching as the duchess, her head held regally high, approached the wild-looking young man. Tears mingled with the sweat on his face as she walked toward him.

"What did you say?"

Alexander squeezed his eyes shut and let out a shaking breath. "Once upon a time," he said in a clear voice, "there was a silent boy."

The duchess raised one shaking hand to her throat. "And how does this story end?"

"This is nonsense," the duke spat.

"It was the boy's job to watch the sheep, for it was the only task he could do. He was to protect them from the wolves, but as there had been no wolves in that area for years, he was never in any danger. But one day, the wolves came and he had to call to the men of the village for help. But, you see, the little boy could not talk when he was very frightened."

"Did he save the sheep?" the duchess asked, as if this were of utmost importance. The church was completely silent, as if the crowd were waiting with a collectively held breath to hear the end of the story.

"He was very frightened, but he knew if he didn't speak, his sheep would be killed. And so he cried out for help and the men came. And he was a hero."

At the last words, the duchess raised a trembling hand to her mouth before throwing herself into Alexander's arms with a cry that sounded more like pain than joy. He held her against him, a long-lost son who had dreamed of this moment for more than twenty years, and Elsie could hardly bear to watch.

"My God, my God," the duchess said over and over, tears streaming down her face. "Alexander, it is you. My God."

She'd been so intent on watching Alexander, Elsie hadn't noticed that Oscar had stepped down from the altar and approached his father. "Is he truly my brother?" he demanded, his voice raw.

Kingston stared at his youngest son, and without a word, sat down heavily in the pew.

"Is he my brother, damn you," Oscar shouted.

As Kingston continued to stare blankly ahead, a low murmur started in the crowd.

"Yes, Oscar," the duchess said with quiet strength, "this is your brother, Alexander."

"But how? He died. Didn't he die?" Oscar looked around at the faces staring blankly at him as if one of them would have an answer.

"I will explain all later," Alexander said, his voice now clear and full of an authority that Elsie hardly recognized. The reverend no longer held her, for there was no need. Through all this, Alexander had not looked at her. Not once. And though she yearned to go to him, she held back, instinctively knowing that he would spurn her.

He bowed toward his mother and gave her the smallest of smiles. "Mother, I shall be in touch." He looked over to his father. "I believe our attorneys are meeting tomorrow. It is my greatest wish that everything be resolved. I do apologize for the interruption. You may continue with the nuptials." Finally, finally, he looked toward Elsie, and she nearly swayed from the force of his heated stare, filled with a terrifying combination of raging anger and unfathomable despair. "My fondest wishes for a happy marriage."

With that, he turned and left, leaving behind a stunned crowd. As the door closed quietly behind him, Elsie collapsed to the floor.

Chapter 24

Two months later

Alexander entered Warbeck Abbey and ripped the black band from his sleeve, crumpling it into his fist.

"Your Grace, a Mr. Crowley is waiting in your study. I explained to him that this would, perhaps, not be a good time for you, but he insisted."

Alexander stared at the butler, who'd been employed at Warbeck Abbey for as long as he could remember, and gave a short, jerking nod. After his father had died, Alexander had been tempted to fire everyone in their country house, but his mother had dissuaded him. In the end, the only casualty of his father's death was his ever-loyal secretary, Farnsworth. It had given Alexander no joy to terminate the man, but he found that each time he looked upon his face, he felt the urge to vomit.

"I will see him, Hawkins. And I would appreciate your directing him to the library. I dislike the study."

"Of course, Your Grace."

Your Grace. How strange it was to hear that title given to him. Two months ago, his father's lawyers had agreed to draw up the necessary papers to acknowledge him as the rightful heir of Kingston, a decision that no doubt brought his father to an early grave. His father's death left him oddly empty; he felt no great happiness and certainly no grief. He'd not seen his father after he'd rushed into the church, nor did he have any desire to. He was Duke of Kingston now; it was what he was meant for, even if he was only just realizing it.

He reached the library only a few minutes before Crowley was let in, giving him a chance to breathe deeply and let the fact of his father's death settle in his mind. He presumed his lawyer was wasting no time in dealing with matters handed over to them from the old firm. It bothered him not at all that whatever this business was couldn't wait until the day after his father's funeral.

"I am sorry to disturb you on this day, Your Grace, but I didn't think you would mind," Crowley said, looking slightly out of sorts.

"Not at all." He held up the crumpled arm band before tossing it on a nearby table. "As you can see, I have officially stopped mourning."

Crowley smiled. "This was delivered one day after your father's death." Crowley handed over a piece of paper. "It is a petition from Lord Huntington, demanding that you make good on his daughter's marriage contract."

Alexander looked down at the paper and back at Crowley in disbelief. Even the thought of Elsie made his gut wrench, and so he'd avoided such thoughts these past weeks as much as humanly possible. The thought of marrying her sent a sharp stab to his gut that was difficult to ignore. He would never forget how it felt to stand at the door of the church and watch as Elsie, looking more beautiful than he'd ever seen her, stood calmly at the altar with his brother.

He'd nearly killed himself getting to that damned church, certain he was on a rescue mission, certain that his beloved Elsie had been forced to wed his brother against her will.

He'd looked for tears, for chains, for any sign that she was under duress. Instead, she'd smiled up at her father and kissed his cheek, and her smile grew when she turned to his brother and offered her hand to his. That was when Alexander realized with a sick twist of his bowels, that he had been a fool to think Elsie would honor her promise to him. A knife to his heart couldn't have been more painful. It was then that he turned his anger toward his father. If his father hadn't treated him like an unwanted horse, it would have been Alexander on that altar, standing next to Elsie, taking those vows. Blind with pain and a rage that frightened him even as it gave him strength, he'd shoved the door against the stone wall of the church as hard as he could, getting certain joy from the loud crack it made when it struck.

And now, Elsie, Oscar's docile, smiling bride-to-be, wanted to marry him. Now, when she'd nearly killed him with a betrayal he could hardly bring himself to examine.

"Surely the marriage contract is not binding."

"Typically, such contracts are not. But in this case,

because of the large amount of money that has already exchanged hands, it's a bit more complicated. I believe his lordship may be acting preemptively in the event you demand repayment of the settlement."

"Ah," Alexander said, finally understanding what this meant. "He fears I will demand the money back and so is making this offer to show good faith. He has no real intention of forcing a marriage." It was a business deal, nothing more, and he felt even a greater fool for allowing the smallest bit of hope into his heart. This business of being cynical was still new to him, but he was quickly learning how.

"That may be the case. Or it could be he is earnest in his request," Crowley said, his voice tinged with doubt. "This is the girl, is it not, who precipitated all the recent events?"

"It is."

"You are within your rights to marry the girl. However, Lord Huntington did prepare a document in case you decided against such a union."

"Oh?"

Crowley pulled out a sheath of paper. "They prepared this agreement, which Lord Huntington has signed already, making him not liable for any money owed and dissolving the contract altogether. Signing this document will make it as if it never existed."

"How very mercenary of him," Alexander muttered. "What is my other alternative?"

Crowley smiled grimly. "You could demand repayment."

"Of the full amount?"

"Yes, your father paid Lord Huntington eighty

thousand pounds for the privilege of having Miss Stanhope as his daughter-in-law."

"It was an insane amount." Repayment of that sum would surely have ruined the entire family. No wonder Elsie had felt so trapped. For some reason, that odd pain that had occurred less and less frequently since the day he'd stormed the church came back in force. He did not want to feel sorry for her; he did not want to think of her at all.

"Of course, you could marry her."

Alexander clenched his jaw painfully, hating the knowledge that this was what he truly wanted. He didn't want the money and he didn't want to dissolve the contract. He wanted Elsie and he hated himself for it.

"But that is not what he wants. Not what she wants, obviously."

"I wouldn't know, sir."

How shocked Elsie would be if he refused to sign this document. Obviously, being a duchess wasn't so important to her, after all.

"I will not sign their paper," Alexander said before thinking. But once said, he would not take the words back, even though the thought of marrying Elsie made him feel as if he were hurtling off a very high cliff. "I intend to enforce the contract as it stands. She wanted a duke; she'll get one. But not the one she apparently intended to marry."

After Crowley left, Alexander sat at a table laden with leases, titles, and financial documents, feeling absolutely no inclination to wade through any of it. His mind was only on Elsie and how she would react when her father's solicitor arrived with the news of their impending marriage and the conditions he'd demanded. Once he had her, he would have everything it was his right to have. Everything his younger brother had thought to have. Oscar had been cordial to him, but had not appeared at a single meal since their father's death. While Alexander had no culpability in what had happened, he still understood that his brother no doubt resented his sudden appearance—and at his wedding, no less. Now that he planned to marry the woman Oscar had thought all his life he'd marry, their relationship could only suffer. He didn't know Oscar at all, had no idea of his life, his dreams, or how their father's death had affected him. He was about to send an under butler to search for Oscar, when his brother appeared at the door.

"Your Grace," he said, bowing deeply, and Alexander wondered if he'd been drinking. The few times he'd seen Oscar, he'd appeared to be slightly foxed.

"Oscar. I was about to go find you. I need to talk to you about a personal matter."

His brother's blond hair was mussed, his brown eyes red-rimmed, though Alexander was quite certain it was due to overindulgence the night prior, not grief over his father. Still, it was possible Oscar was grieving.

"I am at your service, my liege," he said, again with a bow.

"Your highness will do," Alexander said sardonically, which earned him a crooked grin from his brother, who threw himself down into the nearest chair.

"You know, brother, I spent my entire life preparing for the role you now take," Oscar said lazily. "Every moment from the time I was three, I lived knowing that one day I would be duke. Our father, God rot his soul, took his duty of preparing me for that life extremely seriously. Do you not find it ironic that everything he taught me, every mind-numbing task he gave me, is going to be completely worthless?"

Alexander studied the younger man, who appeared more amused by his predicament than angry or bitter. "I'm afraid I am going to add to your list of things taken away," he said. "I have agreed to honor the marriage contract."

Oscar dipped his head and let out a humorless laugh. "Why not?"

"Do you love her?" Alexander asked, his body tense. He wasn't certain he could marry Elsie if his brother loved her.

"No. I never got the chance, you see. From the time we were young, we were paired at dinner, sent to take walks together, all the time knowing we would one day marry. Why should I court her when she was already mine? Why would she pursue me? It was all very planned. Very business-like. Love had nothing to do with it."

"Very well then. You have no objection to my marrying her?"

"Why shouldn't you? You have everything else that was to be mine."

Ah, thought Alexander, there was some bitterness, after all. "This is, none of it, our fault."

"I do realize that. But I daresay it still stings a bit. More than a bit. I feel like a boat that's been cut adrift. Shall I just float away and eventually sink?" Oscar stared up at the ceiling and looked very young and uncertain.

"Too maudlin. As you are no doubt aware, we have very many properties, more than I care to deal with. If you have a favorite, it is yours to do with as you like."

"I'll take this one," Oscar said, then burst out laughing. "Perhaps I'll buy a commission. Or become a vicar. Isn't that what second sons do? Perhaps I'll fade into a life of debauchery and sin."

Alexander gave him a level look. "For now, I could use your assistance here. I confess I need help and no one knows of these matters better than you. You can drink and whore all you want once I am better able to understand all this," he said, sweeping his hand over the mass of papers on his table.

Oscar was silent for a long moment. "You ask much," he said finally.

"I know I do."

"One month. Then marry and I will leave. Or rather, I'll leave, *then* you marry. I don't think I could stomach seeing you with Elsie. I would be spared that, at least."

"Of course," Alexander said.

Elsie sat in her room reading, as she often did these days. She no longer went to the ballroom, for the memories it held were still far too painful. Her father had asked if he should have the mural painted over, but Elsie couldn't bring herself to do that any more than she could bring herself to look at it.

It would soon be over. No doubt Alexander had signed the paper her father's solicitors had drawn up and she would never have to think about him again. Wouldn't have to, but would. Every night until the day she died, she would think of Alexander and the pain and rage she'd seen in his eyes right before he'd turned and left the church.

She lifted her head from her book when a knock sounded on her door. "Enter."

Her father came into her room, his expression unreadable. "Elsie, sit down," he said, and Elsie started. She was already sitting and the fact that her father hadn't noticed alarmed her. A sense of dread began to seep through her veins.

"I am seated," she said, and patted the chair upon which she sat as proof.

"Ah. So you are."

"What has happened? Please don't tell me he is demanding the money. I feared such a thing even as I hoped he wouldn't."

Her father shook his head, but looked even more miserable. "No, no. It's not that."

"Then tell me. Goodness, Father, you're frightening me."

"I'm sorry, my dear. I suppose it's best to just let it out." He took a bracing breath. "He wants to honor the contract."

Elsie felt suddenly weak and was grateful she was seated. "He wants to marry me?"

"He wants to honor the contract," her father repeated significantly.

Elsie swallowed down the ridiculous joy that surged through her, sensing that joy was not an appropriate response to Alexander's decision. "Why?" she whispered.

"I cannot say."

"I don't know whether to be happy or very frightened," Elsie said, her voice shaking slightly.

"Once you are married to him, I cannot protect you. You know that, don't you?"

"Alexander would never hurt me."

"No, perhaps not physically. But there are worse things, sometimes, than physical pain. There's mental anguish and fear, and I have every reason to suspect you would suffer them if you married him."

Elsie tried to imagine Alexander acting so, and could not. Perhaps he wasn't a gentle man, but he had never been cruel. She thought of the way he'd looked at her at the church and she pushed that image away as she had so many times before. "He may be angry at first," Elsie said, slowly. "He's been hurt, badly, as have I. But I have absolutely no doubt that in time, he will learn to love me again. I am sure of it. Love cannot be extinguished so easily."

"Never in my life have I seen a man so full of rage. I know we were unwitting pawns in a terrible game, but what was done to him over the years was unthinkable. Perhaps that is why it was so difficult to believe. And now I am nearly as culpable for his pain as his father."

Elsie shook her head. "I refuse to believe that. You couldn't know he was telling the truth. Even I, in the end, was convinced he was a fraud when the solicitors wrote that they did not represent him. If only I had remembered the right firm. I am as guilty as anyone. But were we to have such blind faith in the face of so much evidence?"

"Hearsay. That's all it was. I believed Kingston."

Elsie leaned forward. "And why wouldn't you? He was a peer of the realm. He was supposed to be a man of honor."

"I knew he was not. You knew it, too. And yet we allowed him to destroy that boy. His *son*. My God, I still cannot believe a man could do that to his own child."

"Father, please," Elsie said, pressing her cool fingers against her temples in an attempt to stem a burgeoning headache.

"I wronged you, too. You loved him and I . . ." He closed his eyes, as if he could keep his thoughts from escaping. "I failed you."

"He will forgive me. And perhaps you, too. Perhaps this is his way of saying he has already forgiven us."

Her father gave her a doubtful look.

"Perhaps not," Elsie said, with a chagrined look. "But if we are married, I have a chance. I suppose we should set a date. A small ceremony, and we'll invite only the local gentry. I'll have to have a new dress, of course. Something subdued, in deference to his father's death."

Lord Huntington shook his head sorrowfully. "I'm afraid there is to be no ceremony to speak of. His Grace has insisted you be delivered to his estate alone. In one month's time, you shall marry in a small chapel at Warbeck Abbey. He gave explicit instructions, one of which is that you are to come alone."

"Alone? And in one month? People will be outraged."

"I hardly think he cares," Lord Huntington said.

"I'll refuse, of course," Elsie said. How could Alexander possibly think they could have a wedding so close to his father's funeral?

"I'm afraid you cannot, my dear. If you refuse to adhere to his demands, he will forfeit the agreement and demand repayment of the loan."

Chapter 25

It was raining, and the old wives' tale, meant to put brides at ease about rain on a wedding day being good luck, seemed a bit ridiculous to Elsie. She was in a ducal coach, surrounded by opulence and luxury, but shivering despite the warm wool blanket the driver had taken from the storage bin in the floor. Actually, sleet was coming down, spattering noisily against the coach's roof, and Elsie idly wondered what the old crones said about sleet. At this moment, she didn't much care. She was nearly as miserable at this wedding as she had been at her first, as uncertain of her choices, as ill at the thought of marrying a man who didn't love her.

Alexander had refused to see her, had ignored her letters pleading that she be allowed to bring her father, a friend, anyone to make this day easier. Aunt Diane was nearly in Bamburgh fetching the Earl of Braddock's stubborn niece, who had apparently refused to leave her home even though it had been sold to someone else. Elsie couldn't imagine such a stubborn girl, but secretly admired her spunk.

Her aunt, on the other hand, who detested long trips, was anything but impressed by the girl's disobedience. Spunk was something that Elsie had always had in short supply, but she wished she had a bit of it this day.

The coach moved noisily up the cobbled drive, but past the main house. Elsie pulled back the velvet curtain and watched, puzzled, as the coach continued around the great manor house, and she wondered if she were to be delivered to the servants' entrance—or worse, the stable. Perhaps a pile of horse dung awaited her instead of a happy groom. The coach stopped, seemingly in the middle of the gardens, and Elsie watched for a time as the sleet beat relentlessly onto the gray cobbles, glazing them with ice. Sliding to the opposite side of the coach, she lifted the curtain and let out a small sound of dismay. They had stopped outside the estate's tiny, ancient chapel, which as far as she knew, hadn't been used in generations.

When she and Christine were young, they had entered the old chapel, even though they'd made up a story about how it was haunted by an old priest. Actually, Christine had made up the story and Elsie had tried very hard not to believe it. Even then, all those years ago, it was in disrepair. Indeed, the small building looked about to fall down. Apparently the old duke had not been a spiritual man, and the current duke had not deemed it necessary to repair.

My goodness, she didn't even know if Alexander attended services. For all she knew, he could be Catholic; Monsieur Desmarais was French, after all, and the French were known for their papist beliefs.

Surely, she wasn't expected to descend from the

coach and go immediately to the ceremony. She wore only a simple traveling gown of blue wool, for she hadn't wanted to ruin any of her nicer gowns in the weather. Her shoes were sturdy practical things, not the delicate creations she'd thought to wear. The coach door opened and she found herself facing a footman in blue and gold Kingston livery, his uniform sprinkled by ice, his face dripping from the melted sleet. He lowered the stairs, then held his gloved hand for her to take, his expression one of supreme patience.

"Where is His Grace?" Elsie demanded before taking a single step. If she was going to be a duchess, she might as well sound like one right away. She ruined the effect by adding, "If you please."

"Inside the chapel, Miss," the young man said. He waited perhaps two beats, his gloved hand still extended before saying, "This way, Miss."

The poor man's hair, exposed beneath his bicornered hat, was growing icy, his cheeks red from the cold, so Elsie really had no choice but to take his hand and step down. He released her and moved back, leaving her to walk into the chapel alone. The cobbles were slick with ice, and she gave the oblivious young man a glare before carefully making her way to the chapel's door, taking mincing little steps. When her boots touched the dry stone beneath the entrance, another footman opened the heavy, thick wooden door, which swung inward soundlessly, revealing a tiny chapel with three rows of benches on a stone floor. Standing in the front of the room was a reverend she did not recognize, the duchess, Warbeck

Abbey's butler, and Alexander, who snapped his watch shut just as she began walking forward.

"Good morning, Your Grace," Elsie said, giving the older woman a quick curtsy.

"Elizabeth," the woman said, nodding serenely, as if this were an everyday occurrence. She didn't smile encouragement or frown disapproval, but simply turned back to face the front of the chapel.

It seemed rather like an awful dream, in which one is not certain if all will turn out right or will spiral into a frightening nightmare. Alexander said not a word, but stood at the altar beside the reverend looking like some sort of clothed statue, his face unmoving, his eyes made of cold granite. This was no nervous groom, no loving man waiting anxiously for his bride, and Elsie's heart fell to her suddenly shaky knees. Truly, this was a nightmare.

"I should like to change for the ceremony," she said, and looked down at her wrinkled gown and sodden hem, if only to hide the sudden tears that burned her eyes.

"No need," he said, and turned toward the reverend and nodded.

"Miss," the reverend said, with an open palm gesture indicating she could come forward. He was a round little man, but without the twinkle one associated with round little men. Indeed, he looked quite put out and impatient to be on with it.

He opened his prayer book and immediately began reading, even before Elsie had managed to step up next to Alexander. Her groom did not reach for her hand; he did not look at her. It was almost as if she was not there at all and she wondered if she could quietly slip away without notice. Perhaps this was a dream, one in which she could fly to the moon if she wanted or close her eyes and return home to play hide and seek with Mary.

The reverend spoke quickly, like a child reciting a well-known verse, with little inflection, slowing down only when saying the lines they were to repeat. When it was Elsie's turn, he glared at her expectantly, and she muttered her lines, feeling her throat close tighter and tighter, until she was hardly able to speak at all.

As for Alexander, he put as much emotion into his tone as a man reading a language he was unfamiliar with, and his eyes never strayed from the reverend. A puddle was still forming around her boots from the melting sleet when he proclaimed them man and wife. Alexander immediately walked to a lectern and signed the marriage certificate, handed the pen to her, paid the reverend, then strode from the church. Elsie stood in her puddle, pen in hand, watching in bewilderment as the chapel door closed, muffling the sound of the sleet hitting the cobbles.

Her cheeks burned in humiliation as the butler cleared his throat and the now-dowager duchess looked at her with pity. "He doesn't care for public displays," she said, with a helpless little hand gesture.

"I think His Grace doesn't care for me," Elsie said, and was slightly gratified when the dowager's eyes widened in surprise. Elsie turned to the certificate and signed her name next to his bold signature. It looked decidedly ducal. Her signature seemed meek and timid in comparison. To offset that impression, she underlined her name, pressing so hard she nearly broke the nib.

After that tiny show of defiance, Elsie had expended her spunk for the moment, and waited for the dowager and butler to sign the certificate as witnesses. She wouldn't dare think how mortifying it was that a butler was one of two witnesses to her wedding.

"If you will, Your Grace," the butler said, gesturing for her to precede him through the door. She was almost certain, though it seemed rather absurd, that he actually winked at the dowager as he said the words. No, he couldn't have. That would have been extremely impertinent of him.

"Your temporary quarters are in the west wing, Your Grace," he said. "His Grace is having your suite refurbished and awaits your opinions on décor."

The west wing was where Kingston had always put the guests. In a way, Elsie was slightly relieved, for it was a part of the huge manse that she was familiar with. Still, it was not what she'd expected. None of this was. What she had expected, she wasn't certain. She only wished she could go back in time and stop herself from walking down that aisle toward Oscar. It didn't matter that even as she'd done it, her promise to Alexander had rung in her ears. That promise, that stupid, romantic promise that she hadn't been able to keep. She should have said, "I will try" or "I will do my best." Instead, she'd promise on her soul that she would wait for him, that she would die before she married Oscar without word from Alexander.

It didn't matter how many times she told herself no other woman would have been as strong, would have resisted for so long, would have stood up to her father and a duke. She'd given in. She'd broken that promise and broken Alexander's heart and there was nothing, absolutely nothing, she could do to make up for it.

Chapter 26

"How long are you going to punish her?"
Alexander ignored his mother's question and continued reading through his estate manager's report. Oscar had done a fine job teaching him about his new duties, but he still had much more to learn before he felt comfortable.
"Alexander."
"Yes, Mother, I heard you," he said, underlining a section about one tenant who needed a new roof. "If marrying me is punishment, then I daresay she should have refused."
He could feel her stare and finally looked up to find his mother frowning at him.
"It's quite clear that she married you because she loves you."
Alexander let out a sound that was more growl than sigh, and continued reading, his pen at the ready. Already he'd authorized a new grain mill to be built, as well as an irrigation system to replace one in desperate need of modernizing. Oscar had already designed the new system, which needed

only the funds to pay for it. He was beginning to gain confidence in his decisions, and starting to realize that being a duke wouldn't be such a burden, after all. However, he was not used to family, not used to explaining himself, and found he did not like this part of having the title.

Loved him, did she? Marrying his brother—or at least being prepared to—did not a devoted lover make.

"Do you remember your father?"

"You are not going to leave this alone, are you?"

Her answer was to perch herself at the edge of a settee, as if in for a long chat. Alexander hated long chats. "He was an exceedingly intimidating man. A bully with a mean streak and he liked nothing better than to take advantage of the weak, or at least people he perceived as weak. He had an uncanny way of finding someone's most vulnerable spot, exposing it, then going in for the kill. Figuratively speaking, of course."

"Mother," Alexander said with forced patience, "I do not wish to speak of my dead father. Or my living bride. If you would simply leave me alone to work, I would be exceedingly grateful."

Her response was to purse her lips and narrow her eyes. "Elizabeth had no chance against a person like your father. No more chance than I did in the thirty years I was married to him. He had a way of speaking that made you feel as if you were an idiot. If I said the sky was blue, he'd make me believe I was foolish for believing it. It made him extremely successful in parliament. Oh, to be set down by Kingston. It was everyone's greatest fear.

"And yet, she stood against him, Alex. Certainly she deserves some credit for that."

"Five days," Alexander said harshly, making his mother flinch. "This paragon of strength lasted all of five days before she trotted down the altar to marry Oscar after swearing to me that she loved me, that she would wait for me. Five days was all she gave me. For all I know, it was five minutes, one word, and she was filled with doubt . . ." He stopped, because he knew the rage he felt should not be directed at his mother. "I apologize," he said, feeling true remorse.

"You always felt too much."

"Oh, please, Mother."

"It's true. Henry, he didn't care when his father yelled at him. Henry would just smile and go on his merry way. But you, you took it to heart. He made you suffer. Sometimes I think he enjoyed it."

Alexander didn't want to talk about it, wanted never to think of his father again. But he couldn't help asking one question. "What of Oscar?"

"He was harsh to Oscar, but never completely cruel."

Alexander scrubbed his face with his hands. "My father has nothing to do with me. Nothing to do with my wife, nor how I treat her."

"You want me to stay out of it."

Alexander gave his mother a look of exasperation tinged with tenderness. "Of course I do. The dowager house is only three miles from here. Out the door and to the left." He was half serious.

"Oh, you are quite awful, Alexander," his mother said, completely unaffected by his words. "But as a matter of fact, I do plan to move there tomorrow."

"You don't have to, you know."

"Yes, I do. And if you don't mind, I'd like to take some of the staff. Would it be all right if Hawkins came with me? And perhaps a few of the downstairs maids? You know I won't be doing much entertaining."

Alexander knew his mother was nearly as uncomfortable in crowds as he was. "We shall be known as the Kingston recluses."

"That would be heaven, wouldn't it?"

They both laughed, sharing their common dislike of socializing. His mother started for the door, but paused before leaving.

"Alexander?"

He lifted his head in question.

"Having a cruel husband is terribly lonely." With that she left, closing the door quietly behind her.

Elsie sat in her room, knitting Mary a lovely winter hat, which would join the mittens she'd already made. Most brides would be doing needle point, some monogrammed handkerchiefs she could give her new husband, but at the moment she had no tender thoughts to spare for Alexander.

Abandoned, alone on her wedding night, her dinner eaten without company in a small room off her bedroom, she'd stared at the steady candle flame before her. Not even the breath of another soul was present to make the candle flicker. She hadn't cried, and as she put the tasteless food in her mouth, she'd grown more and more angry. Would this be their life? Not just separate rooms, but separate wings.

Would they ever have the easy conversation that had passed between them when they thought they'd been in love? Would he ever again share his joy or his pain with her? Would he ever touch her and make her body shake with joy?

She held up the hat, seeking out any imperfections, and was about to continue when she heard the faint sound of music. She cocked her ear but couldn't make out anything but the barest hint of sound. Walking to the window, she pushed it open, bracing against the cool breeze that buffeted her face. She heard only the sound of the wind in the trees, rustling and reminding her of home. The sound must be coming from inside, then.

Elsie put her wrap on and walked to her door, opening it slightly and heard, quite distinctly now, the sound of a piano. Smiling grimly, Elsie walked from her chamber in the direction of Warbeck Abbey's music room, knowing that the source of music could only be Alexander.

The soft carpet beneath her feet was lovely, and a sharp contrast to the icy marble where no carpet lay. She walked down the darkened halls, lit only occasionally by a gaslight turned low. The closer she got to the music room, the more she could identify the sound as a song, though she was unfamiliar with the piece. It was loud, harsh, almost frightening—the music one would hear in a nightmare if that were possible.

Even through the closed door, the music was shattering, as if he were pounding on the keys instead of playing them. And yet, for all the music's chaos, there was a beauty to it, an emotional pull that was impossible to deny. She opened the door silently, feeling an unexpected fear run down her spine.

The room was darkened except for a single lamp on the piano, which shook with the ferocity of Alexander's playing. He looked like a man possessed—his hands a blur on the keys, his face a mask of fury, as if the notes he was playing were somehow transforming him into the devil himself.

Suddenly, he stopped and looked up, his gray eyes filled with fire. His hands went to his thighs and Elsie watched with no little trepidation as he curled them into fists. His fury was nearly palpable.

"My," she said, trying for a light tone but failing miserably. "That was rather . . . violent."

"Go back to your rooms," he said, turning his gaze to the keyboard.

Elsie wrapped her arms around herself and stared at the man she loved, knowing she would endure whatever it took to win him back.

"I am sorry if I caused you pain," she said, her words sounding strangely loud in the deathly quiet room.

"Yes," he said softly, "I suppose getting one's heart ripped from one's chest is a bit painful."

Elsie would have thought he was joking if not for the expression on his face. "You must understand that I . . ."

"Must I?"

Elsie took a sharp breath at his abrupt interruption. "Yes. If this is to be any sort of marriage, you will have to forgive me."

"I cannot."

"Oh, Alexander, you must," she said, taking a few

hesitant steps toward him. "We were both victims of your father's schemes. You far more, but I, too, was hurt by him."

"Really. At what point were you hurt? As you were walking down the aisle or when you happily accepted the new wedding date less than a week after promising me you would wait for me."

"Please, Alexander."

He stood so quickly, the piano seat skidded some way across the room. "You promised to wait. Upon your *soul*," he spat. "You had so little faith in me that you allowed a man you knew was cruel to manipulate you. It was only five days, Elsie, from the time I left you to the time you were walking down the aisle. I can never forgive that."

Elsie felt her heart ache in a way she did not think physically possible. "You're not being fair."

Alexander took a stiff step toward her and the anger in his face made Elsie back away. "I'll tell you what's unfair. Being put in an idiot asylum when you are ten years old is not fair. Watching the woman you love more than life itself walk down the aisle to marry your brother *is not fair*."

Tears streamed down Elsie's face and she felt all her hopes slowly die. "Then why did you marry me, if it pains you so?"

Alexander took a harsh breath and looked away. "I am a man of honor and I dishonored you. The marriage contract bound me to you, and even though I loathe myself for it, I could not bear the thought of you marrying another."

A long silence followed those words, and finally

Alexander retrieved the piano bench with exaggerated calm, then sat back down and laid his fingers silently upon the keys. "You may go now."

Elsie stared at his profile for a moment, before turning and leaving the room, so drained she couldn't even bring herself to close the door behind her.

Chapter 27

Elsie awoke the next morning to bright sunshine streaming into her easterly facing window. The sight gave her unexpected and likely foolish hope. A new day, no matter what had transpired the day previous, always gave her an optimism that the night before was quite missing. As sad as she'd been as she'd drifted to sleep, this morning she clung to the knowledge that Alexander "could not bear" the thought of her marrying another.

And that could only mean one thing: perhaps he loved her still. He might not want to love her, but it was possible he did. At least she hoped he did. Now all she had to do was convince him that she would never betray him again, that she loved him with all her heart. No matter how much she told herself that she had had no choice, the truth was that she had betrayed him. She could have refused to marry Oscar. And from Alexander's perspective, what she had done was unforgiveable. Elsie wasn't so hard on herself that she disallowed the intense pressure exerted on her. She had resisted for days, had been tempted even on her wedding day to refuse. But that didn't matter, obviously, not to Alexander. A list of the facts made her culpable. Not having been born a saint, however, Elsie still felt the need to defend her actions.

A knock on the door startled her, and for a moment she allowed herself to think perhaps Alexander was coming to see her, offering an olive branch. "Enter."

"Good morning, Yer Grace," Missy said, dipping a low and exuberant curtsy.

"Oh, Missy," Elsie said, launching herself into her maid's arms. Over the years, Missy had become far more than her personal maid, and their relationship had grown even closer through the long weeks of her illness.

"You still look like a miss, not a duchess," Missy said, stepping back and wiping her eyes with her apron.

"I don't feel like a duchess," Elsie said, her eyes shining. "How is Mary?"

"Oh," Missy said, turning quickly to survey Elsie's rooms. "She's well enough."

"She's heartbroken, I take it."

"Yes, ma'am. A regular watering pot yesterday when I left. His lord said that the duke could refuse to let me accompany you, but he couldn't refuse you your personal maid. I do hope it's all right that I came."

"I'm certain His Grace won't mind. And if he does, I shall overrule his decision."

Missy grinned. "These are grand rooms, aren't they? I'll feel like a princess working here."

"These aren't my rooms. Mine are being renovated and I'm using these only until they are ready. This is a guest suite."

"Oh, Miss, I mean Yer Grace."

"It is a bit strange, isn't it?"

Missy nodded, glancing through the window that overlooked the gardens.

"Are your rooms satisfactory? I fear I haven't had a chance to tour the entire house yet."

"Oh, yes, ma'am. They're larger than Mrs. Whitehouse's," she said, referring to the housekeeper's rooms at Mansfield Hall. "She'd be pure green with envy. You're feeling well, are you?"

Elsie knew Missy was asking about more than just her health, but she nodded. "I'm almost back to normal. I scarcely even remember being ill."

Missy gave her a level look. "May I do your hair? Something special for your first day as a duchess?"

"That would be lovely."

Elsie spent the day with Mrs. Billings, Warbeck Abbey's amazingly efficient housekeeper. Though Elsie was already quite familiar with the house, there were many areas she simply hadn't been privy to when she was a guest. After meeting with the chef, a brusque man with a Scottish burr who'd studied in Paris, to go over the week's menu, she followed Mrs. Billings to her suite so that she might be inspired to decorate it in her taste. She had five rooms to herself, a home within a home, including a bedroom, sitting room, bathing room, private dining room, and a lovely study. Everything had been stripped bare, and her footsteps echoed on the marble floor.

"It's rather grand, is it not?" Elsie asked, slightly bewildered by the rooms. One could live in them alone and have no need to leave. She wondered if the dowager had done just that unless forced to socialize. Instead of feeling happy to have such an opulent space, she felt a depressing sense of loneliness. As lovely as this home was, it was oppressively silent. There were no sounds, no voices, no little girl laughter.

"The house is so quiet," she said, almost to herself.

"Yes, Your Grace. Quite a change for you," the housekeeper said. "If I may say so, we find His Grace to be a good master. He allows us to do our tasks without interference."

"It is a mark of a well-run house that everything continues on so well," Elsie said, making Mrs. Billings blush.

"The staff here is very dedicated to His Grace. Some of us were here, you see, when he was just a boy. The things that happened . . ." She stopped, closing her mouth like a door closing on a room full of secrets.

"I am aware of His Grace's turbulent youth," Elsie said. "Where are His Grace's rooms?" she asked, hoping Mrs. Billings didn't notice the blush staining her cheeks.

"This way."

Elsie followed Mrs. Billings, unexpectedly surprised by this turn of events. She hadn't thought to see them, only to discover where they were. Nodding to the right, the housekeeper said, "The old duke's rooms were down there," she said. "But His Grace had another suite set up on the other side."

She took a key from her massive ring and opened the door, allowing Elsie to precede her into the room. The first thing Elsie noted was the pungent smell of paint, the second thing she noticed was the pure beauty of the room. Masculine beauty, to be sure, but it had to be one of the most soothing, lovely rooms she'd ever been in. The walls were the color of tea with milk, the trim stark white, the furniture done in rich browns and deep maroons. The suite was very much like her own, with a small sitting room at the entrance that led to a large bedroom. Elsie found herself staring at the bed with a longing that manifested itself with an ache deep in her core. She missed his touch, the way he made her body soften for him. She had the sudden and rather embarrassing image of Alexander and her naked and tumbling about the massive canopied bed.

Elsie was about to enter a room off the bedroom, when Mrs. Billings stopped her. "Oh, we're not allowed in there, Your Grace."

"I see. But I'm certain I am. If you will." Elsie smiled inwardly, thinking she sounded very much like a duchess at the moment when in reality, it was only her childish curiosity that had her demanding entrance.

Mrs. Billings hesitated just a moment before pulling out a key and turning the lock. Alexander actually kept one of the doors to his inner sanctum locked? She was more than intrigued—and felt only a bit guilty for entering. Mrs. Billings, loyal servant that she was, stepped back and did not enter the room.

Elsie knew, even before she stepped inside, that Alexander was using the room as a studio. The smell of paint, so faint in the main rooms, was quite strong now, and immediately brought her back to those magical nights when she'd watch Alexander painting. The first thing she saw when entering the brightly lit room was herself . . . and Mary.

Her heart, which was already quite fragile, nearly dissolved in her chest and she nearly dropped to her knees as she stared at the large canvas. The painting captured a moment so rare and beautiful it took her breath away. Mary was hiding, an impish smile on her face, behind a wispy bush, giggling as only a three-year-old can when she thinks she is outsmarting her favorite adult. And Elsie was standing on the opposite side of the bush with an expression so real, so much like the reflection in her mirror, it was striking.

"What are you doing in here?" came a deep and angry voice.

Elsie snapped her head around as Mrs. Billings started to explain herself, but Elsie interrupted. "It is my fault entirely, Alexander. I insisted she open the door."

Mrs. Billings bobbed a curtsy and hurried away, but not before giving Elsie a look that seemed to say "I told you so."

"You frightened her nearly to death."

"My servants have been given specific orders not to enter this room."

"And it is your prerogative to issue such an order. I, however, am your wife and not subject to your whims."

Alexander's jaw twitched. "As my wife, you are more subject to my whims than any other person in this house. They may quit. You, my dear, are bound to me until death."

"Is that supposed to frighten me? I daresay, you must work on your methods of intimidation, for I fear my heart hasn't picked up a single beat," Elsie said with far more bravado than she was feeling.

He pressed his jaw even tighter, and Elsie hoped it was humor he was trying to suppress, not anger.

"The painting is lovely. More than lovely."

"I didn't realize you were so vain," Alexander said, and Elsie found herself trying not to smile. She wasn't quite certain whether he was being sincere or simply teasing her. His stern expression gave her no clues. It seemed Alexander had already learned the haughty stare that was second nature to the aristocracy.

"You captured our joy, a moment I shall treasure. It's the most wonderful gift you could give me."

Alexander let out a sigh. "It is not for you."

Elsie's heart gave a slight stutter. "What is it for, then?"

"I have never painted on canvas and thought I would practice with human subjects I knew. As much as I admire Monsieur Desmarais, he would not make a very appealing subject of a painting."

"Even so, I do like it and if you are finished, I would like to have it in my rooms. I miss Mary."

"You may bring her here any time you like."

"Can I?" Elsie asked, overcome with happiness.

"Do you think I would deny you your own sister?" Alexander asked, anger in his tone.

"You deny me my husband," Elsie said, lifting her chin.

"That is an entirely different matter. I like Mary's company."

Elsie narrowed her eyes, but ignored his comment. "Can I have the painting?"

"If you wish."

"I do."

"I'll have it framed and delivered to you."

Elsie bit her lip, but decided spontaneously to forge ahead. "And when may I have my husband?"

His gaze suddenly sharpened, sweeping her body as if against his will. "When I believe I can touch my wife without throttling her."

The days passed slowly—and with exceeding dreariness—inside and out. It seemed as if it had either misted or rained or deluged each day since her marriage, and no matter how optimistic Elsie tried to remain, she was becoming downright depressed. Never had she been so bored, so restless. This house was too well-run, the staff too efficient. She found herself looking for even the smallest infraction just to have something to say to someone. Unfortunately, even finding a bit of dust in a forgotten corner was impossible. No corner was forgotten in Warbeck Abbey, and Elsie was quite certain it had nothing to do with Alexander and everything to do with his father. She had nothing against a well-run household, but this home was so sterile, so quiet, it was unnerving. Even Missy had little to do once Elsie was dressed and her hair was done. There were no gowns to prepare or clean, no ribbons to organize, no outings to accompany her mistress to. She had no gowns to be repaired or made, no correspondence to deliver. Missy would never complain, but Elsie could tell that even her industrious and usually cheerful maid was unhappy here.

On the fourth day of her marriage, Elsie stared morosely out her bedroom window, a letter to Aunt Diane forgotten on her secretaire. She didn't know what to say, for the truth of her marriage was so disheartening, she couldn't bring herself to write it down. She and Alexander did not share meals, conversation, or a bed. Not even the painting that now graced one wall of her temporary quarters made her feel better. In fact, it made her long for the days when she and Mary had romped around their gardens, playing for hours on end.

She turned away from the window, hating that she was letting herself dissolve into self-pity. Perhaps Alexander was content to have such a marriage, but she was not. She had seen him only once in the past several days, meeting him in the hallway as he'd returned from a ride, all flushed and smelling of the outdoors and horse. It was an intoxicatingly male combination that had given her an intense jolt of longing. She'd nodded to him, noted he looked exhausted and miserable, and carried on down the hall as if he were nothing more than a stranger. It had taken all her will not to turn, to call back to him, to ask him why he looked as if he were being haunted by some malevolent ghost. To throw herself into his arms and beg him to forgive her—even though she wasn't entirely to blame for anything that had happened.

Today, she would talk to him. She would force him into a conversation if for no other reason than to break the interminable silence of this house. Elsie left her chamber of self-pity and wandered toward the main part of the house, stopping the first servant she saw.

"Do you know where I might find His Grace? Anne, is it not?" she asked, trying not to look as pathetic as she felt. She had no idea where he spent his time or even if he was in the house at all.

"Yes, Your Grace," the girl said, flushing a bit. "In the library."

Elsie thanked her, then stopped, realizing she didn't know where the library was. In all the times she'd been in Warbeck Abbey, she'd never seen the room. It had been that kind of house; one in which one did not wander freely about exploring. Seeing her hesitation, the maid bobbed a quick curtsy and said, "This way, Your Grace."

"Thank you. I still get quite lost here," she said.

Anne led her to a large, carved door, gave her yet another curtsy, then went back the way she'd come, no doubt ready to efficiently complete some task. And there she came upon yet another servant. Elsie had grown up with a household of servants, but even she was unused to the number of servants

Kingston employed. The footman, smartly dressed in livery, gave her a quick bow, then knocked on the door, his head cocked slightly so he could hear his employer's command.

Elsie clearly heard Alexander calling for him to enter, and so she did, just as the young man was opening the door, flustering him and causing him to leap back or bang into her. "Thank you, James," she said, and walked directly to the desk where Alexander sat glowering at her. He had also, apparently, mastered the art of the glower.

One look at his desk, and Elsie determined that the reason he was glowering was not because of her visit but rather because he had such an immense amount of work in front of him.

"You need a secretary," she announced, eying the mountain of paper on his desk.

"I'm quite aware of that," he said, sitting back and staring at her. "To what do I owe this interruption?"

Elsie beamed a smile at him, recognizing already he was trying to be difficult. "The expression, I believe is, 'to what do I owe this pleasure'."

Ignoring her, he scanned his desk with his gray eyes. "As you can see, Elsie, I am quite busy."

"Perhaps I can help."

"I doubt it."

"I used to help my father all the time, especially after my mother passed away. My father did not have, and did not need, a secretary, having far fewer holdings and interests than you. However, he neglected his duties for several weeks, and I helped him quite a bit." Elsie walked over to his side of the desk, idly looking at the piles, noting that Alexander stiffened as she approached.

"What is all this?" Elsie asked, pointing to a rather large pile of expensive-looking stationery. It, in fact, looked like a large pile of invitations. She picked one up before he could protest and saw the unmistakable seal of the Duke of Newcastle. She gave Alexander a pensive look before snapping the seal and revealing a lovely invitation to a ball and house party during the House of Lords' Easter break in just three weeks. *The Duke of Newcastle.* It was an amazing honor, one that they absolutely must accept. Oh, to be invited by Newcastle, to dance at Clumber Park, to be part of a house party there. It was something most young girls only dreamed of. Elsie, despite her informal engagement to Lord Hathwaite, had never garnered an invitation to any of Newcastle's events. A small thrill went through her and she smiled, thinking how absolutely green her friends from Mansfield would be if they knew she was going . . .

But, of course, they couldn't go. Of course not. She looked up at Alexander and found him studying her face, before he quickly looked down again.

"These are all invitations, are they not?"

He nodded, his jaw set as he stared at the document before him. "They began arriving as soon as the announcement of our wedding appeared in the *Times*." When Elsie raised her eyebrow in question, he said, "I assumed it was your father's doing."

"Ah. That does explain the pile. Even if we do not attend any of these events, we must send our regrets. I will do so, if you don't mind."

"I do not."

Elsie went through the pile, her heart plummeting at the invitations she saw, all from the highest level of the *ton*, all of which would have to be rejected. It was not that Elsie was a shallow woman, one who only loved parties, some frivolous belle who flitted about from ball to ball. But she did adore socializing, and realized this was one thing she had not considered when she'd married Alexander. It had seemed the least of her concerns at the time.

Now, she faced a marriage of silence and a life of isolation and it seemed almost more than she could bear at the moment.

"How popular you are," she said, trying to keep her voice light.

Alexander closed his eyes slowly. "Even seeing that stack of requests makes me feel slightly ill," he said with more than a touch of self-loathing.

"It's not important. Goodness, most of those people who attend such amusements are rather dull, aren't they? I daresay I'd send my regrets to most of these out of hand simply for that reason alone."

"Don't," he said sharply and Elsie's false smile disappeared.

"Perhaps we can select one. Just one . . ." She stopped when his expression closed. She gathered up the invitations, pressing them to her chest, and hurried toward the door.

"One," Alexander called, sounding as if the Devil himself had ripped that syllable from his throat.

Guilt assaulted her. She knew more than anyone how difficult it was for Alexander to attend social events. She shouldn't—and wouldn't—ask it of him even if it meant becoming a recluse. "No, it's perfectly fine, Alexander, and perfectly wretched of me even to ask. Please."

"Pick one or I shall," he said angrily. "Perhaps the least offensive of the bunch. The shortest event?"

Elsie smiled at him, feeling her heart lift a bit. Not only at the prospect of going somewhere, but at the fact that her husband was actually talking to her and obviously cared enough to put himself through torture simply to please her.

"If you insist," she said, guilt warring with real pleasure at the thought of appearing in public for the first time as a duchess.

"I do," he said, staring at her. "And, of course, you may attend anything you like without me. Attend them all if you like."

Her brow furrowed. "You don't mind if I go alone?"

"I would not want to keep you from your fun. You should not suffer simply because your husband is a hermit."

"While that is quite thoughtful of you, I really wouldn't want my friends to think my marriage is an unhappy one. We really should keep that truth close to the vest, don't you think?" With that, she did leave the room, even when she heard what sounded like a growl coming from behind her.

Alexander felt his lips tug into a smile, wondering how his wife could evoke such an emotion when she was clearly insulting him. When she'd smiled at him, he'd felt that smile to his very soul. It was the kind of smile that could heal a different sort of man than he. Elsie's smile, instead, was just another knife to his heart.

What the hell had he done, forcing her to marry him? How could he have sentenced her to such a life? He knew it had nothing to do with revenge and everything to do with his own selfish heart. And now, he'd done it. He'd said he would attend some social event at which he would no doubt make a complete ass of himself and embarrass Elsie.

But he knew he'd go, if only to see her smile like that just one more time.

Chapter 28

The ducal carriage was third in line when they arrived at the one and only social event Alexander would be forced to suffer through. Suffer was a rather apt description of what he had been going through since Elsie had barged into his library not an hour after he'd given her license to find a social event that would not kill him.

"A concert," she'd announced, holding the offending invitation in hand. "Lord and Lady Brower, in two weeks, at their home, which I personally know cannot hold more than twenty people at a time. Apparently they have lured Camillo Sivori, the violinist, from London for the night. How does that sound?"

"Do you want the truth or a lie?"

"A lie, please."

"Then I'm delighted." He had not been delighted, but being a man of his word and frankly sick to death of his all-consuming fear, he would take his bloody wife to this bloody concert whether he bloody liked it or not. For two weeks he'd suffered through episodes of anxiety so violent he'd thought he was literally dying. What the deuce was wrong with him? What masochistic bent had prompted him to promise his wife that he would gladly take her to the concert?

He knew the answer and didn't like it. His ridiculous efforts to remain detached from Elsie were killing him as surely as the thought of attending the concert. She was ever smiling, ever coming into his library and reading a bit of a letter she'd received or one she'd written. She insisted that they at least eat together since they were man and wife—stressing "at least" without even the subtlest attempt to disguise her meaning. It wasn't as if he didn't want her. God knew that was yet another thing that was slowly killing him—not having his wife in his bed. He wanted her, yes, good Lord yes, but he didn't want to want her.

And so he sat in the carriage with his beautiful young wife, who was bubbling over with happiness, waiting in line to disembark into a roomful of people he'd never met and frankly never wanted to meet. He would smile and nod and lift old ladies' hands for a charming kiss. He would make polite conversation and pray no one noticed he was drenched in sweat, his heart was pounding painfully in his chest, and he was on the verge of vomiting on their highly polished shoes.

He could do this. It was simply a matter of mind over matter. In fact, he was so successful at masking his terror, that when the evening was over and they were safely in their carriage again, Elsie looked quite angry.

"You were quite charming tonight," she said, narrowing her eyes at him.

"Thank you."

"Many people noted it. How handsome the new duke is. How charming. What a nice smile he has."

"And yet you're angry."

Elsie put her hands on her hips even though she was sitting on the leather bench seat and such an action wasn't at all easy. "Of course I'm angry. You didn't seem the least bit nervous."

"Come here," he said.

She was immediately suspicious. "Why?"

"Please come here," he repeated. With some reluctance, Elsie moved to sit next to him and he grabbed one hand. Though she resisted a bit, he placed her hand on his shirt beneath his coat. It was wet—so wet it felt as if he'd doused himself with water. Elsie knew immediately what she was feeling was sweat, cold sweat that plastered his fine lawn shirt to his skin.

"Oh," she said, her voice small. "I must say you hid it well."

"I did try, though it was one of the most difficult nights of my life."

"Truly?" she asked, feeling dreadful.

He held his hand up as if to stave off her sympathy. "But I did survive and proved something to myself. I can do it. I can pretend my way through almost anything and I don't think I would have been able to a short while ago. These past months have made it easier for me to deal with my affliction. I will never enjoy socializing, but I do believe I won't become violently ill each time."

Elsie gave him a weak smile. "That's nice to know." She was quiet for a while, her hands in her lap, feeling rather small at the moment. Were parties, concerts and balls more important than her husband's well-being?

"In London during the Season, we shall attend one ball of your choosing," he said. Elsie began shaking her head. "We must. I worked hard to obtain this title and I will not have it disgraced in any way. If I must attend some events, I will. I think I realized tonight that it can be a vital part of my position."

Elsie smiled and kissed his cheek, noting he immediately clenched his jaw as if the kiss were somehow offensive. "I will help in any way I can," she said, wishing that jaw-clenching had not hurt quite so much.

"You need not concern yourself," he said, his voice clipped, as if he were angry.

"I'm just acting like a good wife."

"There is no need," he repeated. "You need only concern yourself with selecting a social engagement and appearing by my side as a dutiful wife should."

Elsie stared at him, wondering why he was suddenly being so cold. "So I am a well-dressed escort and nothing more?"

"Precisely."

Elsie quickly crossed over to the opposite side of the carriage and sat there, fuming, for many long minutes. "You are being hateful," she said, unable to keep her anger to herself.

"I am being practical."

"Practical," she shouted. "Is that what this is, this marriage of ours, practical? Is that all this is to you?"

She got her answer when he jerked his head in a sharp nod, then proceeded to stare out the window.

That night, Elsie sat at the edge of her bed having a fierce debate with herself. Her brave self had decided she would march into her husband's room and demand her wifely rights. Her angry self had decided that pigs would fly before she set one foot into his room. And so she sat, conducting an internal battle with those two sides, clutching the edge of the bed and swinging her legs back and forth.

She stood suddenly, and just as suddenly sat back down. And then she stood again, slowly, thoughtfully, and walked out her door quietly and headed toward his rooms. Alexander had not acted coldly to her until she'd kissed his cheek. She was not foolish enough to believe he didn't want her physically. She'd caught him looking at her quite often, a brooding, dark look that was so filled with desire she would shiver from it. But if that was true, why had he been so hurtful on the way home that evening? Did he still hate her so much for almost marrying Oscar?

The house was quiet; no violent piano music marred the silence. When she reached Alexander's rooms, she found no light lining the edges of the door and wondered if he were already abed. Perhaps she would tip-toe in and look at him while he slept. He couldn't scowl at her if he were sleeping.

As quietly as possible, Elsie opened the door and

slipped inside, listening intently for any sound that would indicate he was awake. The rooms were completely dark, the door to his bedroom open. Her heart pounding in her chest, Elsie moved silently toward the shadowed outline of the door and peeked inside to the bedroom.

"Why are you here, Elsie?" he asked calmly, and she nearly jumped out of her skin.

Recovering quickly, she went to his bed, where she could now see he lay with his hands tucked beneath his head, as if he'd been waiting for her. "I want to know what I need to do to make you love me again," she said. It was not what she'd meant to say, not what she'd planned, but there it was, the agonizing truth of why she needed to sneak into his room in the dead of night.

"I never said I did not love you," came his low reply.

Elsie sat down at the very edge of the bed, balancing rather precariously. "Then why are you making this so difficult for me?"

"Difficult. For you."

"Yes. Because there is nothing I can do to prove myself. You have made your judgment and found me guilty and now I must endure this sentence." She reached out and clutched his hand.

"Please," he said. "Don't do this. Not now." Though he sounded angry, he did not remove his hand, and in fact pressed her fingers against his palm.

"Why?"

He released her hand abruptly and swung his legs over the opposite side of the bed so that his back faced her. She could see only his dim outline, his head turned slightly toward her in profile. "It may kill me the next time. Do you understand what I'm saying?"

"No. I don't."

"I don't want to discuss this now, Elsie. I'm not ready."

"And yet you were ready to marry me."

"Only to prevent you from leaving me," he shouted, turning half toward her, making her cringe at the violence in his voice.

"I'll go, then," Elsie said, feeling like a child running away from a darkened room with hidden demons inside.

"Elsie. Stop."

She did, her breathing heavy, as if, indeed, she had been running.

"I'm sorry," he said. "Please come back. Come here."

Elsie stared at the entrance to his room for a long moment before turning slowly back to face her husband, this man who seemed to hate her but professed to love her.

"I'm not angry. I am frightened," he said so softly she wasn't entirely certain she'd heard him right. "I cannot bear to lose you again."

"You won't have to."

"You don't understand," he said harshly.

"Then help me. Tell me."

He hung his head and kneaded his neck with one hand as she stood at the foot of the bed. "Two days after your thwarted wedding, I sat in a hotel room with the barrel of a pistol jammed into my mouth."

She couldn't stop the gasp of horror. "No, Alexander."

"The only thing that saved me was a knock on the door. My solicitor bearing a legal document declaring me heir to Kingston. I looked at my father's signature and realized if I killed myself, he would win. And I couldn't let that happen."

Elsie padded over to him and sat down next to him on the bed, not touching, her hands folded on her lap, hurting so much for him it was almost beyond bearing.

"I know, more than anyone, my father's power, his arrogance. I know you had no chance against such a man, never mind your own father. I understand it was difficult for you. But at that moment, when I held that gun, it didn't matter. I just wanted it to be over. I just wanted the pain to end."

They sat silently for a long moment before Elsie launched herself against him, pressed her face against his neck, breathing in his familiar scent, as tears coursed down her face. "Don't you *ever* contemplate such a thing again, do you hear me, Alexander?" she said fiercely. "You cannot leave me. You cannot."

He did not embrace her, did not even acknowledge that she held him.

"You needn't worry," he said, sounding dull and unconvincing. "I've been fighting this thing my whole life and it hasn't won yet."

"Alexander, look at me," she said, pulling his face 'round forcefully. "I love you. I have always loved you. If I had married Oscar, I still would have loved you. My heart was broken that day. I felt nothing as I walked down that aisle except complete and utter despair. But I've been taught well to hide my feelings, to put on my best face in public. I could not disgrace Oscar with tears, even though it hurt so badly I could hardly walk. All this sadness and fear and despair has done one thing, Alexander." She held his face between her hands and gave him a small shake. "It has brought us together. *We* have won. We still love each other and we are married. It's what we wanted. No matter how bad things are, there is always a light. Always. And that's the one thing you should always remember when you feel that blackness. It passes. It does. Just look at us. We're sitting in the same bed, married. Of course, I am crying and you are terribly angry and sad, but we're together just as we planned. Don't you see? Don't you see that everything passes?"

"You do like to talk, don't you?" he said, with the barest hint of a smile.

Elsie let out a watery laugh. "You do see, don't you?"

"I see you," he said. "For now, that's enough."

With a low sound, he pulled her to him and kissed her, pressing his mouth almost painfully hard against her lips. He pulled back and rested his forehead against hers, his hands on her shoulders.

"Make love to me, Alexander," Elsie said. "You're my husband and I love you. Let me show you how much."

She wanted so much from him, his Elsie. She wanted him to throw away that thick, black blanket of despair that had become so familiar to him it was almost a comfort. To do as she asked, to make love to his wife, would be to open himself up again, to take the terrible chance of being swallowed up by that blanket once again.

"I love you," she said, peppering his cheek with kisses, kisses he'd missed and longed for so desperately. "Let me love you. Let me be your wife."

Oh, God, he could never refuse her, and probably never would. If she told him he could fly to the moon, no doubt he'd believe it because that was what she did to him. She was his light and his darkness, and that was too, too much. But, he realized with a tinge of fear, he really had no choice in the matter. He'd never really had a choice when it came to Elsie.

"Shhh," he said, pressing a finger to her mouth. "You don't have to ask, my love. I'm sorry you felt you did." He took his finger away and replaced it with his mouth, kissing her deeply, devouring her, showing her with his body and hands and mouth how much he loved her. God, he'd missed her, the sounds she made, the way she moved her body against his when he aroused her. He smoothed one hand along her thigh, letting out a low moan when he found her completely naked underneath her nightgown.

"Let me see you," he said, and she lifted her arms and let him remove the nightgown, revealing herself to him without one bit of reticence. "I forgive you," he said, smiling, as he brought his mouth to one nipple, sucking deeply. She arched against him, and he heard her chuckle.

"Are you saying that all I had to do was remove my nightgown and you would have forgiven me?"

"Instantly," he said, turning to her other nipple and flicking his tongue against it. She brought his head up to hers and they kissed deeply as she moved her hand over his chest and around to his back, pulling him closer and closer, as if she were trying to pull him inside her. He moved his hand between her legs, feeling her slick and warm, finding the spot that made her cry out, made her move her hips involuntarily against his hand. She was the most beautiful woman when she was aroused. The complete darkness of the room only enhanced the intense feeling of arousal when she began jerking herself against him in abandon, seeking her release.

Alexander moved between her legs and tasted her, inserting one finger deeply so he could feel the spasms that meant she was coming.

"Oh," she said, right before she was completely overcome, her body pulsing against him, her hips jerking erotically.

She was still pulsing her release when he entered her, and stopped, savoring the miracle in his arms. At that moment, the world was right and beautiful. He moved because he could not bear to stay still any longer, and she drove her hips up to meet him.

"I've missed you. I've missed this," she said, kissing him.

She was slick and tight and lovely, and she was his wife. *His* wife. Elsie, the girl who wouldn't stop talking, who captured his heart even though he had tried so hard to protect it. God, he loved her. Loved her. In his head, he said it over and over as his rhythm increased, as his release grew ever closer. Her legs drew around him, holding him close as she matched his thrusts with her own, as she let out the sounds that told him she was close, as close as he was. And when he felt her contract around him, he was lost to a place he never wanted to climb out of.

He lay, spent and out of breath, atop her, bracing on elbows so she wouldn't take the full brunt of his weight. "I finally figured out how to stop you from talking," he said, feeling rather pleased at the moment.

"Hmph," she said, but she was smiling. "You know, Your Grace, you have found a perfect match. You are silent. I am talkative. You are morose and I am interminably cheerful."

"Like comedy and tragedy?"

She nodded. "One cannot exist without the other."

"I do believe I am figuring that out." He lay on his side, but pulled her close. "I . . ."

When he hesitated, she pulled herself up onto one elbow and looked down on him. "Yes?"

"I need you," he said simply.

"Well, of course you do, silly. And I need you. So we are a perfect pair, the two of us."

"Elsie, don't make fun. Living with me will not be easy. I am prone to despair, I don't like people, and quite often I am rather not very much fun to be with."

She kissed his cheek. "But you're very handsome and that can make up for quite a lot, you know."

Despite himself, he let out a laugh. "I've a feeling you won't let me be serious, even when the situation calls for it."

"I'm not as shallow as all that. But I will make it my life's work to keep you giddy with happiness."

He let out a sigh as if the prospect of a giddy life was not such a good thing. "And what shall my life's work be?"

"To make very certain I feel loved."

"I do believe," Alexander said, kissing her on the very tip of her nose, "that is something I can do."

Epilogue

"Where is the artist?" Lord Smythe-Kingsley asked, looking at one of Alexander's finest works on exhibit at the Royal Academy of Arts. "I'd like to express my great admiration of his work."

"His Grace is somewhere," Elsie said, pretending to look around the crowded gallery and lying through her teeth. "You must have just missed him." And so it went through three days of the wildly successful exhibit of the Duke of Kingston's oils.

Alexander loved to paint but absolutely abhorred the public adoration he received during his exhibits. His annual shows drew huge crowds, who he claimed attended as much to view his paintings as in the hope of viewing the artist himself. Elsie adored walking among the crowds, hearing accolades about the man she loved most in the world. He was touted as a great master, and his paintings now sold for thousands of pounds.

"It's the mystery more than the mastery," he said to Elsie, after his exhibit closed. The two stood before his favorite piece—the one of Elsie bending over their son's ornate crib and looking lovingly down into his smiling face. Christopher Wilkinson, Lord Hathwaite and future Marquess, was nearly always smiling and had already begun to talk, obviously taking after his beautiful mother.

That particular painting was not for sale, though many wealthy members of the ton had made exorbitant offers.

"I don't know how it has happened, Alexander, but you are the most popular member of the peerage in all of England. How very ironic," Elsie said.

"Painfully ironic."

"And no one but me knows you can play the piano like a virtuoso. Imagine the invitations we'd receive then."

"Are you trying to torture me? We attend far too many social events as it is."

"Two a Season is not far too many."

"It's one more than I agreed to," he pointed out.

"Yes, but that was before I realized how much you love me. Now I have such a wonderful weapon to use at my will."

"You are a devious wench," he said, pulling her against him and kissing her soundly.

Alexander called for his carriage, not quite believing how his life had changed in the past two years. He was starting to realize that this feeling—this strange and wonderful feeling that had started the night of the violin concert—was, oddly enough, unrestrained happiness.

"Why are you smiling?" Elsie asked, a smile of her own on her face.

"Because, my love, I have so much to smile about."

She nodded thoughtfully and placed her hand in his. "Yes," she said, her eyes filling with tears as they often did when she took the time to think about how very happy she was. "You do." It appeared her life's work—to keep him giddy with happiness—was succeeding, after all.

Did you miss Jane's other books?
Go back and read those as well!

MARRY CHRISTMAS

A Christmas wedding to the Duke of Bellingham. Any other socialite in Newport, Rhode Island, would be overjoyed at the prospect, but Elizabeth Cummings finds her mother's announcement as appealing as a prison sentence. Elizabeth has not the slightest desire to meet Randall Blackmore, let alone be bartered for an English title. Her heart belongs to another, and the duke's prestige, arrogance, and rugged charm will make no difference to her plans of elopement.

Against his expectations and desires, Randall Blackmore has inherited a dukedom and a vast estate that only marriage to an heiress can save. Selling his title to the highest bidder is a wretched obligation, but to Randall's surprise his intended bride is pretty, courageous, delightfully impertinent—and completely uninterested in becoming a Duchess. Yet suddenly, no other woman will do, and a marriage in name only will never be enough for a husband determined to win his wife in body, heart, and soul . . .

A CHRISTMAS SCANDAL

Dashing, debonair, and completely irresistible, Edward Hollings has all of Newport buzzing—and to Maggie Pierce's surprise, she alone has caught his eye. But when the handsome earl returns to England without proposing, a devastated Maggie knows she must forget him. Life only gets worse for Maggie, as all her dreams of happiness and love come crashing down around her. When Maggie receives an invitation to go to England for the Christmas birth of her dear friend's baby, she accepts—vowing to keep her devastating lies and shameful secrets from the one man she has ever loved . . .

Edward vowed he'd never marry, but he came dangerously close with Maggie. She's beautiful, witty, indescribably desirable—and Edward can't forget her. When Maggie visits mutual friends for Christmas, Edward can't stay away. In fact, he finds himself more attracted to her than ever—a desire fueled even more by Maggie's repeated snubs. With the love he never thought he'd find slipping away, Edward is determined to make Maggie his own, no matter what the cost . . .

A CHRISTMAS WALTZ

To Lady Amelia Wellesley, it seems utterly romantic to surprise her dashing fiancé at his home in Texas so the two can marry by Christmas. But Amelia's surprise goes awry when Carson Kitteridge calls off their wedding as soon as she arrives, leaving Amelia in disgrace . . .

With nowhere to turn, Amelia finds an unlikely savior in Carson's brother, Dr. Boone Kitteridge. Boone offers to marry Amelia, sparing her the shame of returning to England unwed. But Boone isn't just protecting Amelia's honor; secretly, he finds her irresistible, and the thought of indulging his desire for her is too tempting to ignore. As Boone and Amelia forge a fragile bond, something goes terribly wrong—and it will take nothing less than a Christmas miracle for Amelia to discover who she is destined to love . . .